au
pair

viveka tolf elworthy

FpS

Greenville, South Carolina

Published by:

FpS

1175 Woods Crossing Rd., #5
Greenville, S.C. 29607
864-675-0540
www.fiction-addiction.com

ISBN: 978-1-945338-93-9

Cover & Book Design by Vally Sharpe
Cover image created from photographs licensed from www.Shutterstock.com

Printed in the United States of America.

To Alfred

au
pair

1

The moment Birgit Svenson saw the ad in the *Swedish Daily News*, she knew that her life was about to change.

Even at the young age of twenty-two, she was not an impulsive girl. Born in January, she had typical Capricorn characteristics, caution and realism being two of them. Still, here she was, cheeks flushed, and with a heart beating a mile a minute the moment she read the ad: "Au pair wanted by an American family."

She worked as a nurse's aide at the hospital and during her lunch break had picked up a discarded newspaper. The sandwich counter in the cafeteria was, as usual, crowded, so instead of standing in line for a pick-up meal, she grabbed a cup of coffee from the vending machine and headed to a nearby park.

Birgit lived in Västervik, a small town south of Stockholm. Driving time to the capital should be no more than four hours, she thought, but with notoriously-safety-conscious Swedes at the wheel, it might take longer.

As people, Swedes value safety, order, and, most of all, privacy. When movie actress Greta Garbo uttered the famous words, "I want to be alone," she could have spoken for all her countrymen. Swedes dislike crowds and will walk for miles to find that one lonely spot on the beach. The country is roughly the size of California, but sparsely populated, only seven million inhabitants in the 1960s. Plenty of room to be solitary.

If the world were an elementary school with every nation having their own classroom, Swedes would be the least stressful to teach. Willing to learn and take direction, respectful of authority, exhibiting no desire to talk back or rebel. What else could a teacher want from students?

Boring? Maybe! But if you crave flash and drama, you'd teach the French, who strike and protest for no good reason, or the boisterous Americans with their demands for "rights." Swedes believe they have all the rights they need. The right to carry arms? Why? In an orderly society, who needs it?

High taxes and harsh weather are negatives, of course, but Swedes generally take the good with the bad. The nation has no desire to bother anyone else, nor do its citizens want to be bothered.

Swedes like to think of themselves as uncomplicated, but in reality, are a paradox—conventional and traditional but with only a lukewarm interest in organized religion. Tolerant of pre-marital sex, not exactly condoning it, but not raising a big fuss over it either. Young people were expected to handle this issue responsibly.

Socialists, but still royalists. Weekly magazines with young Crown Prince Karl Gustaf, Sweden's future king, on the cover, sold out immediately. One of Europe's most eligible bachelors, the prince was handsome, sporty and likable. His subjects devoured gossip articles about him and his more or less blue-blooded girlfriends. Parades, visits from other royals, uniforms, plumes, horse-drawn carriages, benevolent waves from His Majesty. Spectacles like that had even socialists in the crowd cheering.

Who doesn't enjoy a fairy tale?

Many others had the same idea for lunch—finding an available seat in the park turned out to be a challenge. Only one bench in a shadowy corner was free. Birgit understood quickly why that was the case—two infamous town drunks enjoyed a picnic nearby. Their liquid breakfast was gone, and they were working on a similar lunch. A passer-by in a business suit sent a disgusted look in their direction. Mothers made sure to keep their children at a safe distance.

The two alcoholics wore good quality coats. *Most likely provided by the local government services*, she thought. Birgit didn't feel charitable. Her father, Torsten, was a fisherman, who'd worked hard all his life, but had little to show for it. Still, Birgit knew that her dad would be the first to defend the men. "Tone it down girl," he would say, "the poor bastards aren't as able as some of us. Life is unfair that way."

The Social Democrats, Sweden's governing party, had made it their motto to take care of its people from 'cradle to grave' and they'd succeeded. Many taxpayers were not at all happy about supporting people who wouldn't help themselves but tolerated it grudgingly. This attitude of acceptance often irritated Birgit.

She looked toward the pond where ducks were circling, fooled into believing that spring had arrived. For early April, the temperature was surprisingly pleasant. This time of the year the weather in Sweden was unpredictable. On the country's east coast, the changes were seldom for the better. Today was an anomaly—the sunshine was a gift. Maybe the long dreary winter had finally come to an end.

Birgit placed her coffee on the bench and searched her handbag for a pen. She found one, skimmed the newspaper, located the page she wanted, and circled the employment agency's phone number. She gave the rest of the paper a quick glance. The headlines warned that Sweden's wolf population was soon to be extinct. Further down, in much smaller print, was a reference to the Vietnam War.

"I live in a duck pond," Birgit mumbled to herself, "No sense of priorities."

She finished her coffee and dumped the cup in the nearby garbage can. Stupid of her not to bring a sandwich from the cafeteria—strong coffee on an empty stomach was not a good idea.

Birgit looked again in her handbag, this time for the coin purse. The number to dial was in Stockholm, and she needed change for the call. Outside the hospital was a pay phone and her next shift didn't start for another half hour. She'd have plenty of time to contact the agency. Before tucking the paper under her arm, Birgit used the pen to underline the date—Wednesday, April 12, 1967. She would remember this day.

The two men watched her and drunkenly snickered as she left. Birgit didn't look their way, but her blue eyes turned dark and icy. She flicked back her shoulder-length dark blond hair, and with chin up, she passed them with strong, confident strides. One of them made a lewd comment about her shapely legs. The other one loudly hiccuped while fumbling for the top to the liquor bottle in his hand.

Their laughs sounded hollow and sad. *Poor bastards*, Birgit thought, *I'm going places, and you're not.*

§

"Borden's Employment Agency, Marianne Dahl speaking."

The voice on the phone had a slightly nasal Stockholm accent. Before responding, Birgit made a mental note not to roll her "r's" and give away her southern Swedish origin. That should not be a problem, she thought, since

Mom was born and raised in the capital and insisted that her two daughters didn't speak like "country bumpkins."

Birgit introduced herself and explained the nature of her call, making a point to sound professional. The interviewer asked her a battery of questions.

"Do you speak English, Miss Svenson?"

"Yes, I studied English for four years in school, and after that, I took some evening courses…"

"Did you ever travel abroad?"

"Just to Denmark and once to Germany."

"Never to the U.S.?"

"No."

"Do you have any experience with children?"

"Yes, I worked one year as a teacher's aide."

"Just one year?" The tone of the question sounded like a reproach.

"Correct."

Birgit decided not to elaborate. *No need to over-explain. Sometimes you get yourself in more trouble that way.*

The truth was that she had yet to find what she liked to do. Teaching and nursing had been equally disappointing. Birgit enjoyed children—most of them anyway—but she much preferred connecting with them one on one. A large unruly group didn't appeal to her. Her work as a nurse's aide had not been as fulfilling as she had hoped for, either. Running from one place to another, changing bedpans and doing menial tasks hadn't give her much chance to interact with patients.

Her father, as usual, understood her restlessness. "She just needs time to find herself," he had said. Her mother, Vera, critical by nature, hadn't agreed. "She's a 'hopper,'" she said, nodding knowingly to Ruth, Birgit's nine-years-older sister. Ruth had produced a smug, little smile in agreement.

It had always been like that—Ruth and Mom, Birgit and Dad. Birgit had sometimes wondered if her birth had been an accident. A child her mother hadn't wanted. When she had mentioned her thoughts to her father, he'd dismissed the idea. "Nonsense," he'd said. "They're just a better fit. Has nothing to do with love."

Birgit still wasn't sure he was right, but Ruth and Mom definitely had more in common. Ruth was a younger, taller version of Mom—dark haired and intense with a similarly restless energy. They enjoyed the same romantic books and movies and had the same taste in music—sentimental and a little syrupy. Both had sharp tongues and neither liked to have their opinions questioned.

Physically, Birgit resembled her father more. Like him, she had what Mom called the Scandinavian look—tall, blond, blue-eyed—but in personality, she was quick to be critical and judgmental like her mother. Her father lacked those traits. It was one of the reasons he was so well liked. "A handful, your mother," her father had once said, chuckling. "But that might be the reason I fell for her. God help me."

The agent interrupted Birgit's reverie. "Well, all that's left to do for you now is to send in your application, and please, don't forget to include a photo." She paused. "Of course, there are no guarantees. We have quite a few applicants. So many young girls are interested in spending a year abroad these days."

Ms. Dahl was reluctant to give out information about her clients, but the family in Greenwich looked like a perfect fit. The Fillmores had one daughter, Elizabeth, eleven years. Mrs. Fillmore was an artist. She had a studio in the house where she did her painting. Mr. Fillmore worked as a stockbroker in New York. Perhaps Birgit was overly optimistic, but she had a good feeling.

"Where do you get all that confidence?" her father often asked. He should've known it came from him, Birgit thought. Torsten Svenson might be one to struggle financially but he had a quiet presence about him that demanded respect. He was the union representative for fishermen in the area, and you wanted him on your side in disputes.

Sending her resume didn't concern her, but the requested photograph did. Would Lindsey and Brad Fillmore of Greenwich, Connecticut find her too plain-looking? In American movies, the actresses looked so glamorous with flawless make-up and never a hair out of place. Maybe Ruth, who owned a beauty parlor in town, could give her some help. No, she thought. She wouldn't ask her sister for advice. It was too early to discuss her plans anyway.

She knew if the job came through, Dad wouldn't fuss but Mom would lecture. Her sister was simply too small-minded to understand anything. But talking to Bengt, her boyfriend…*that* would be hard!

How do you tell somebody who loves you that you plan on leaving him for a year or more? Not just to go to another town close by, but to another continent?

Bengt was beloved by her family and for good reason. He was polite, pleasant, and easy-going, with an infectious grin. Just the past Saturday, he had grabbed her hand outside the jewelry store and asked her if she wanted to go inside to look at rings. When she'd laughed it off and continued walking, he hadn't been mad. He'd just put his arm around her and nodded. "I get it," he'd said. "Not ready for serious stuff just yet."

Birgit looked at her watch. It was time to go back to work. She decided it made no sense to think about what might happen—she would just send in her paperwork and let things fall where they may. Besides, she already had a mental picture of the Fillmores, especially of the daughter. She and Elizabeth would be good friends—about that she had no doubt.

2

One year had passed since Birgit moved from her parent's house on Händelöp Island to an apartment in Västervik, the neighboring town. It hadn't been a big move—she still had her parents nearby. But, it was a step toward independence. To have her private phone and mailbox was a relief, especially now with her future in limbo.

She'd lucked out, finding an affordable place in the historic district of town before the renovation of the area escalated the rental costs. Her mother had objected to the move. Birgit couldn't figure out why. Maybe it was a habit—her mother objected to most of her plans. The two of them never got along, so having her youngest daughter out of the house should have made her mom happy, but it hadn't.

In the year 1200, Västervik was located deep in an inlet of the Baltic Sea called Old Bay. Two centuries later, in order to make maritime traffic and commerce easier, King Erik of Pommern had ordered the town to move further out, closer to where the Bay and the Baltic Sea meet. Despite being burned to the ground by the Danes in 1667, the town rebuilt and prospered, reaching its high point in the 1800s, when it became one of Sweden's leading seaports. When the era of the clipper ships ended, Västervik lost its prominence and turned back to being a sleepy little town.

Lately, however, tourists had discovered the area's beautiful archipelago. Travel magazines referred to Västervik as the pearl of Sweden's east coast.

When Birgit was growing up, foreign visitors to Sweden were rare. She and her father joked about a stop they'd made to the country store many years before. The shop, the only one of its kind on the island, was crammed with goods—mostly fishing gear, garden tools, and camping and boat supplies. Boots and nets hung from the ceiling. A pleasant smell of canvas, rubber, and kerosene met customers as they walked in. To Birgit, that scent was the scent of the island.

Mr. Thorner, the store's owner, a short, middle-aged man with thinning hair, was involved in a transaction with her father when he became flustered. Red spots showed up on his cheeks. "Two Danes are in the store," he whispered excitedly, "and they are speaking Danish."

Her father had chuckled. "Makes sense," he said. "That two Danes would speak Danish, I mean." Seeing that the store owner was unable to concentrate, he added, "Sven, go ahead and take care of your international customers. I can wait."

Mr. Thoren had flashed a grateful smile and walked off in a hurry. Dad had winked at Birgit and said, "Girl, seems we've entered the big world now."

Now, visitors from other countries were no longer a rarity. Quite a few yachts, with foreign flags, docked in the harbor. People who didn't mind roughing it put up their tents on the camping ground near the beach.

Swedes' anticipation of the summer season was spiritual in nature. They dreamed, wrote, and sang about those short summer months. How could one forget boat trips to the outer islands on mornings when the water lay still in silent obedience? Who wouldn't be enchanted by the "white" summer nights, so full of fragrance and light that the thought of sleep never enters the mind?

Of course, more often than not, the summer rained away or the days were too cold to enjoy, but when right, it was achingly beautiful. The rainy weeks and the nasty wind blowing in from the sea were things you just put up with. But why not talk about the good times instead? How about the summer of '56 for instance, when the temperature equaled Africa's? And hadn't '59 been another scorcher?

The tourists didn't care about what "used to be." With long faces, they listened to the weather reports on crackling transistor radios. "Outlook for tomorrow. Low pressure is moving in over the Baltic. Increased cloudiness, rain likely, at times heavy. Cold…."

Wimps. That's what the residents called the ones who, after weeks of rain, packed up their damp tents and left. "You have to take the good with the bad," they muttered defensively. "Last summer the sun was out every damn day."

§

Birgit had begun dating Bengt Lindgren in the spring of the past year. Bengt was a year older and had dated a sister of one of Birgit's friends. They had known each other since high school but had never really talked. She remembered him once holding the door for her at the school entrance. She had liked the way he had done it—gentlemanly, no flip remarks, just a polite smile.

And, he'd played hockey for the high school team. Once, when Birgit watched a match, he had assisted on two goals. Not the best or the fastest, but he played a smart game and was precise with passes. To set a teammate up for a score seemed to please him almost as much as scoring himself.

She hadn't seen Bengt since high school, but they would meet again, by chance, at the track. Arriving for a jog one April morning, Birgit had found the place almost deserted. A youth soccer team, done with practice, gathered up balls in a large mesh bag. On the track, a lonely figure circled the oval, running with an easy stride.

She recognized Bengt the moment he came around the bend. His shirt was soaked—it was obvious he had been running for a while. As he got closer to where Birgit stood, he slowed down, checked his stopwatch, and then headed in her direction. Birgit ignored him, finished her stretching exercises, and removed her warm-up pants. Not breathing hard at all, Bengt had paused in front of her and given her long legs a quick, approving look.

"Five miles," he said, reading her mind. "Care to do a few laps with me?"

Birgit glanced up at him. He had an engaging smile, though one of his front teeth was chipped—probably from playing hockey. His hair was reddish blonde, and he stood maybe a couple of inches taller than Birgit's five feet, six inches—not tall for a Swede, but sturdy and athletic. When he spoke, he looked directly at her eyes. She'd noticed *his* eyes were gray and calm.

They ran around the track in comfortable silence. Even so, Birgit learned a few things about Bengt. He was easy to be with, straightforward, smart, and seemed to have no hidden agenda. "He's just nice to be around," her mother would say later. High praise from Vera Svenson, who didn't approve of many people.

As they ended the run, Bengt stopped and turned toward her. "Any plans for Valporice Day?" he asked. "I'm taking a boat ride to Gamleby to watch the bonfire on the mountain. Like to come?"

Birgit had no plans she couldn't change, so she decided to say yes.

Valporice Day is celebrated on the 30th of April and marks the beginning of spring in Sweden. Choirs sing and bonfires are lit, supposedly to drive out evil spirits, an ancient tradition from pagan times.

"Bundle up," Bengt told her, and luckily, she had followed his advice. The wind, coming from the east, brought a heavy dose of winter.

His old wooden motor boat handled the waves well and they arrived earlier than planned. "She is a dependable little thing," Bengt said, stroking the side of the boat affectionately. "I bought her second hand, but she was built over there." He nodded at a large building on the shoreline. "That's Tore Holm's shipyard. That man makes some of the finest boats in the world."

"Really?" Birgit wondered why someone with that kind of reputation would live in a small village like Gamleby, but she didn't doubt Bengt's words. He struck her as the kind of person who wouldn't speak unless he had the facts.

Bengt nodded. "Tore's boats—especially his sailboats—are world famous. It's a shame that so many of his finest sea crafts end up abroad." He tied the boat and helped Birgit up on the dock. "The guy won two gold medals in Olympic sailing, Antwerp 1920 and Los Angeles 1932. Don't think he's much of a businessman, though. More interested in building something beautiful than making money, I've heard."

Birgit shook her head. If you build the best, they should pay you accordingly! Holm, having seen the world, had still chosen to live here. So had her father who, once a sailor, had also settled in the area. Birgit did not understand their reasoning but kept her mouth shut. Instinctively, she knew that the boat builder, her dad, and Bengt were kindred spirits.

§

Just before the lighting of the bonfire, a student choir moved to a podium at the square. The songs they sang were traditional, sung for generations, professing the Swedes' love of nature and the beauty surrounding them. They sang optimistically about the arrival of spring.

Standing next to Birgit, Bengt mouthed the words to the songs. He caught her looking at him, and smiled self-consciously. "What?"

She smiled. "Nothing, You're kind of sweet, that's all…"

After the singing, people mingled for a while, catching up with friends and neighbors. Older folks and families with small children stayed down in the square to watch the bonfire, while the younger crowd headed for the mountain for a better view.

A winding trail led to the top portion where the lighting of the fire would take place. Bengt grabbed Birgit's hand firmly, leading the way, making sure she didn't stumble and protecting her from thorny bushes on the way up.

Within minutes, a roar went up from the mountain. The bonfire was ablaze. Bengt pointed to the plateau where the fire was burning. "See how smooth the rocks are here? I bet this whole area was under water at one time."

Birgit looked at the rocks and saw several giant boulders. A huge one with a flat top was surrounded by four smaller rocks. *Maybe once an eating area?* "Where do you think *these* came from?" she asked.

"Not sure," answered Bengt. "This formation might have been here since the Ice Age. Blows your mind to think of all the people who might've sat here—Vikings, pagans, robber barons. See the opening over there?"

Birgit followed Bengt's eyes to the side of the mountain.

"That's the entrance to a cave," he continued. "There was a tunnel once going all the way to the other side of the mountain, but it collapsed. You can still walk inside. I have a flashlight…"

"No, thank you!" Birgit was usually fearless, but the thought of entering a dark cave didn't appeal to her. "I'm more of a sea and sky kind of person," she said, regretting the words as soon as they came out of her mouth. Who talks like that? I sound uptight and stuffy.

Bengt watched with amusement as she turned and stepped away from the fire with her head held high. "My lady, did you lose your tiara?" He was right behind her, teasing her, putting his arms around her.

Birgit smiled and leaned up against him, relaxing. "I'm afraid it fell over the cliff. Would you mind retrieving it?"

On the water below, flaming rafts lit up the sky and a group of teenagers broke the spell with loud chants. They had gathered on the ground and, based on the beer bottles lined up in front of them, they were far from sober.

A strikingly handsome boy, dressed in faded khaki pants and a black sweater, stood up. A bit unsteady, he held a tree branch in one hand. Moving his feet around for balance, he dipped the end of the branch into the fire, waited until it burst into flame, and then raised the torch to the sky. Cat calls, whistles, and claps erupted from his friends.

With his left hand, the boy searched his pocket and pulled out a wrinkled piece of paper. Tossing back his long blond hair, he began to read. His voice was powerful, but Birgit had a hard time making out the words. The language he spoke was Swedish, but the words originated from another era—a tribute to ancient Nordic gods perhaps.

Against her will, Birgit became intrigued. The boy, grandstanding now, continued in dramatic fashion. Despite his antics, and possibly due to the setting, the words echoed powerfully against the mountain. As the reading continued, she saw a change in him, hardly perceptible at first. The boy's eyes were still shining from beer and youthful arrogance, but his tone had changed. Instead of sounding like someone in charge, he became a messenger.

The noise from his group quieted down, and suddenly, out of nowhere, a strong gust of wind ripped over the mountain. The tall pines bent and moaned in protest, the flames from the fire danced madly, but, as if in a trance, the boy continued speaking.

The moment he finished, the torch flickered and died. Looking as if he couldn't get rid of it fast enough, the boy tossed the paper in the fire, and, holding his head, sank to the ground. A friend leaned over, mumbling something, but there was no response. The group seemed suddenly sober—no comments or laughter were heard as they quietly began cleaning up, putting the empty bottles in their backpacks.

One by one, they left, with the boy who'd held the torch the last one heading down the slope.

Birgit felt Bengt's arms around her tighten. "Did you know," he whispered, "this supposedly is the time when the natural and supernatural meet. The pagans picked this date for a reason." He cleared his throat. "No wonder Christianity was such a hard sell in this part of the world."

§

It was just a first date, too early then to even think of a relationship, but what happened on that old worn mountain made an impression on Birgit. Walking back to the boat, she'd had a premonition that life was about to change…and perhaps not for the better.

One thing she knew for sure—Bengt would not be part of it. Some other lucky girl would have him. The thought made her sad.

3

Almost a month had gone by and there had still been no contact from the employment agency in Stockholm. Birgit tried to put it out of her mind, but her dream of America continued to surface—at work, while spending time with family and friends, on dates with Bengt, but mostly late at night when she was alone in her apartment. The day Birgit finally decided to put the idea to rest was the day the letter arrived.

She didn't rush to open it. First, she took the phone off the hook and brewed herself a cup of coffee. She kicked off her shoes, curled up in the apartment's only comfortable chair, and tore open the envelope.

It was brief and business-like. First came an apology for the delay, and then the important part. The Fillmores had taken their time evaluating Birgit's references and compared hers to others they had received. They'd decided that she was the best fit and were looking forward to having her join their family. Now it was up to Birgit to get in touch with the American embassy in Stockholm to get a visa, green card, and other necessary documentation.

Birgit read the letter a second time and absently wiggled her toes the way she always did when she was excited. It was overwhelming—her dream was coming true. So much to think about and plan for.

What about Bengt…and her family? She would have to tell them—but not yet. Something might change, she thought. It is better to wait.

Then she shook her head. Face it, she told herself. Nothing will change. You're just too chicken to deal with it.

§

She had some vacation time coming and would use a day or two for a visit to Stockholm. To make the trip short—and inconspicuous—she would take the early morning train, arrive in the city by afternoon, go to the American embassy, come back on the evening train, and be ready for work the following day. Another less stressful option would involve spending the night with Aunt Lola, her mom's sister, and returning home the next day. But that would start an inquisition, she thought. Lola finding out before her mother would not be good.

Birgit got along fine with her aunt, although she sometimes thought Lola to be an insufferable snob. If Birgit avoided certain subjects, she could be both fun and entertaining. For instance, Birgit's grandfather—her mother's and Lola's father—had once been a prominent businessman and part of Stockholm society, but had fallen on hard times. Lola glossed over the bad days as if they'd never happened, causing Vera to sneer when the subject of Lola and their father came up in conversation. "She skipped about ten years in the process," she would say.

Neither Birgit nor her father would comment. They both knew when the sisters were on the warpath, it was better to stay away.

By marrying a colorless heir to two umbrella factories, Lola had reclaimed the life she thought she deserved. Her husband, who had passed away some years ago, had left her with a sizable income, plus a seven-room apartment in a brownstone in Östermalm, one of the city's more upscale areas.

Birgit's mother's marriage to a fisherman from a small island off the coast had disappointed Lola. She hadn't openly disapproved, but her feelings had been well known. Birgit didn't want to add to her aunt's silent disapproval of her. "Call it au pair if you must," she could hear Lola saying, "but all you'll be is a glorified maid."

No, she thought. Involving Lola wouldn't work.

§

From past visits to Stockholm with her mother, Birgit knew her way around downtown, but "Diplomat City," the hub for the embassies, was not familiar. At "Centralen," Stockholm's railway station, she bought a map and got directions to Djurgården, the island where Diplomat City was situated.

Stockholm was, as always, delightful. Built on islands and surrounded by water, it had a crisp breezy feel. "The most beautiful capital in the world," Mom claimed. Birgit seldom agreed with her mother, but when it came to Stockholm, she did. The city was, if not the most beautiful capital in the world, certainly one of them.

Streetcar No. 7, sky-blue and noisy, rattled and shook its way toward Diplomat City. The ride was bumpy and the seats uncomfortable. At each stop, passengers bounced forward and then sharply back when the trolley started up again. Despite the rough ride, Birgit enjoyed the scenery from her window seat, She watched as the city changed, almost undetectably, from buzzing inner-city to green, unhurried tranquility.

A young man sitting a row in front of her pointed out the Nobel Park to his girlfriend and Birgit looked too. Lush and idyllic, the Park seemed the perfect place for joggers and dog walkers. She smiled at a horse with a young girl on his back trotting along on a riding path near the water. To keep pace with the trolley, the girl, smart-looking in her riding outfit, brought the horse to a gallop.

Birgit realized too late that she'd missed her stop. The directions had said to get off before Djurgården Bridge and she'd passed it. No big deal, she thought. Just a few minutes' walk back. The day was sunny, the stops were close together, and she'd thought to wear sensible low-heeled shoes.

She got off the next time the trolley came to a stop. An imposing cathedral-like stone building on the right looked vaguely familiar. And then she remembered. Of course—how could she forget? It was the Nordic Museum. The domes looked different from what she remembered—the once shiny copper roofs had turned green from verdigris.

How old had she been when she visited last? Eleven? Twelve? She wasn't sure, but she knew both her mother and Aunt Lola had been with her. After a day of sightseeing, they'd ended up at the Nordic. Mom had been pleased that her daughter preferred museums to department stores.

Lola had taken charge and guided her guests through Stockholm, ignoring the fact that her sister had also grown up in the city. At the museum, Lola had enthusiastically grabbed Birgit by the arm, pointing things out, while Mom had tagged along behind. Her occasional snorting told Birgit that she was more than a little annoyed. Lola, just as intense and energetic as her sister, had rubbed her the wrong way again.

As she always did when angry with Lola, Mom had said, "She drives me crazy! Next time we'll stay in a hotel."

Maybe it had to do with finances, thought Birgit, but as many times as

Mom had said it, they'd never booked a hotel room. Afterward, she would stay angry for a few weeks and then, out of nowhere, she and Lola would begin talking again, making plans for future get-togethers as if nothing ever happened.

Despite the two sisters' ongoing squabbles, Birgit's appetite for her favorite museum hadn't been curbed. History had been her favorite subject in school, and the Nordic Museum was a place where the country's bloody and turbulent history came to life. Constant wars, glorious victories, crushing defeats, mighty kings, weak kings, betrayal, and treachery—all was on display.

Birgit remembered moving quietly from room to room, searching for her favorite kings. She'd stopped in a room dedicated to Gustaf II Adolph. The king's clothing, his armor, and a bloody shirt were on full display; you could clearly see where the bullet that killed him had entered. "1632, the battle of Lützen," Birgit had announced. Her mother had shushed her.

In another room was a pair of muddy boots that had belonged to Sweden's warrior king, Karl XII. The young king, a master strategist, had defeated the Russians, and, in the 1700s, made his country into a great power.

Birgit had seen a statue of Karl in the King's Garden, where disrespectful seagulls took turns resting on his head. People commented that the king's outstretched arm pointed a warning eastward—toward Russia.

§

On Djurgården Bridge, three tourists leaned against the railing—a husband and wife in their forties and a teenage son. An expensive looking camera hung around the man's neck. The legs sticking out from his wrinkled shorts were knobby, pale and thin. The couple's body language suggested there had been an argument. "I bloody well know where I'm going," Birgit heard him mutter.

The wife looked unconvinced. She called out to Birgit in a high-toned British accent. "Excuse me, do you by any chance speak English?"

Birgit nodded and stopped. Her hope had been that they were American, but British would do. She welcomed an opportunity to test her language skills.

The woman continued. "You wouldn't happen to know where the English Church is? We seem to be lost."

Birgit nodded. "I know exactly where it is."

The English Church was one of the landmarks near the American embassy and she had memorized the directions. "Turn on Strandvägen; stay on that street a short distance. You'll see the church. The embassy will be right behind it."

She explained to the tourists that she was heading to the American embassy to apply for a work visa and that the English Church would be on the way. "Do you want to follow me?"

The wife gave her husband a commanding look. He reluctantly walked over and introduced himself. "Howard Brooks." He nodded in the woman's direction. "My wife Margaret and our son Will."

The boy, still slouching against the railing, looked bored. A stern look from his mother made him straighten up and he raised his hand in a half-greeting.

The mother sighed. "Teenagers."

Birgit noticed that all three of them wore heavy walking boots and had the same thin legs. "We have taken a walking tour of Scandinavia," continued the mother. "An unforgettable experience that Will, I'm afraid, wasn't quite ready for."

Mr. Brooks chuckled. "So, you're visiting the colonies, eh?"

Birgit was confused for a second. Colonies? Of course. America…once a British possession…the American Revolutionary War. She smiled politely at his joke.

Mrs. Brooks tapped her husband. "Look, love!" She pointed to the canal, where a sleek rowboat with eight young men moving the oars rhythmically, knifed through the water. "Didn't you row one of those once?"

He grinned. "I most certainly did. At Cambridge, an eternity ago." He looked back at the bridge and dug out a dog-eared guide book from the pocket. "An educational tidbit," he said, glancing at his son, who said nothing but looked uneasy.

Mr. Brooks continued, unaware. "The three-span steel bridge we just stood on was built in 1897 for the Stockholm World Fair. On the granite beams supporting it are statues of four Norse gods. Odin, Thor…"

Will sent his mother a pleading look.

Mrs. Brooks interrupted her husband. "Let's carry on, shall we? Ms. Svenson must get to the embassy. We're holding her up."

Birgit translated the Swedish street name into English. "We have to turn right on Beach Avenue."

Mr. Brooks smiled and translated it back. "Strandvägen!" She noted his Swedish pronunciation was surprisingly good.

Mrs. Brooks interrupted her husband again to talk with Birgit. "You must be quite courageous, traveling to the U.S. on your own. Doesn't it worry you with the Vietnam War and all the crime over there?"

Birgit shook her head. "Not at all. I've always wanted to see the U.S."

"Oh dear! How thoughtless of me. I didn't mean to scare you. It's just that Sweden seems like such a beautiful, safe place."

"Yes, but it is so…" Birgit searched for the right word in English but couldn't find one. "It is so small."

She felt a bit disloyal. It was one thing to rat on your country with friends, but to do it in front of foreigners was different.

Mr. Brooks pointed to a church steeple showing behind the trees. "Here it is, just like I said it would be." Again, out came the guide book and he began to read. "The English Church was moved from downtown, stone by stone. Probably to be closer to the British embassy."

Mrs. Brooks dutifully looked at the church. "Lovely, absolutely lovely." Birgit too spent a few minutes admiring the charming little church before excusing herself. "So nice meeting you," she said.

Mr. Brooks bowed. "The pleasure is ours."

Mrs. Brooks reached for Birgit's hand and gripped it firmly. "You are a delightful young woman. So wholesome. Don't let them change you."

As she walked away from the small family, Birgit thought about what Mrs. Brooks had said. Don't let them change her? She couldn't wait to be swallowed up by America—this vast new country. She wanted nothing more than to have a chance to be different, to be more than a girl from nowhere… with a boring name like Birgit.

4

The building was disappointing. The American Embassy was modern, boxy and large, but also uglier than the other embassies and villas in Diplomat City. Birgit didn't let that bother her. She was there, and that was all that mattered.

On top of the roof, the American flag waved a welcome in the breeze. Birgit had studied up on America and picked up some trivia along the way. She had learned that the flag was affectionately called "Old Glory."

It had been cool when she'd left her apartment, but the temperature had risen. The suit she'd worn was a nice, strict, navy-blue tweed, the only business-like piece of clothing she owned. The skirt was short, but not too short. Just below the knee.

She had been happy with her choice initially, but now she worried that her outfit might look fall-like warm. She stopped, searched her purse, took out her compact, opened it, and checked herself in the mirror. Did she look *eschaufferad*? She suppressed a giggle. "Eschaufferad," a word borrowed from the French, meant hot and bothered, according to her mother.

Birgit's mom and Aunt Lola were in the habit of mixing highbrow French words into their conversation and Birgit had made a conscious effort not to use them. She knew that her mother was probably out to prove that despite living in the boondocks, she was no common Svenson. In fact, she and Lola had found a family genealogy paper that said their last name—Gramse—had come from a family of Swedish nobility.

"For crying out loud," Birgit's dad had grumbled. "I guess *my* real name is Torsten von Svenson. What idiocy will the two of you come up with next?"

Birgit could feel the pantyhose digging into her waist, its lining unpleasantly moist. Pantyhose were a new and supposedly wonderful invention for women, said to be an improvement over the hated girdle. They were, but they were still uncomfortable.

A trickle of perspiration dribbled from Birgit's neck, made its way down into her bra, and settled in the cleft between her breasts. She pulled out a handkerchief from the pocket of her jacket, discreetly put it inside her blouse, and dabbed. Her actions didn't go unnoticed—a group of young demonstrators watched her from under a tree. They carried signs with anti-war and anti-American slogans. Their angry messages contradicted their peaceful appearances.

Nobody seemed terribly engaged. Birgit again marveled at her countrymen's lack of passion. To protest, to storm the barricades, doesn't come naturally to Swedes. Still, the demonstrators looked right out of central casting, she thought. Their hippie-like clothes and their long hair fit the bill, but something was wrong. They seemed more like kids dressed up for a costume party.

She felt sympathetic. Some years before, a friend had talked her into marching in a demonstration against apartheid in South Africa. She'd carried a sign that demanded a boycott of South African oranges. To protest apartheid was right, of course, but to march down the street with hundreds of strangers had made her feel foolish and terribly self-conscious.

A kid with a red bandanna wrapped around his head stood up. He looked sleepy or stoned. Birgit went out of her way to avoid him. "Peace," the kid called out to her, spreading two fingers in the well-known sign. She nodded and hurriedly opened the door to the embassy.

She was met by a receptionist with a big smile, showing lots of white teeth, who led her into a room where an embassy employee—a Mr. Jackson, the receptionist said—would interview her shortly. Would she like a glass of water, and did she need an interpreter? Birgit said, "Yes, please," to the water, but "no" to the interpreter. She could handle the questions in English without any help, or so she hoped.

The room was quiet and empty. She sat down at a table and waited. A portrait of President Lyndon Johnson hung on one wall flanked by two American flags. The president looked to Birgit like a tired old basset hound. He probably sometimes felt lonely and anxious too, she thought. The way he was thrown into the presidency, and then immediately had to cope with a terrible war...what a burden that must have been.

Birgit remembered also the outpouring of emotion after the assassination of President Kennedy. It seemed as if all of Europe had gone into mourning. Even Swedes, usually stoic, had cried on the streets. It was not so much what the man had done, her father said. It was the loss of the hope he had offered.

The door opened and a man Birgit assumed was Mr. Jackson entered the room. Slightly built, he was dressed in a dark, well-tailored suit. Appearing to be in his thirties, he looked official but not terribly important.

As she observed him, Birgit realized how insignificant she was. Fine with me, she thought. That can change.

She pushed away all her negative thoughts. Americans, she'd heard, valued confidence and optimism in people.

Mr. Jackson spoke kindly and slowly, but some of the questions he asked were strange. Did she have any plans to overthrow the American government? Did her relatives have ties to the Communist party? She was shocked, but since Mr. Jackson wasn't smiling, Birgit suppressed her feelings and, of course, said "no." If she had any such plans or Communist relatives, did he think she would tell him?

The rest of the interview went smoothly. The fact that Birgit had a sponsoring family in America helped. She swore an oath to uphold the American Constitution, and that was that. The two chatted briefly and then it was over. Relieved, Birgit shook Mr. Jackson's hand enthusiastically. Her grip was firm and she thought she saw the man wince. He wished her well in America, and then looked at his watch, said a quick goodbye and disappeared through the door.

Before she left the room, Birgit glanced once again at the portrait of Lyndon Johnson and her spirit was restored.

"Mr. President," she whispered softly, "here I come."

5

The time had come to tell her parents about her plans, so on Sunday morning, Birgit rode her bike to her childhood home on the island. Her mother slept late on weekends. She hoped she would catch her father first—talking to him would be easier. She wasn't particularly worried about her mother either. The conversation she dreaded most was with Bengt, her boyfriend. Not that he'd heap guilt on her. He didn't have to. She felt bad enough as it was.

§

The town was not yet stirring. A lone jogger looked surprised as Birgit sped by him. An emergency? In a way, it was.

At the bridge connecting the island to the mainland, she stopped to catch her breath. Down below, a fishing boat chugged its way out to sea. Most times, Birgit might've tuned out the familiar sound, but today was different. A whiff of wildflowers on the bank, pine tar from the bottom of a skiff—the sounds and smells were magnified before they squeezed her heart.

Birgit's dad sat alone on the dock, a broken net on his lap. She leaned her bike against the boathouse and soaked in the peaceful scene, wishing life to stay like this a bit longer.

Apparently hearing her coming, he turned around and waved. Birgit waved back. She sat down on the dock next to him and looked at his gnarled hands. One held a gray enamel coffee cup that his family, unsuccessfully, had tried to replace over the years. "That nasty old thing must go," Mom had said, but even she had known that some things are better left alone.

He saw Birgit eye the mug. "Just made a fresh pot. Want some?"

"Thanks…maybe later. I was just looking at the mug…"

He swirled the coffee around. "What about it? It's a bit dented perhaps, but perfectly fine."

"So what happened to the striped one we gave you for Father's Day and the one with the funny handle Mom surprised you with on your birthday…"

"Haven't the slightest idea…"

Birgit grinned. "Sure, you don't!"

She loosened the laces of her sneakers, bared her feet, and lowered them into the water. The splash disturbed the minnows circling around the dock—sleek, elongated forms darkened the surface and sudden flashes of silver exploded out of the water.

As a child, she'd liked fishing. To use minnows as bait, to thread the hook through their tiny squirming bodies had made her squeamish at first. Later, as she'd became more callous, the minnows no longer mattered. Her desire to hook the "big one" overshadowed any compassion she might have felt.

The "big one" was seldom that, and her dad had ordered her to throw the first fish she'd caught back in the water. "Bad sportsmanship to keep something that tiny," he had said.

Birgit had stomped her feet and thrown a tantrum. A visit to the boathouse had cooled her off.

They sat in silence until her father spoke. "You didn't come out this early in the morning just to chat. What's up?"

When she told him, he looked out over the water. "Will I see you again?" he asked softly. Birgit knew that if her mother had asked the same question, her tone would have been different—accusatory. Dad's wasn't at all, but his response bothered her just the same.

"Of course," she said. "I'll be back within a year."

Her father nodded. "That's what they all say."

"How do you know? You never had anybody leave!"

He glanced at Birgit and smiled. "Sure did."

"When? Who? How old were you?"

"It was ages ago. I was only eighteen, but don't belittle puppy love. Your feelings in these years are as strong as they'll ever be." He paused again. "Her name was Emma. She went to visit an uncle in America and never came back."

"You loved her?"

"Thought I did. When I found out that she was leaving, I thought my life was over. Drove the motorboat straight out to sea until I ran out of gas. Your uncle Nils chased after me in his boat. The wind was blowing like crazy that day. Nils yelled, 'Either you'll let me tow you back or I'll jump aboard and beat the shit out of you.'

"I remember acting crazy, crying and swearing, but somehow Nils got me home. Your mother never knew."

"But she had boyfriends, didn't she?

"Yep, but she made it clear that her past was out of bounds. None of my business."

"And yours?"

He chuckled. "Well, now, that's a different story. If Vera knew, I'd never hear the end of it."

Birgit leaned back on her hands. "Is she up yet?"

"Probably." He stood up and reached for his daughter's hand. "Be ready for some fireworks."

Birgit waited in the kitchen as Dad poured himself a second cup of coffee. The lines on his face suddenly seemed more pronounced. Maybe it was just the early morning light.

Again, there it was, this new keen observance, this focused attention on things she seldom noticed. Why was she staring at everyday objects as if she would never see them again? The geraniums, so well-tended by her mother, blooming in clay pots on the window sill—no dead flowers, not even a crumbled leaf. An old copper pot hanging on a hook near the stove—useless, but decorative. A blue and white tablecloth ironed to perfection...

The grandfather clock in the parlor struck nine and Birgit's mother wandered into the room. She wore her silky pink robe, a gift from her sister. A sticker from the Nordic Company, Stockholm's finest department store, was still attached. A lone roller hung from her hair. Seeing it dangle, Birgit felt a wave of tenderness surge through her. It was short-lived, however. Sensing that something in her appearance wasn't right, her mother reached up, annoyed, and snatched the roller from her hair.

Birgit felt the warmth drain out of her.

She wanted her mother to understand her reasons for leaving, but the words didn't come out right. It was not until she mentioned Bengt that Vera Svenson even flinched.

Birgit felt the old resentment bubble up. Her mother was more concerned about someone else, a young man she'd just known for a short time. The fact that she was leaving wasn't important.

The anger felt good—it wiped out the guilt from before. She started to accuse her mother of not caring, but she felt her dad's hand on her shoulder. "Birgit…" If the warning tone in his voice hadn't stopped her, the look in her mother's eyes would have.

Birgit once again felt a peculiar sensation of seeing things more clearly. What she'd seen in her mother's eyes wasn't anger or rejection—it was hurt and bewilderment. It all made sense. Bengt was the son-in-law Mom desperately wanted for her. He would've kept her home, close to her family, and given her a good, stable life.

Her sister Ruth, on the other hand, had made two serious mistakes: having sex at an early age, resulting in a pregnancy at seventeen, and choosing the wrong man to father the baby.

Arne's father owned a Saab dealership in town, so money wasn't an issue, but he was a bore—loud, opinionated and prone to drink too much. Not husband material and not a good influence on Ruth's son, Gunnar.

In her mother's mind, Arne was a failure. Bengt was not. Bengt's easy way and sense of humor had instantly won her over. For her birthday, he'd called in a request to her favorite radio program. The family—in on the secret—held off the celebration so she would listen to her show. Then, at the very end, the host had gushed, "This last request comes from Bengt to Vera Svenson on Händelop Island. Are you ready to swing, Vera? This one is for you!"

She had let out a scream of pure joy as Bengt waltzed over, took her in his arms, and danced around the room. Her eyes had sparkled and the smile never left her face.

Now, again, Birgit would disappoint her. No blond or redheaded grand-children would dive from the dock or eat Grandma's home-baked cookies. Vera loved her grandson Gunnar, but he was too much like her—he didn't fit in and had trouble making friends.

A fly buzzed around in the kitchen and landed on the table. Instead of jumping up to locate a flyswatter, Birgit's mother absentmindedly shooed it away. Her voice was flat. "When do you leave?"

"Three weeks…"

Birgit heard herself begin to babble. "I have given notice at the hospital, and Karin is taking over the lease to the apartment. You remember her, right? A tall girl with glasses—"

"And when will you tell Bengt?"

Birgit looked away. "Next weekend. He and his brother are away fishing and won't be back until then."

Her mom fingered the tablecloth, swallowed hard, and started to speak but changed her mind. Birgit stood and awkwardly put her arms around her—unfamiliar territory for both. Her mother tilted her head slightly, just enough that her cheek touched Birgit's arm.

It isn't much, thought Birgit. But it was something.

6

"Catch!" The line from the mooring flew down. Birgit snatched it in the air and rolled it up. Agile as a cat, Bengt leaped from the dock and landed on the boat deck with a light thud. "Couldn't ask for a better day."

Bengt's expression was one of satisfaction, as if the glittery water and the cloudless blue sky had been ordered and delivered by him. Illogically, Birgit had hoped for rain—bad news and lousy weather fit together, she thought.

She curled up on the seat, pulled her knees up to her chest, and hid behind her sunglasses, while Bengt busied himself with checking the engine. Everything seemed in order. There were no hacking noises, as the well-tuned motor turned over on the first try. Bengt rose up, a little-boy grin showing on his face.

Birgit looked on amused. At times like this, she felt nothing but love for him. Even when his lips didn't smile, his eyes did. To be serious was a challenge for him. The brilliant silvery flecks in his eyes never stopped dancing. He wasn't movie-star handsome but didn't need to be. Once Birgit was gone, the girls would start to line up. *Why did that thought bother her so?*

Bengt shouted over the noise of the engine. "We're heading to Last Island today. Okay?" The island was the farthest one away in Västervik's archipelago. After that, as far as the eyes could see, were just water and sky. On the nautical chart, the name "Last Island" didn't exist. Bengt had made it up. It's official name was Bussan, but as far as Bengt was concerned, that moniker had no ring to it.

Bengt's whole family was just like him—likable, happy-go-lucky people. The Lindgrens' owned the largest, best-run, busiest hardware store in the area—a true goldmine. If the item you were looking for was out of stock, they found ways to locate it for you. "Salt of the earth, backbone of the country" were expressions used to describe them. They all saw themselves as ordinary, but they demonstrated qualities that the town folks admired: kindness, contentment, and decency.

Bengt's dad—tall, lanky, and good-natured—was a strict disciplinarian when it came to his sons. Jan, his older son, was a taller copy of Bengt, with the same pleasant disposition. Their mother, with her mop of frizzy red hair, was a Swedish version of Raggedy Anne. Bengt had inherited her coloring. His hair, with its reddish hue, didn't bother him, but his failure to tan was a source of frustration. He openly and unapologetically envied the way Birgit's skin darkened to a gingerbread brown in the summer.

Halfway out in the bay, Bengt changed the route, and instead of going straight out to sea, he headed to the other side, where vacation homes dotted the shoreline. "Let's check out the cottages," he shouted. "Someday, we'll own one of those."

Birgit pretended she hadn't heard. He'd said "we" without hesitation and she wasn't ready to destroy his certainty. She nodded and managed a weak smile in response, but guilt clawed at her stomach.

Owning a summer home—or at least a summer *cottage*—was a dream that most Swedes shared. It didn't have to be anything fancy—getting hold of one of the little timbered cottages called "torps" was enough. "Torps" were once given to retired soldiers as thanks for their loyal service to the Crown.

Typically, the small cottages remained red as tradition required, with corners and windows trimmed in white. They were quaint fixer-uppers and highly sought after. If you had a dock, a few knotted apple trees, and maybe a lilac bush or two, the value was enhanced. People bought charm and nostalgia, not comfort.

To "rough it" in the summer was something people did regardless of income. Embracing adversity was an appreciated trait and many lawyers and doctors who easily could afford better bought the cottages and gladly lugged water and spent their summer months without electricity. A certain stigma was attached to owning a vacation house with too many creature comforts.

As soon as one moved in, the custom was to raise the flag and keep it up every day. Foreigners watching the sea of blue and yellow flags wondered if there was a special celebration or holiday. But Swedes didn't need a special occasion to raise the flag. It was something you did out of habit and national pride. "Patriotism shouldn't be a lot of fanfare," Birgit's dad had once said. "It should be a gentle song within your soul." His speech was seldom emotional or flowery but after a *schnapps* or two, the romantic side of him showed up.

Bengt abruptly changed direction and turned the boat away from the shoreline. There was no more mention of the cottages. *Perhaps he had sensed her apprehension.*

The wind picked up as they headed out to the open sea, leaving the sheltered bay behind. Grayish waves topped with whitecaps rhythmically rose and sank, gaining strength on every roll. Gulls and sea-swallows followed for a while in the boat's wake. Further out, the birds slowed down, altered their courses, and returned to the safety of the bay.

Birgit closed her eyes and let the sweet clean air rush over her. Telling Bengt was inevitable. She had practiced the words for weeks. But for now they were gone, swept away, her head blank.

The boat made a sudden turn, tipping sharply, the railing almost level with the water line. Water splashed over the side, and Birgit was instantly soaked. She opened her eyes and stared at Bengt and he laughed happily. "Just checking that you're awake."

She sat up and looked at the navigation chart. Bengt had handed it to her before they left, but Birgit knew it was only a formality. He knew this part of the Baltic Sea like the back of his hand.

On the starboard side, the lighthouse seemed to appear out of nowhere, water crashing against its base. There were plenty of dangerous shoals in the surrounding area, but Birgit always felt a dark sense of foreboding when they approached this particular spot. Bengt gave her a reassuring smile—he was back to being all business now. No more joking around.

The island consisted mostly of smooth flat rocks. No vegetation, except for a few windblown bushes fighting to stay alive in the crevices. Wind was a problem and finding a sheltered area on the island was a challenge to most. But not to Bengt.

Birgit couldn't help but be impressed with his efficiency. He turned off the engine and coasted in, maneuvering between the rocks with a boat hook. Before throwing in the anchor, he hung buoys over the sides of the boat to protect it. It was probably an unnecessary precaution—they were nowhere near the rocks.

Once the boat was secured, Bengt put a blanket, a transistor radio, a thermos and two mugs in a large canvas bag, and then stripped down to the swim trunks he wore under his shorts. He swung himself over the railing, grabbed the bag from the seat, and waited for Birgit in the waist-high water. "Bring what you need, okay!"

"You go ahead," she said. "I'll just change into my bathing suit."

The yellow polka-dot bikini she'd just bought was in the cabin. The frivolous purchase was so not her. Nothing had been wrong with her old bathing suit, but three days in a row she'd passed the store window hoping the bikini was there. "Only a fool would spend a large amount of money on something so small and skimpy," she'd told her friend and shopping companion, Karin.

Karin read her friend the way only another woman can. "It doesn't hurt to try it on."

Once she'd donned the suit, Birgit opened the door to the fitting room. "How do I look?" The question was rhetorical. The bikini looked sensational on her, and she knew it.

"Wow," said Karin. "I bet Bengt will go gaga when he sees you in *this* one."

Birgit had laughed off the remark, but now, as she slid into the water, it crossed her mind that maybe this was not the best time to be sexy. She caught her breath—the water was shockingly cold but clear. She walked gingerly—kelp and sea grass made some of the rocks slippery and others covered with barnacle hurt her feet.

Bengt, already on the shore, had spread out a blanket and turned on the radio. The volume was low—he knew Birgit hated music blaring outside. When she was almost to land, her feet slipped under her, and she yelped as she slid down between the rocks. He was at her side immediately.

"Can I be of assistance?" he said, with a twinkle in his eye, but she wasn't in the mood for bantering. One of her feet was stuck between the rocks.

Bengt knelt and gently freed her. "Steady now?"

She carefully stood up. "Yes, I'm okay."

Bengt held her close and didn't let go. His eyes burned with a deep, dark wanting as his hands slipped underneath the clasps of her top and loosened them. Instinctively, Birgit tried to cover her breasts, but Bengt held her arms down. "Don't do that," he whispered. "They are beautiful."

Birgit disagreed—it was in vogue to be flat-chested à la the fashion model Twiggy. "They are too big," she mumbled.

Not taking his eyes off her, Bengt shook his head. "Who wants to make love to a beanpole? Not me. I like a full-bodied woman."

"Well, you haven't made love to me yet."

"No, but I'm going to." Bengt's voice was calm, all playfulness gone. He touched her breasts tenderly, without urgency, as if he had all the time in the world. Birgit let her body respond to the touch, ignoring the warning bells in her head. Soon the only sounds came from the waves and her own beating heart. *How could something so wrong feel so right?*

Up until now, she had resisted making love to him, but not because of religious or moral reasons. To do "everything but" made one a fake in Birgit's opinion. She saw no virtue in that at all. She wasn't at all sure why, but suspected it had to do with Ruth's getting pregnant and "stuck," or perhaps an unconscious fear of commitment. If her friends had known, they'd have rolled their eyes. It was, after all, the era of "*free love.*"

Fortunately, Bengt hadn't pressured her. Well, sometimes a little bit, but he had always been respectful of her feelings.

On the blue blanket he kept in the cabin of his boat, which smelled of sea and summer, he made love to her in the same way he did everything else—unhurried and competently—while seagulls screeched overhead.

Afterward, Birgit lay silently, just being, for once—no thoughts, just staying in the moment.

And then she told him.

She watched as the light in his eyes went out and tears ran down her cheeks. On the radio, Sinatra sang, *"The summer wind came blowing in from across the sea…"* After that day, she would never listen to the song again.

7

Birgit's father didn't persist when she declined his offer to drive her to Arlanda, Stockholm's international airport. One of her father's best qualities, she thought, was that he left things alone, did not probe or pressure. He too understood that no matter how painful it was, the time had come to cut the cord. Besides, his old Volvo truck, with a zillion miles of wear and tear was still dependable, but even "Ol' Faithful" had a lease on life.

The emotional turmoil was over. Birgit had said goodbye to the people that mattered. Her feelings, at least for now, were neatly tucked away—her ability to do that amazed her. What was left now were the mundane aspects of travel—loading her suitcase, deciding what should go in a carry-on, checking and rechecking to make sure nothing important was missed.

She'd ruled out flying. It was too expensive, and the tiny eight-seat commuter plane to the capital didn't fill her with confidence. Her remaining options were to either travel by bus or by train. The train ride was prettier, with a long section of the journey snaking through the coastal area, but the changeover in Linköping meant having to drag her luggage from one train to another. The bus was usually cramped and the ride bumpier, but it was a direct connection. Once Birgit weighed her suitcase on the bathroom scale, the choice was easy. It had to be the bus.

Tomorrow, she was leaving Stockholm and flying Scandinavian Airlines to New York, where the Fillmores would meet her outside the baggage claim. Her plane would not take off until noon, but since she had to be at the airport a couple of hours before departure, she had no choice but to spend the night in Stockholm. Aunt Lola was away at a spa in Ischia, Italy for treatment of her arthritis, but she'd said that Birgit was more than welcome to use her apartment.

The "goodbye" meeting with Ruth had gone as expected—no better, no worse. There was not much love coming Birgit's way, but at least her sister had kept her negative comments to a minimum. Later on, no doubt, she and their mother would get on the phone to pick apart Birgit's decision.

Birgit and Ruth had met for afternoon coffee and pastry at Café Unique on Main Street, a place they both enjoyed. Two dotty sisters named Doris and Eva had bought the café years ago and changed the interior and the ambiance to suit their eccentric tastes. Initially, the town people had smirked behind their backs, proclaiming that it would never work. However, twenty years later the sisters were the ones laughing—all the way to the bank. They were thought to be slightly mad, and possibly were, but their place had a certain quirky allure that was hard to resist.

The Cafe was a jungle, crowded with exotic plants, stuffed animals and a few live ones too. A parrot in a cage delighted the customers by crying out, "Doris, pick up!" in a hoarse, urgent voice each time the phone rang.

Mirrors and art—some religious, some of a darker nature—covered the walls. The old sisters dressed in turn-of-the-century clothing and served coffee in small antique cups and delicious pastries on gold-rimmed plates.

Ruth had seemed rushed, as usual, her dark hair teased and sprayed into a stiff glossy helmet. How much she takes after Mom, Birgit thought. There was the same energy, yet something was amiss the way even the best-made copy never quite measures up to the original.

The meeting was strictly a courtesy, as the two seldom had much to say to each other. Birgit asked questions about Gunnar, who was away at camp. Despite the rocky relationship between the sisters, Birgit had always been close to her nephew. Arne, her brother-in-law, was a different story and Birgit avoided the subject. The lines in her sister's face were telling; her marriage was on shaky grounds.

Ruth had also offered to drive her to Stockholm, but Birgit knew that her sister didn't like to drive long distances, which meant that Arne would be at the wheel. That thought made her cringe. To hear them argue all the way up was not a pleasant thought, but she really didn't have to worry. Although the offer was made with a polite smile, Ruth's eyes told a different story. Birgit returned the favor and cordially turned down the offer, giving her sister the chance to act offended, a role she liked.

Conversation stalled as usual. To pump some life into the conversation, Birgit brought up her upcoming trip. Ruth asked no questions, but sat straight and silent across the table, a well-rehearsed smile plastered on her lips. Birgit knew her too well to be fooled—in her sister's eyes, she saw regret and naked envy.

§

Dark clouds and heaviness in the air telegraphed the coming rain. Birgit had packed her jacket hoping the rain would hold off until she was inside the bus. She checked her watch. There would be another fifteen-minute wait. By being early, she hoped she would have a chance for a window seat. A few people with the same idea started showing up.

A group of teenagers made their presence known. Pencil-thin little girls giggled, chomped away at their gum, and pretended to ignore the two boys riding their bikes around. They weren't travelers, but the bus stop was a good place to hang out. Thirteen tops, Birgit thought, almost babies, but still old enough to play the pick-up game.

Doing wheelies to show off, one boy circled the assembled luggage. His friend tried the same trick, but without the same skill crashed to the ground, letting out a stream of profanities. Two middle-aged women in line behind Birgit spoke in unison. "Brats!" They maintained a few seconds of outraged silence before resuming their gossip about a neighbor's alleged infidelity.

"Bonjour tristesse!" Birgit's Francophile mother might have said. *Hello, sadness.* Birgit smiled to herself, grateful to be leaving. Small town boredom was something she couldn't wait to escape.

When the bus pulled in, Birgit was first in line. The door opened, and the big, burly driver leisurely made his way down the steps. He motioned for her to let go of her suitcase. Country-strong, he effortlessly picked it up, grabbed another woman's luggage with his other hand, took them both to the back of the bus, opened the hatch, and loaded them inside.

A light drizzle turned into a steady downpour, and Birgit was glad to get inside. She picked a window seat in the middle of the bus, sat down, and watched the rain streak through the dirt on the glass. Most passengers had family or friends waving goodbye.

Birgit, who had not wanted anyone to see her off, suddenly felt a pang of loneliness. She picked up a book and made an effort to read. After reading the same page twice, she put down the book and closed her eyes.

Her dad had asked what time her plane was leaving. She knew that at noon the next day he would stop wherever he was, whatever he was doing, and look up at the sky. Because he wasn't a churchgoer, Birgit wasn't sure that her father ever prayed, but tomorrow, she thought, he would. Tomorrow, her father would ask God to take care of his little girl.

The bus doors closed with squeaky finality. She opened her eyes and looked out the window, hoping against all odds that Bengt would be there. She pressed her nose against the glass, willing him to appear, but all of the faces looking back at her belonged to strangers. The rain increased and the small crowd outside dispersed, heading for shelter. Moments later, the depot was empty. "Have a good life, Bengt," she whispered.

She leaned back in the seat and turned to the next page in the book.

8

Birgit couldn't decide whether she had slept or just dozed during the flight. The cabin, a sleeping animal a few minutes before, was waking up and people slowly began to reclaim their space. In the front row, a baby cried and, as if on cue, the passengers began to stir. They yawned, stretched, and smiled sheepishly at people they'd accidentally bumped into during the night.

We must be getting close. Birgit checked her watch but realized that the time shown was wrong. *Six hours back, or six hours forward?* As if he had heard her, the captain's chipper voice came over the loudspeaker, reminding passengers first in Swedish and then in English to set their clocks back. He continued the announcement to say that the weather in the New York area was clear and that no delay was expected. Arrival would be in approximately an hour and a half and the flight attendants would come around shortly to deliver forms that had to be filled out before entering the United States.

The baby's cry rose a few decibels—from a soft whimper to a persistent scream. "I wish I had lungs like that," said the elderly lady sitting next to Birgit. From the southern part of Sweden, she was visiting her granddaughter in the U.S.A. for the first time. Her knowledge of English was minimal, so Birgit help her fill out the entry form.

When they reached the section about fruits and plants and the fact that they were not to be brought into the United States, Birgit panicked. What happened to the banana she'd purchased at the airport? Had she finished it? She stood up and pulled her carry-on down from the overhead. Sure enough, the banana was still there. With a couple of quick bites, it was gone.

The voice of a young man boomed from across the aisle. "Good girl!" A bit of a "know it all," he had flirted with Birgit on and off during the trip. He spoke with the certainty of a world traveler, but his English had an unmistakable Stockholm accent. "Americans act relaxed, but they go ape over the smallest things," he said.

Birgit gave him a curt nod, leaned back in the seat, and closed her eyes. Her sleep the night before had been fitful. Aunt Lola had told her to make herself at home, but it hadn't happened. To visit with her aunt present was one thing; to be there alone was another. The large brownstone corner apartment with its high windows, elaborate moldings, and tall ceilings had seemed eerily quiet.

Most of the tenants in the building must have been away on summer vacation because when Birgit entered the foyer and walked toward the elevator, the only sound she heard was the echo of her footsteps against the marble floor.

The elevator was tinier than she remembered. She managed to shut the antique brass door only by stacking her pieces of luggage on top of each other. Her aunt had told her that the tenants had wanted to replace "this piece of nostalgia" with a more up-to-date elevator, but a proposal to modernize had been voted down. Money was not the issue—in this part of the city, appearances often trumped comfort. Birgit pressed the button, and, with a dignified rattle, the elevator labored its way to the third floor.

On a small table in the hallway, Lola had left a monogrammed envelope dotted with a hint of her favorite fragrance. Inside were an encouraging note, a few instructions, and fifty American dollars. Birgit smiled. Her aunt was self-absorbed, as her mother had always been quick to note, but she was also generous and thoughtful. That she had gone to the trouble to exchange Swedish crowns for dollar bills for her was touching.

Birgit felt a pang of homesickness. "You still have options," said a little voice in her head but, of course, she didn't really. What could she do? Not get on the plane? Take the bus back? Never! It was just a case of cold feet.

In a weak moment, she had thought of calling her family, but had decided another goodbye would only make it harder on everybody. Sleep in any bedroom you want, Aunt Lola had written, but Birgit picked the smallest one and falling asleep had proven to be impossible. Tossing and turning until midnight, she'd finally gotten out of bed and gone to the kitchen.

She sat with a cup of tea and gazed out the window. Dim streetlights lit the park below. A young couple, arms around each other, sat on the ledge in front of a fountain. Birgit watched them for a while and then returned to bed.

Then, the noise from garbage trucks on the street had woken her at dawn. It had been too early to leave for the airport, but she had decided to do it anyway—the silence of the apartment had started to unnerve her. She'd straightened up, written a thank you note, made sure the gas to the stove was turned off, and returned the apartment key to the superintendent.

As she stepped out onto the street, the invigorating morning air mysteriously managed to sweep away all of Birgit's negative feelings. By the time her bus arrived at the airport, her anxiety was gone and her excitement had returned.

The overhead speaker crackled and a stewardess spoke. "Fasten your seatbelts. We'll be landing in just a few minutes." Birgit turned to her travel companion and smiled.

The elderly woman looked worried. "What if my granddaughter isn't there?"

Birgit patted the old lady's arm. "She'll be there. Bet she has been looking forward to this moment as much as you have."

The whole terminal vibrated. Birgit had expected it to be different, but not this much. By comparison, Arlanda Airport in Stockholm seemed quaint, small, and sane—JFK was anything but. Birgit took it all in—the sounds, the smell, the energy. Never in her life had she seen so many different people or heard so many languages.

She gripped her customs forms firmly as the crowd pushed forward. A big-bosomed black lady in uniform yelled for her to step back behind the yellow lines. "Airport Nazi," the young Stockholmer behind her muttered. "See what happens when little people get authority?"

Birgit clenched her teeth. He had sneaked up on her again. She didn't want to be seen with him when she met the Fillmores and scoured her mind for ways to get rid of him. With a hopeful smile, he continued. "Are you staying in the Big Apple? I'll give you a tour."

Fortunately, Birgit was next in line at the pass control. Whisked through quickly, she hurried to the baggage claim. She hoped her old suitcase, not so lovely to begin with, had not taken a beating. She was relieved when it finally appeared on the luggage belt, but disturbed to see a large rip in one of the corners.

Her first attempt to pull the suitcase from the belt failed. When it came around the second time, someone lifted it off for her. The annoying young man had shown up again. "You need brute strength to handle that baby!" He put down the suitcase and leaned over to check the nametag.

"Birgit Svenson? From Västervik! What's a little girl from the sticks doing all by herself in the US of A?" Birgit gave him a look that could kill. Willing herself to make it look easy, she grabbed hold of her luggage and hurried off toward customs.

The tear in her suitcase upset her. So did her wrinkled dress. The dress had seemed perfect for travel but had not held up as well as she'd hoped. The wrinkles weren't the only problem—she'd also managed to put a spot on it during the flight. Rubbing it with soda water hadn't helped. It was still there—quite noticeable—right above the belt.

Her head was spinning. The long trip, the lack of sleep, the stress of the last couple of months hit her all at once. How in the world would she be able to speak intelligently in English?

In what seemed an eternity, Birgit was through customs and out to the waiting area where a sea of people had gathered. In the crowd, she caught a glimpse of the elderly lady she'd met on the plane. The woman was too busy laughing and hugging her granddaughter to notice Birgit's wave.

She turned back to see two people approaching—a blond man and a dark-haired little girl. The man's stride was purposeful. He had already guessed her identity. "Brigitte Svenson, I presume. I am Brad Fillmore."

His voice was an attractive baritone, his smile pleasant, and his teeth perfectly white. He appeared to be in his mid-thirties. Birgit had pictured him as older. Above average height, trim and athletic looking, face tanned, from golf or sailing, Birgit guessed, or maybe both. A straight nose, hazel eyes, a dimple in his chin. Movie-star handsome in tan slacks with no wrinkles, he wore a casual but expensive-looking striped shirt. In contrast, Birgit realized how crumpled she must look.

The little girl scolded her father. "Dad! You said her name wrong. It's *Bir-git*, not Brigitte."

The man shrugged. "Sorry. To an English-speaking person Brigitte flows a bit easier…"

"Oh, it's fine. Many of my friends call me Brigitte. Actually, I prefer that name…"

Birgit was surprised at how easily she lied. Nobody in Sweden had ever called her Brigitte, but she actually loved the sound of it. Here in this new country, she could be anything she wanted. The thought was exhilarating.

She looked around for Mrs. Fillmore. For some reason, she had not been part of the welcoming committee. Perhaps it was because she was an employee—not a guest.

The man smiled his easy smile again, but the little girl's face remained expressionless. Tall for her eleven years, the girl's body had a coltish quality, but the gaze of Elizabeth Fillmore's large green eyes was startlingly direct. Birgit had the distinct feeling she was being sized up.

Birgit held out her hand to the girl's father. "Nice to meet you," she said. He took it after what seemed a moment's hesitance. The official at the embassy had done the same. *What was wrong? Didn't American women shake hands?*

Sensing her confusion, Mr. Fillmore was quick to explain. "Just a golf injury." He turned to his daughter. "Elizabeth, where are your manners? Aren't you going to say hi to your new nanny?"

"Hi." The girl's voice was unenthusiastic.

Birgit sensed that the girl might be a handful, but it didn't put her off. She'd always hit it off with kids and Elizabeth Fillmore would be no exception.

"Birgit…over here!" The booming voice was familiar.

Mr. Fillmore eyebrows rose. "A friend of yours?"

Birgit rolled her eyes. "Another passenger from Stockholm…" She watched in horror as the Swede jumped up behind the crowd, waving both arms.

Mr Fillmore grinned. "I had no idea Swedes were this exuberant."

Exuberant. Birgit frowned. The English word didn't register in her tired brain. "Lively," said the little girl in a serious grown-up voice. "It's a synonym for exuberant." She didn't return her new nanny's grateful smile but in her green eyes was a hint of approval. Maybe the young man's shouting her name had made Birgit more acceptable in the girl's mind.

"No," said Birgit, "normally they aren't this…*exuberant.*"

Mr. Fillmore looked amused. "Well, we'd better move on before your admirer hunts us down."

The heat outside JFK was stifling, a dusty kind of heat Birgit hadn't experienced before. "This is the worst time of year," Mr. Fillmore explained. "Out in the country, where we live, the temperature will be cooler."

The rest of the trip was a blur. Birgit tried to stay awake in the back seat of Mr. Fillmore's large comfortable car, but she laid her head back on the seat and closed her eyes. She felt the car slow and turn and opened her eyes. At the end of a long driveway was a large white farmhouse.

"This is it." Mr. Fillmore pulled in front of the house and shut off the engine. "By American standards, it's a rarity. Built in the late 1800s, early 1900s, we think. Of course, we've made improvements, but the structure is still intact. I hope you'll enjoy it here. We certainly do."

Birgit knew instantly that she would. She had hoped the Fillmores' residence wouldn't be like a house in a Hollywood movie. Here she would feel more at home.

Elizabeth skipped to the front door with Birgit behind her, suddenly acting more like a typical child. "Mom, we're back!" she called.

The door opened, and Birgit found herself eye-to-eye with a woman in a long dress that was woven in a geometric pattern. The agency had told her that Mrs. Fillmore was an artist. Her complexion was pale and flawless and her jet-black hair was arranged in an elaborate braid, in itself a piece of art Birgit knew she would never be able to duplicate.

Lindsey Fillmore had the same remarkable green eyes as her daughter but they had been enhanced with expertly-applied makeup, making them even more a focal point. "Welcome, Birgit," she said in a smoky voice. "Please come on in." Her pronunciation of *Birgit* was perfect. She seemed to be a person who didn't make mistakes.

"So nice to meet you." Birgit parroted her greeting to Mr. Fillmore, but this time she didn't offer her hand. *What if Mrs. Fillmore had the same reluctance to shake hands as her husband?*

Mrs. Fillmore solved Birgit's problem by reaching for her hand. The woman's fragile look was deceiving—her handshake was like a man's. "I hope your trip wasn't too strenuous."

Strenuous. Birgit understood the context but wasn't sure about the word. One more thing she needed to look up in a dictionary.

The girl saved her again. "Strenuous is like tiring!" She looked at her mother. "With a foreigner in the house, we should simplify the language, right?"

Maybe the tiredness had made her extra-sensitive, but Birgit felt the word *foreigner* sting. Of course, that's what she was—there was no denying it. She'd lived her whole life in one place, where what she did—and said—was perfectly acceptable. To be foreign was okay, as long as it wasn't confused with inadequacy.

Mrs. Fillmore seemed to sense her discomfort. She waved her daughter away. "Thank you, Elizabeth. If we need a translator in the future, we'll certainly call on you. Run along now so Birgit and I can talk. Zoë is waiting for you." She turned back to Birgit. "Zoë is our Bassett hound. An absolute dear, but not terribly bright, I'm afraid."

The smile was still there, but Birgit was conscious of the woman's green eyes taking an inventory of her appearance—registering, she thought, the wrinkles and the spot on the dress.

Mrs. Fillmore turned to her husband. "Dahling, please bring Birgit's luggage upstairs." He studied his hand for a second, flexed his fingers, and then picked up the suitcase and ascended the stairway, taking them three at a time. Birgit found herself wondering if Mr. Fillmore's star power was offset, even diminished, by the strength of the women in his family.

Only time would tell, but she knew one thing for sure. Life with the Fillmores might turn out to be a lot of things, but *boring* would not be one of them.

9

She's not much of a housekeeper, thought Birgit. The perfect woman had a chink in her armor!

"Mother doesn't do menial things," said Elizabeth. Birgit stopped herself from saying it, but she guessed that this was another reason she'd been hired. She didn't mind—physical work never bothered her. Besides, she had already fallen in love with the old house. The signs of neglect didn't bother her, either. They were an inspiration.

"After Ilse left, things kind of fell apart," Elizabeth explained. Birgit's German predecessor, Ilse was, according to the girl, an unpleasant "neat freak" who after a two-year stay had left for a hotel job on the Virgin Islands.

It became increasingly obvious that Elizabeth was right about her mother. Lindsey Fillmore didn't seem to have the slightest idea of how to run a household or of what Birgit's duties should be. "Do whatever you feel needs to get done. Just leave my studio alone," she said, waving dismissively at her and walking away. The house wasn't dirty—just crowded with pieces of furniture bunched together and in the wrong places.

After she'd been there a couple of weeks, Birgit stopped asking questions and began doing things her way. In her childhood home, clutter had been a no-no. "Every item must have its place" was Vera Svenson's motto.

Some of Mom's preaching must have rubbed off on me, thought Birgit. She started straightening one area after another, waiting for someone to stop her. When nobody did, she continued her effort.

Mr. Fillmore was the first to comment. "I'm not sure of what you did," he said, "but the house feels much roomier and airier now." His approval made Birgit pick up the pace even more.

§

Elizabeth leaned against the wall in the upstairs hallway, legs pulled up against her chest, arms wrapped around them, chin resting on knobby knees. Her large eyes were focused on Birgit, who was up on a ladder dusting the artwork, most of which was her mother's. "Why do you work so hard? Are you trying to please Mom or trying to stay busy because you're homesick?"

It had not taken long for Birgit to learn that any question, any comment, might come out of the girl's mouth. Birgit was also now certain that the Elizabeth's curiosity was more clinical than personal. Even so, it was nice to have questions directed her way. The hardest part of her new job was to be both invisible and useful—available, but not in the way.

Birgit stepped down from the ladder, moved it a few feet, and turned to face Elizabeth. She knew the girl was perceptive and very smart. To give her anything but a straight answer wouldn't work. "Not sure what to tell you," she said truthfully. "It's a little bit of both, I guess."

"Well, you can forget pleasing Mother. She is *unpleasable*. Believe me, I have tried. It won't happen."

"And why is that?"

"If I knew, I'd tell you. Dad says Mother's just one of those artsy, creative types who lives in a world of her own." Elizabeth bit her lower lip and switched her gaze from Birgit to the wall. The silence lasted only seconds. "She likes you better than Ilse, though. I even heard her tell Dad that you've classic cheekbones." The girl paused and made a stern face. "Ilse used to yell, *'Aus! Sitzt not hier! I must wasch these floors schnell!'*"

Birgit stifled a giggle at Elizabeth's throaty imitation of a German accent, and the girl looked pleased. She seemed badly in need of attention and Birgit assumed that making outrageous remarks was a way for her to be noticed. School would not start for another month, but boredom wasn't the only reason the girl acted the way she did. She was still a child with a child's needs who was treated as an adult by her parents.

Birgit had seen her curl up like a kitten in her mother's lap, only to be rebuked. "Don't be clingy, darling," her mother had said. "You know I don't care for that." Gently, but firmly, Mrs. Fillmore had shooed her daughter away.

The scene was all too familiar to Birgit. To watch Elizabeth try to connect with her mother brought back painful memories. Vera Svenson hadn't been the hugging kind, either. Whatever hugs Birgit had received had come from her dad.

Birgit had also watched for a reaction from Mr. Fillmore, but none had come. He'd looked up for a second from his *Wall Street Journal*, opened his mouth as if to say something, but then closed it, apparently changing his mind.

Birgit screamed in her head. Don't sit there like a lump! Your daughter needs you! She tried to telegraph her thoughts to him, but Mr. Fillmore's attractive face remained blank and impassive.

Elizabeth recovered like a seasoned actor. If she was hurt, it hadn't shown.

Instead, a bright smile, not quite reaching the eyes, appeared, followed by a witty comment. Controlling her feelings was not Birgit's strong suit, and her expression must have shown her frustration because Mrs. Fillmore looked up as if a houseplant had suddenly come to life. Her voice was silky when she spoke—dangerously so—Birgit thought.

"Please, *do* take Elizabeth to her room. It's getting late."

"I'm a big girl. I'll take care of myself."

Elizabeth's tone was light, but Birgit knew the effort behind it. The tears would come later.

§

Elizabeth sat watching Birgit work. "Are you a virgin?"

For weeks, Birgit had tried not to snap at the girl, but the memory of Bengt and that day on the island made her blush. "That's none of your business!"

The girl missed nothing. "Thought so! I've always thought Europeans were much more sophisticated about that sort of thing. Here everything becomes such a big deal."

Her blush finally fading, Birgit turned to look at her charge. "Why did you want to know?"

Elizabeth sighed. "Well, there is this boy in my class. He's cute, but never says anything bright. Still, I want him to look at me. That makes me straight, right? I used to worry about being a lesbian." She quickly changed the subject. "Can't wait for school to start. There is nothing to do around here."

Brigit paused to look at her and then out the window. "This is farmland, isn't it? Are you growing anything on the land?"

"Nothing! Dad likes to think of himself as a gentleman farmer, but he can't tell the difference between a turnip and a cantaloupe."

"Why don't you and *I* plant something together?" Birgit regretted the question before it came out. *What a dumb idea—Elizabeth was not the type of girl to muck around in a garden.* But, to her surprise, the girl's eyes lit up. Birgit paused. "Then again, your mom might not like the idea."

Elizabeth shook her head. "No, she would be fine with it. She likes the *concept* of earth, digging, getting down and dirty, as long as she isn't the one doing it. But wait…" Elizabeth stopped. "You plant in the spring, don't you? It's August…"

"We can plant a vegetable garden and…" Birgit searched for the right word, but couldn't come up with it. "The ones that come back year after year."

"You're talking perennials," said Elizabeth. Her face brightened. "When do we get started?"

Leaping up from a sitting position, she raised up on her toes, did a cartwheel, landed in perfect balance and went down in a split.

Birgit noted that Elizabeth's overall form was good, except for the split, which didn't reach all the way down to the floor. The girl looked up expectantly, but Birgit had already learned not to act overly impressed. Elizabeth knew when she did well and when she didn't. Praising her for anything less than perfect wouldn't do.

"Good!" exclaimed Birgit. "You just need a few more centimeters …"

Elizabeth stuck out her tongue. "Ha! Bet you can't do it better."

Birgit laughed. "Bet I can!"

Gymnastics had always come easily to Birgit. All through school she had gotten straight A's in the subject. Her father had even hung up a set of roman rings in an oak tree outside the house for her exercises.

Birgit lifted her skirt up high and did a split herself, amused at herself for competing with an eleven-year-old.

A shrill laugh erupted from Elizabeth. "I saw your undies!"

"So what! They are clean, aren't they?"

The two of them laughed in unison.

"It sounds as if you girls are having fun." Mrs. Fillmore stood at the bottom of the stairs. Birgit pulled herself up from the floor and picked up the dust rag on top of the ladder.

"Mom, Birgit knows how to do a perfect split!" said Elizabeth.

Mrs. Fillmore nodded, but no smile appeared on her face. "Birgit is clearly a girl with many hidden talents."

"We are going to make a garden!" Elizabeth exclaimed. "You don't mind, do you?"

"Don't be silly. Of course not. There is a place behind the barn where the past owner had a vegetable garden. Birgit can decide if it is usable." She paused and looked over at Birgit with a quizzical expression. "For some reason, I had the impression you came from a family of fishermen."

Birgit nodded. "I do. My dad is a fisherman but he also likes to garden."

"Wonderful! Well, then, I guess you'll need some equipment—shovels, rakes, fertilizer—that sort of thing. We can visit the hardware store tomorrow. It's a short distance and not much traffic, so Birgit, why don't you plan to drive? That would give you practice."

When Birgit said nothing, Mrs. Fillmore frowned. "You *do* know how to drive, don't you? You must get an American license." She thought for a moment. "Do Swedes drive on the right or the left side?"

"Left. We'll switch to the right just a month from now."

"Then you'll need all the practice you can get. Ilse used the Volkswagen parked in the barn. Elizabeth, you'll show Birgit the car. It might need a tune-up. I'll talk to my husband about that."

Birgit could tell from the woman's voice that her interest was waning. Still, it was encouraging. For the first time, they had had an actual conversation.

10

Unlike her mother, Elizabeth didn't just *like* the concept of gardening—she embraced the whole process of planning and preparing—everything from digging to weeding to watering and planting. Birgit had not for a moment believed the interest would last, but she was wrong. The enthusiasm the girl showed would not die out like it had for so many other projects.

The "garden," located behind the barn, was a patch of hard dirt overgrown with crabgrass. To prepare the area for planting would demand time and effort. The soil had to be loosened and turned, and the weeds removed. The first week, Birgit helped Elizabeth out, offering tips, before handing her the reins. No longer did the girl sleep late in the morning—every day, she was up early, ready to go. Since Mrs. Fillmore had shown support for the garden project, there were no complaints about Birgit missing out on other chores.

Elizabeth had definite ideas on what kinds of vegetables to grow. "No broccoli and Brussels sprouts," she said.

"Vegetables you plant yourself always taste delicious," replied Birgit, but Elizabeth would not be swayed. Her mother's suggestions to plant *arugula* and *radicchio* were also turned down. "Never heard of those veggies," Elizabeth later told Birgit. "Just the names make me think of something preppy and weird—Mom's kind of food." Birgit promised her that they would plant only "normal" stuff, like potatoes, carrots, beans, and tomatoes.

After Birgit had left her in charge and returned to her other household chores, Elizabeth worked alone every afternoon with Zoë the basset hound as her only companion. When she came in at the end of the day, she was dirty and tired, but happy. Around noon, unless it rained, Birgit made it a habit to take lunch to her, so they established a routine. Birgit showed up with the lunch basket and Elizabeth stopped what she was doing, washed her hands with water from the hose, and sat down on the bench with her drink and sandwich. "Just peanut butter and jelly for me," she said. "No surprises, please."

Elizabeth had had enough surprises from her mother. Mrs. Fillmore was an excellent cook who enjoyed whipping up exotic dishes, but neither her husband nor her daughter appreciated her culinary talents. The plates brought back to the kitchen were evidence enough—the food on Mr. Fillmore's plate was spread out to hide the amount left, while Elizabeth's was brimming over. Mrs. Fillmore's attempt to make the family into gourmets had failed miserably.

Birgit customarily served coffee after dinner. One evening when she was headed to the dining room, Mrs. Fillmore's angry voice stopped her in her tracks. "Finish the food!" Birgit heard her shout, but it was Elizabeth's response that made her cringe.

"I wish Birgit was the one doing the cooking," the girl muttered.

A loud thump was heard. *Was that a chair crashing to the floor?* Then the French doors flew open and Mrs. Fillmore stormed out. "Peasants! Why do I bother?" Birgit held her breath for a moment, unsure what to do.

"Brigitte," said Mr. Fillmore, as if nothing had happened, "Sorry about that display of artistic temper. I think I'd like my cup of coffee now."

§

When Birgit had first arrived, she had been invited to join the family for dinner. "But," Mrs. Fillmore had said, "I fully understand if you prefer to eat alone in the kitchen."

The offer had been polite, but not exactly welcoming. *Was it a test? A challenge?* Birgit still wasn't certain. *Maybe she was supposed to turn down the offer, but how could she do so without being rude?*

In any case, Birgit had formulated her answer carefully. "I don't want to intrude on your privacy." *Had she said it right? Did that sound too prim and proper?* Mrs. Fillmore had looked amused but made no comment. Her only response was a "suit yourself" shrug. The "situation," as far as she was concerned, had been resolved, and there was no need for further discussion.

Birgit continued to find that some words she used didn't quite fit what she was trying to say. Her options were either to risk embarrassing herself or say nothing. While her school English covered the basics, it was clear her vocabulary had to improve—the nuances of the language were the tricky parts. She mentioned her difficulty to Elizabeth.

"Take some evening classes," suggested the girl. "It's not what you say that is all that wrong. You just sound terribly foreign."

The next evening, Mrs. Fillmore wasn't feeling well and asked Birgit to make dinner. Everyday food was all Birgit knew how to cook, but she thought that might be what Elizabeth and her dad wanted. She welcomed the opportunity for something new. Doing the same work day after day had become boring. She had learned to iron Mr. Fillmore's shirts to perfection and to drive on the right side of the road, but other than that, she had added no new skills to her repetoire.

Birgit asked Elizabeth to go with her to the store to help with the groceries. They took off in the blue Volkswagen that Ilse had driven. Mr. Fillmore had taken it to a garage to be checked out as his wife had requested. Birgit had assumed he would work on the Beetle himself like her father would have, but in America, apparently, you hired it done.

To travel on the "wrong" side still felt awkward to her, but she'd passed the American driver's exam without problems. In Sweden, her instructor, a stickler for rules and regulations, had hounded her for months with tests and lessons. Here she was asked to just drive around the block and park. That was it. Amazing!

Birgit's meatballs turned out well. Since she knew the recipe by heart, there had been no need to convert from Swedish to American measurements. Elizabeth, a notably picky eater, had asked for seconds and Mr. Fillmore had seemed pleased. He'd wiped his mouth with a linen napkin and leaned back in his chair. "That was excellent, Brigitte."

As soon as Mrs. Fillmore was well again, she took over the cooking again, but a few of her more unusual dishes disappeared from the menu. There would be no mention of the Swedish meatballs.

Whereas Elizabeth was normally gabby, she was quiet when she worked in the garden. Life in the Fillmore household was often intense and chaotic and, for Elizabeth, mucking around in the soil was therapy. Her mother was either *involved,* with phone calls, visits, and fundraisers, or *inspired,* which meant that she locked herself in the studio and painted for long periods, not to be disturbed by anything or anybody.

Birgit and Elizabeth were finishing lunch in the garden. Elizabeth swallowed the last sip of her lemonade, "Do you have to go? Can't you hang around for a while?" Her eyes were pleading.

"Sorry, honey. Your mom is having a luncheon for some ladies and needs my help."

"One of those dumb Democratic fundraisers...for Bobby Kennedy, right?"

Birgit nodded. "That's what I heard."

"Mom is so involved with the Party. She just loves the "common man." As long as he doesn't try to live next door, of course." Elizabeth's laugh, too cynical for an eleven-year-old, reminded Birgit of her sister Ruth's.

"Your dad—is he involved in politics too?"

"No. All he cares about is work, golf, and sailing. Mom says he lacks passion, a WASP thing maybe." Elizabeth noticed Birgit's blank stare. "Oops! Sorry! WASP stands for White Anglo-Saxon Protestant..."

When she spoke again, her voice had an edge. "Well," she said, pouting, "Run off then! Your employer needs you!" Her mood, as usual, had soured at the mention of her parents.

She is neglected, too, just like the garden, Birgit thought. The difference is that Elizabeth is *cared* for and has most things a little girl might want—except her parents' attention.

Elizabeth turned from Birgit and focused instead on a bee that insistently circled the glass in her hand. She didn't shoo it away—just slowly put the glass down and watched the bug crawl inside. She pulled away when Birgit softly placed her hand on her shoulder.

§

Mrs. Fillmore had worked for some time on a watercolor painting—an "aquarelle," she called it. Her plan had been to raffle it off at a fundraiser, but somewhere in the process, she'd lost both her inspiration and creativity. "It's a total failure," she complained. "I'll have no choice but to auction off some of my other junk."

None of Mrs. Fillmore's artwork qualified as "junk," but this one she had wanted to be special. Mr. Fillmore knew better than to protest. He had gone through this before. Then, almost magically, her inspiration returned a week before the luncheon. Except for a few finishing touches, the painting was ready. The brush strokes danced on the canvas, light and flowing, abstract, but still vividly real. You could see the morning mist roll in over the water, a reddening sky, and the vague outline of a boat making its way out in the sound.

According to Elizabeth, her mother didn't know how to swim and didn't care for sailing. Still, she was able to capture the very essence of boating and water. Birgit was no art expert, but she instinctively knew that the painting was excellent. It touched her heart. She wondered what had made the creative juices flow again. Had the outburst at dinner unleashed something? She concluded that with artists, it just happened for no known reason.

§

"Birgit." The voice was cheerful and the footsteps coming towards the kitchen were quick and light.

"Yes, Mrs. Fillmore."

"That is exactly what I wanted to talk to you about." Mrs. Fillmore hung her paint-dotted smock on a hook and walked over to the sink to wash her hands. "Mrs. Fillmore this, Mrs. Fillmore that—it's getting on my nerves. We are too close in age to be this formal. Just call me Lindsey."

Not quite, thought Birgit. She was twenty-two and Mrs. Fillmore, a few years older than her husband, must be close to forty. Not that it mattered. Perhaps she should feel good about Mrs. Fillmore wanting her to call her by her first name, but she didn't. The "Mrs." factor created a separation between them that felt safe and comfortable.

"All right," she said cautiously, "but…but what about your husband…*he* still wants me to call him Mr. Fillmore, right?"

Mrs. Fillmore shrugged. "Well, yes, but that's *his* business. Brad can be stuffy—but I insist that you call me Lindsey… agreed?" She turned and exited as quickly and abruptly as she had arrived.

§

The weather forecast for the day of the fundraising luncheon was not promising. The August heat, stifling for several days, had Lindsey concerned about thundershowers.

"Some of the ladies have to park on the grass," she muttered to herself. "The driveway can only hold so many cars. If it rains, they'll drag mud all over the house. It just absolutely can't rain!"

The guests seemed to arrive all at once. Birgit recognized none of them except for Ethel Hirschberg, Lindsey's older sister. At first glance, the sisters looked alike. Both were thin and tall with eyes the same color, but where Lindsey's were a startling jade, Mrs. Hirschberg's eyes were a murkier green. Also unlike her sister, Mrs. Hirschberg had the lined, tanned face of an avid golfer. Of the two, she was the better athlete and walked with long strides and a swagger. When she'd first met her, Birgit had liked her immediately—although she was not nearly as attractive as her sister, she was more open and friendly and less complicated.

When Mrs. Hirschberg saw Birgit, she called out to her. "There she is! My Swedish friend!" Her strong hand gripped Birgit's arm. She winked and tipped her chin in Lindsey's direction. "Hope she isn't working you too hard!"

As they approached a group of guests, the ladies stopped chattering and focused on Birgit. "Your new au pair, Linn?" asked a woman in a flowery summer dress.

Another lady butted in. "Lovely," she said. Birgit couldn't help but blush.

Lindsey's smoky voice filled the room. "That's enough. You're embarrassing her." Birgit was relieved to have the attention turned away from her.

As usual, Lindsey controlled the room. It was clear that most of her guests—privileged, well-to-do women in their own right—were in awe of and somehow diminished by her. Whenever Lindsey spent a little extra time with one of them, others looked on jealously, waiting their turn. The only one who seemed relaxed was her sister.

"They follow everything she does," Elizabeth had informed Birgit. "They travel in packs, and only shop for clothes at Saks or in upscale boutiques." She smiled wistfully. "One time, Mom called their bluff. She came to a party dressed in something she'd picked up in a thrift store. A 1920's type of dress, black with a low waistline, and lots of fringe. She'd spent just a few dollars on it, but on her, it was sensational. They all went gaga over her how *chic* she looked. That night, when she came home, she woke me up and we laughed like crazy about it." Birgit thought it sad that one of the few quality moments the girl had shared with her mom had come at the expense of others.

The ladies moved to the veranda and Birgit followed, carrying a tray with margaritas. The door had closed behind the women, and she balanced the tray on her knee while pushing the door open with her shoulder.

The noise inside the room was deafening. Birgit tiptoed in, trying not to make noise or bump into anybody. As she entered, she overheard the woman in the flowery dress say to Lindsey, "That cute au pair of yours... Does she speak any English at all?"

Lindsey nodded her head. "Of course, she does." Her smoky voice changed dramatically, picking up a singsong intonation. "*She speaks like this…*"

Her imitation of a Swedish accent was brilliant and she followed the act with her typical belly laugh. The rest of the women laughed, too, almost on command.

Birgit felt her cheeks burn and turned to leave when Lindsey noticed her. "Oh, there you are." She knew that Birgit had overheard her, but there was no hint of apology in her voice. She took a puff on a slender cigarette. Birgit realized she had not seen her smoke before.

In her normal voice, Lindsey spoke again. "You can put the tray down. I'll take it from here." Eyes of steely blue and emerald green met on a collision course. Birgit had a sudden desire to dump the tray in her lap.

There would be no more chumminess, no more first-name familiarity. Birgit proudly took back her servant status.

"Yes, *ma'am*."

11

Everybody in Birgit's family stayed in touch with her, but Dad, to whom she was closest, wrote the least—he just added a few lines to Mom's letters. Birgit could tell from his labored writing that he had a hard time gripping the pen. Arthritis ran on his side of the family, and years of working outdoors in the rain and cold hadn't helped his joints. He didn't say he missed her but he didn't need to. She'd never doubted her father's love the way she had her mother's.

Aunt Lola frequently wrote in her precise, elegant style. Just like her mother, she wanted to know everything about America. Had Birgit been to New York City yet? Visited the museums, the Statue of Liberty, the Empire State Building, shopped on Fifth Avenue? Was the family treating her well? How did Americans feel about the war, and why did the protesters dress so sloppily?

Her sister wrote dutifully. Ruth's letters oozed of obligation. From Bengt, there was only silence. What else could she expect?

Ruth was the only one who'd brought up his name. She had apparently run into him on the street, and they had spoken briefly. Bengt had been with a young woman Ruth hadn't known, probably from out of town. Another blonde! Quite attractive, she wrote. Birgit wasn't sure what bothered her the most—that Bengt had gotten over her so quickly or that her sister seemed so eager to report it.

Birgit had found that her mother communicated much more easily in letters than in person. Although face to face she and Birgit had often rubbed each other the wrong way, in the letters her thoughts flowed freely, with no sign of tension. For instance, in her dark humor, she had described the failure of her annual crawfish party:

We missed you and Bengt and as long as I've hosted the party, it never flopped until this year. Everything that could go wrong went wrong, including the weather. Because of the cold and the wind, eating outside on the veranda didn't work, but by moving inside we lost the ambiance.

Domestic crawfish has been sparse this season, and we had to settle for imports from Yugoslavia. The fish looked fine, the right size and everything, but as far as taste, couldn't compare with the ones your father used to catch.

The real problem, though, had been her son-in-law. No surprise there, thought Birgit. Arne always stuck his nose where it didn't belong. He'd managed to convince Ruth that this was his year to prepare "*kräftorna.*" Ruth, who'd always fixed the crawfish dinner to perfection, couldn't stand to argue anymore and gave in.

The party had turned into a fiasco. In the vegetable garden, Arne mistakenly had picked parsley instead of dill for the marinade, which had given the shellfish an unusual flavor. Instead of owning up to his mistake, Arne had angrily criticized the family for not daring to try something different. He also had added a new wrinkle: one should down a schnapps for every claw one ate—a crawfish party etiquette unfamiliar to the rest of the family.

When it had been time for the guests to leave, Arne had been too intoxicated to operate the boat safely. Dad, who'd been pretty worked up at this point, had forced Arne away from the dock, back to the house, where he spent the night sleeping it off on his in-laws' couch. Dad ended up having to drive his daughter and grandchild home. Ruth had been devastated, and Gunnar, who was there only because his babysitter called in sick, had started to cry. Arne had shown some remorse in the morning, but not nearly enough.

"We had such a great time last year…remember?"

Had they? Birgit tried to think back. If they had a great time, it had more to do with Bengt's presence than anything else. He'd proven to be the outside catalyst the family needed.

That party had started with high expectations. She and Ruth had helped Mom decorate for the party, hanging man-in-the-moon lanterns on the veranda, putting crayfish bibs, tongs, and napkins on the table, and having a friendly disagreement on where to place the vases of wildflowers. The temperature had been cooler than normal, but not too cold to sit outside. *When was it ever in Sweden?*

It was not yet fall, but the days were shorter—darkness came early and the salty breeze from the sea had an ominous chill. Mom, who'd already shown off her youthful figure in a sleeveless dress, asked Dad to bring her an old wool sweater instead of her lightweight cotton one.

Mom's red and yellow dress, with a wide belt accentuating her small waist, had been perfect for the occasion. The vibrant red had matched the crawfish on the table, the bright yellow the color of the full moon—which on that night in August had accommodated them by showing up.

A sudden breeze had made the lanterns sway and the chill that followed was a grim reminder that summer—beautiful, but shockingly short—was about to end. Aquavit and drinking songs couldn't keep a sense of melancholy from creeping in. Arne had raised his glass. "Skoal, folks!" The lull in the conversation had made him nervous. "Why is everyone so damn quiet?"

After that, he'd emptied his glass. Mom had glanced over at Dad and they'd exchanged looks in the wordless communication of long-married couples. Dad had pushed the cork back in the bottle, gotten up from the table, and taken the bottle with him to the kitchen.

Arne looked like a child whose toy had been taken away. He muttered something obnoxious about guests having their drinks rationed. But his comment hadn't started the trouble it might have because Bengt had stepped in. Skillfully, he had deflected the remark and maneuvered the conversation back to safe grounds. Birgit remembered giving him credit, but grudgingly and jealously. *He wasn't part of the family. How much easier it would be for him.*

Dad had put away the hard liquor but returned with a couple of beers, enough to placate Arne and keep the party from going sour. As he'd passed Ruth, his hand had rested for an instant on her shoulder. She'd looked up at him with a tight smile and had patted his hand affectionately.

After that, the conversation at the party had picked up again. But if it not for Bengt, who knew what would have happened?

§

Birgit could tell from the letters that her mother avoided subjects she thought might worry her. In her last correspondence, however, there had been a reference to Dad working too hard and of the fishing in the Baltic drying up. And brother-in-law Arne's declaration about the fishing: "*It's all that crap coming from the East. The fish are dying because the damn Commies are polluting our waters.*"

Birgit had thought that moving away from home was a saving grace, that it would cause her less worry, but so far, she'd found that not to be true. Perhaps, she'd realized, family follows you no matter where you go. Here she was, an ocean apart from them, still thinking about the fishing in the Baltic and how it affected Dad; experiencing a new, less tension-filled relationship with her mother; maintaining the lifelong arms-length connection to her sister. And still thinking about Bengt and wondering if she had made a mistake in leaving him.

Birgit picked up Ruth's letter and read it again. *"Bengt has met someone else..."* it said.

She laid the letter in her lap and looked out a window. The day after tomorrow was her day off. She would go to New York as Aunt Lola had suggested and see the sights. The idea of it lifted her mood.

"Good for him!" she said out loud to herself. And with that, she crumpled Ruth's letter into a ball and, with perfect aim, tossed it into the wastepaper basket.

12

"I'd like to visit museums in the city...in my spare time, of course," Birgit told Lindsey. "Are there any you would recommend?"

Her employer looked neither curious nor surprised, but raised eyebrows were a telling sign. She is assessing me, Birgit thought, trying to figure out if I'm serious or trying to impress her. Maybe au pairs in America are not expected to be culturally inclined.

"What are your interests?" Lindsey asked coolly.

"Art...history..."

"Hmmm."

"Mom quickly makes up her mind about people," Elizabeth had told Birgit. "She labels you and puts you in a box. Dad is the 'trophy husband, handsome, but predictable,' I am the 'bright child,' who sometimes amuses her."

Birgit was almost afraid to ask. "And what am I?"

"Oh, you're the *help*." Elizabeth, as expected, hadn't tempered her response. "Mom doesn't *see* you." Maybe the girl had been right early on, but for now, at least, Birgit had been taken out of the box, brushed off, and "noticed."

"The Guggenheim is my personal favorite," said Lindsey. "You might have heard of the builder. Frank Lloyd Wright?"

"I have."

"Another must see is the American Museum of Natural History—so massive, so much to explore. One visit is not nearly enough." Lindsey turned back to the magazine she was reading.

The audience was over, but Birgit felt encouraged. Lindsey had taken the time to give her pamphlets, a guidebook, and a city map.

§

Thursday was Birgit's day off. Dressed in casual clothes, slacks, a cotton top, and sensible walking shoes, she took the Long Island Railroad to New York City. As the train pulled up at Grand Central Station, she watched passengers rush out, scatter, and vanish in the crowd. Some stopped to catch announcements over the loudspeaker; others surveyed the area for familiar faces and found them, their concerned looks replaced by smiles. Hugs and handshakes followed, and they too were on their way.

Did all these people have places to go, appointments to keep? Today was her day to savor—her first visit to the Big Apple—and she refused to hurry. She leisurely stepped onto the platform, adjusted the strap of her shoulder bag, and began walking. Her bag held the things she needed—sunglasses, a map of Manhattan, an inexpensive camera, a bottle of water, a pocket-size guidebook, and most importantly, the money she'd saved from her last paycheck.

She had not asked Hilde, Mrs. Hirschberg's live-in housekeeper, to join her. A broad-shouldered Austrian girl with a thick accent and a wheat-colored braid hanging down her back, she was good company—a nice girl, but, in Birgit's opinion, not someone she'd take to a museum.

Dad would've said that I make awfully snap judgments about people, thought Birgit. And he would've been right. I must work on my failings—just not today.

On 42nd Street, the heat rose from the pavement and the blinding sunlight turned the street into a fluorescent white. Birgit stopped and drew in a long breath. How long had it been since she'd felt so relieved and happy? Memories flooded her consciousness before disappearing. She waited for the right one, and when it came, she snatched it.

The dive from the dock had been her first. She'd been seven years old, and her parents were watching. Going headfirst was new—thrilling, but scary. To avoid the dreaded belly-flop, she went straight down. The plunge had been too steep and would not have won many style points. Reaching the surface had been a struggle. With her lungs hurting, she'd exploded from the water, coughing and gulping for air. Relief, pride, and excitement followed, just like they had this morning.

It was early, and the city was waiting. Birgit put on her sunglasses, looked around, and couldn't stop smiling. "What's the matter with that Svenson girl?" people back home would've said, but here, in this huge city, nobody watched her or cared. How wonderful to be invisible!

A cab slowed down beside her, but Birgit continued walking. Her plan was to explore the city on foot. A section of the street had been roped off and two hardhats watched as their co-worker drilled. The jackhammer shook and roared and the pavement broke up bit by bit.

For a moment, the young man operating it disappeared in a cloud of grime and dirt. The screeching noise stopped, the dust settled, and he appeared again, coughing and wiping sweat from his face. Seeing Birgit, he whistled softly, smiled, and gave her a thumbs-up. She smiled back, no longer wishing for anonymity.

The shape of the Guggenheim was dramatically different from other museums. Birgit, who dutifully studied her guidebook, learned that the inspiration came from a pyramidal Babylonian temple. The building process had not been smooth—Wright and Guggenheim had clashed about several things, but mainly about the location. New York, in Wright's mind, was too crowded and noisy, but the closeness to Central Park and its green natural charm had eventually won him over.

Heading next to the American Museum of Natural History, Birgit checked her watch and realized she had to skip the ferry to the Statue of Liberty. Her family, not sharing her fascination with museums, would be stunned. *Why not visit the symbol of America first?*

Talk about being overwhelmed! The natural history museum was larger than any building Birgit had ever entered. Lindsey had been right—to see even a fraction of it would take many more trips to the city. Visiting the Hall of American Mammals and the gem exhibit was all she had time for. The rest would have to wait.

Her next target would be the Empire State Building, but hunger pangs reminded her that all she'd eaten since morning was black coffee and toast. She was not looking for anything fancy—a hamburger would do fine.

It was past two before she found a restaurant that fit her budget. By then, the luncheon crowd had thinned out. After hours of walking, her legs needed a rest. A few stragglers hung around, and she found a seat at the bar.

The hamburger tasted delicious, but the coffee was lukewarm *and* the color of dirty dishwater. Birgit enjoyed most everything American, but not the coffee. How she missed the full-bodied Scandinavian coffee! She grimaced, pushed the cup aside, and asked for a glass of water.

The waitress was a thin woman, most likely years younger than she looked. Her hair was a faded red, a dye job in serious need of a refresher. As the waitress bent over, ready to pour, Birgit could tell that her dark roots were winning the battle. "Honey, d'ya want me to heat it up?"

Birgit quickly placed her hand over the cup. "Thanks. I'm all right."

"You're not from around here, are ya?" The waitress had obviously noticed Birgit's accent, and with not much of a crowd, she seemed ready to chat.

Birgit told her that she was from Sweden and where she was staying.

"Oh, yeah, my granny had one of those cuckoo clocks from Switzerland..."

Birgit grimaced again. "I'm not Swiss...I'm Swedish."

The woman pinched her lips, unwilling to debate. Geography was clearly not her strong suit. "Whatever," she said, waving generally to the east. "They're both over there. Right?"

Birgit asked for directions to the Empire State Building, which she probably didn't need. How can you miss it?

"Bet you won't find a building like that where you come from," said the waitress with a hint of pride.

"Nothing even close," Birgit answered truthfully. She was itching to mention a few things they had "over there," like Versailles and the Sistine Chapel just for starters, but chose not to. Birgit admired the waitress's spunk and loyalty to country.

In their brief conversation, the waitress, without self-pity, had shared glimpses of her life. Birgit had learned that her mom helped watch her three kids while she worked and about her struggles with debt and a deadbeat husband. Other than her children, the waitress's only other pride was America.

Birgit looked at the check, and dropped some bills and coins on the counter, knowing that she'd probably over-tipped. The unfamiliar currency still gave her problems. To try to figure out the percentages would take time, and the woman looked like she could use an extra dollar anyway. "Keep the change!" she said, with a flair that would've pleased her mother and her Aunt Lola.

"Thanks, honey," the waitress said, sweeping up the money with one hand while absently wiping the counter top with the other. "Have a nice day."

13

Tall, straight, and sterile, Manhattan's skyscrapers dominated the skyline. From a distance, they reminded Birgit of the toy blocks she had played with as a child. Up close, they were formidable. The tallest, the Empire State Building, was also the one with the most pleasing classical façade.

Sweden had no skyscrapers. Even in the larger cities, buildings were seldom over eight stories high. By European standards, Sweden is a good-sized country, just sparsely populated. With plenty of room and few metropolitan areas, the need for highrises wasn't there.

Even so, Birgit was not easily bowled over, but standing at the top of the Empire State Building, she felt like pinching herself. Years ago, a movie house back home had shown the classic "King Kong" and, on the screen, she'd watched the big gorilla climb this very building. She'd been sure it was trick photography. Nothing could be that high. But it was! From the observation deck, a quarter of a mile up in the air, all of New York City was there for her to see.

It was a bright day, and many tourists, domestic and foreign alike, were milling around on the deck, jockeying for the best viewing spots. Loose sentences floated in the air. "Wow, isn't this grand? Look! There she is, the Statue of Liberty!" merging with, "*Wunderbar, Magnifique, Maravilloso,*" and other enthusiastic exclamations from foreigners.

Birgit, an avid people watcher, noticed that American and European tourists seemed to travel in pairs or small groups. The Japanese, on the other hand, arrived by the dozens. As soon as one of them showed up, eleven others magically appeared! While other tourists stopped to admire the scenery, the Japanese took control of the best spots at the railing.

Sophisticated cameras began pointing at the sights, ready to shoot. Birgit, tall enough to see over their heads, followed suit with hers. She snapped away, not sure that her inexpensive camera would do the view justice.

Birgit thought of her family. Who would have enjoyed this experience the most? Definitely not Ruth. Much too negative. Not Dad either. He would never be comfortable in a city this size. Mom was the one! She'd fit right in, loving the energy and the action.

Suddenly, Birgit felt sad. Was it the height that made her feel so insignificant and lonely? Was it because she was there by herself? How nice it would have been to have shared this moment with someone—why hadn't she asked Hilde to come along?

A cheerful voice brought Birgit out of her self-judgment. "Isn't this view something? Let me have your camera—I'll be happy to take your picture."

A stout, middle-aged woman with her husband in tow smiled pleasantly. The couple wore matching purple caps with "Kansas" embroidered in white letters. The man, who had both a camera and binoculars strapped around his neck, waited patiently as his wife struck up a conversation.

"Bess McCauley," the woman said, introducing herself.

Her accent had a twang that Birgit didn't recognize. Growing up, she, like most Swedish kids, thought all Americans sounded like John Wayne.

The movie star was an icon, especially among the boys. Their imitation of his slow drawl frustrated their English teacher. "In my classroom, we speak the *Queen's* English," he would say. The boys made faces behind his back. Why talk like a prissy Brit, when you could sound cool, like an American cowboy?

"We're here for our 25th wedding anniversary," said the woman. "This is my hubby, Herbie." She motioned for her husband to come closer. Herbie stayed put after a polite hello to Birgit, clearly not wanting any part of what could become a lengthy female conversation.

Bess made a face. "He's getting antsy," she said. "Ready to go home." She spoke of her husband as if he were a child. She reached for Birgit's camera, asked Birgit to pose, made sure the sun was in the right place, and snapped a picture.

Since arriving in the city, Birgit had gradually lost her "I want to be alone" attitude. Small talk, even with complete strangers, made her less lonely, so she hung around. The man stepped closer to the railing, removed his cap, carefully patted down a few strands of hair, put the cap back on, and pointed. "Seven people have jumped from here." He spoke with the authority of a trivia expert.

His wife interrupted him. "Remember, it's our anniversary, honey. Let's not discuss sad things. Okay?" She looked at Birgit and rolled her eyes. "The glass is always half-empty as far as he is concerned," she whispered.

The husband continued. "Nineteen-forty-five, a plane crashed into this building. Took out the whole north side. Fourteen people killed."

"See what I mean?" said the woman, lowering her voice. "He gets gloomier day by day." She removed two bananas from her tote bag. "Want one?" she asked.

"Thanks, no," said Birgit. "I just ate…"

"Well, let's just split one then. Herbie thinks it's tacky to bring sandwiches, so I only brought fruit." Bess put one banana back in the bag and peeled and broke the other in half. She called to her husband, who had squeezed himself between two young Japanese men at the railing. "Honey, what's out there? Anything exciting?"

"Nope." The man focused his binoculars on a spot in the distance. "But I'll bet you that's Hoboken over there!"

The woman shook her head in mock frustration and giggled. "See? With all these sites around…what does he do? Looks at New Jersey!" She shook her head again. "That man kills me."

§

To shop seemed like the perfect ending for Birgit's trip, even if it was mostly window shopping, which was the only thing she could afford. To buy something in the exclusive boutiques along Fifth Avenue was out of the question, but she enjoyed the displays in the windows. In front of Saks, she hesitated. The temptation to enter the famous department store was too great—after all, a peek wouldn't hurt.

The store reeked with the intimidating ambiance the "have" customers craved. The category Birgit belonged to, the "have nots," usually had the good sense to shop at Caldor and Korvette, the lower-end department stores where the goods were sufficient and far less expensive.

As soon as the large doors closed behind her, Birgit knew she was at a place where she didn't belong but she continued anyway. "Okay, Svenson," she said to herself, "you have as much right as anybody else to be here." She straightened her back and turned up her nose like she had seen Lindsey do in places like this.

At the cosmetic counter, a young flawlessly made-up clerk treated a customer to a facial makeover. When she was almost done, she took a few steps back to admire her work. Foundation, powder, contours on the cheekbones, shimmer on eyelids, mascara on the lashes…everything was in place. Now all that was needed was the finishing touch. She rummaged through a drawer for the right color lipstick. A pale pink didn't make the grade. Too bland. A fire engine red was also rejected. Too loud. Finally, a subdued shade of purple called "Blushing Plum" prevailed.

"Quite a transformation, don't you think?" Her professional voice took on a smooth, persuasive tone, as she handed her customer a mirror. The woman inspected her face from all angles and nodded. She turned expectantly to a person beside her. "How do I look?"

"Marvelous," said her friend, who, bored, barely glanced at her. Instead, she was passing the wait by spraying perfume on herself from the test bottles on the counter top. She gave her wrist one last squirt, shut her eyes, brought the wrist to her nose and sniffed. An exotic aroma filled the air. Birgit breathed in the scent, loving it. She had no clue what fragrance it was, but she knew it was nothing she could afford.

In store windows back home, manikins stood in plastic tranquility, demure and obedient. Most of them were leftovers from the fifties, and in some cases, even the forties. Their duty was to display clothes, not to make statements. The ones on Fifth Avenue were more superior "clothes hangers." Lifelike, with provocative postures. Pelvises thrust forward, heads tilted back in perceived ecstasy. One of the "dolls" had beads in different colors dancing around her neck. Birgit wondered if invisible strings held them up, creating an image of frenzied movement. The doll's dress, a green mini, had small white polka dots and a wide white belt. Birgit touched the fabric. It felt like cotton but was mixed with a stretchy material.

A woman, fifty-something but well-preserved, stopped in front of the manikin too. "Not for me!" she said to no one in particular. Birgit, on the other hand, had no problem imagining herself in the dress, but the price tag brought her back to reality.

She sighed and moved on to the accessories. The woman behind the counter gave her a quick glance and then looked away. Birgit detected a hint of condescension in her eyes. Was it her accent? No, she hadn't opened her mouth. And even if she had, what was to say that she wasn't a European aristocrat in the U.S. on vacation? She knew it wasn't the way she was dressed—Lindsey, in her "relaxed" attire looked more casual than Birgit did today—sometimes downright sloppy. Even so, sales personnel everywhere fawned over her. *It must be something else*, thought Birgit. *An aura maybe.* She had pulled fish from the water with more intelligence in their eyes than this sales clerk. Still, the woman had reached the conclusion that Birgit didn't belong.

The young au pair gave the elegant Italian silk scarf a long, last look before putting it back in the bin. It was overpriced. For the same money, she could buy two dresses at Caldor's. "Not quite what I had in mind," she said out loud with her head held high. Then she turned and walked toward the exit.

§

The Fillmores' blue Volkswagen was still waiting for Birgit at the railroad station. It had been a long day and it was getting late, so she climbed in and started the engine. She had asked Lindsey not to count on her for supper. She'd find something to eat in the fridge later, she'd said.

Elizabeth was at a friend's house on a sleepover, and the house was silent.

Birgit stuck her key in the lock, expecting to hear the clicks of Zoë's claws on the hardwood floor, but the old basset only barked—once out of habit and a second time for emphasis. The last one was really just a drawn-out growl.

Birgit assumed the dog was in the family room stretched out in her favorite position, with her head in Lindsey's lap. Not wanting to talk, Birgit quietly tiptoed to her room. She kicked off her shoes, massaged her legs, and curled up on the bed.

What a day! She closed her eyes and replayed the day's events in her mind: The arrival at Grand Central Station, the whistling hardhat on 42nd Street, the museums, the waitress. By the time she reached the Empire State Building, her thoughts were fuzzy, and shortly thereafter, she drifted off to sleep.

Hours later, still fully dressed, she awoke feeling hungry. In the kitchen, she found a leftover meatloaf in the refrigerator, made a sandwich, and poured herself a glass of milk. On her way up the stairs, she heard sounds from the master bedroom—agitated voices, Lindsey's in particular. "Brad, why don't you just fuck off!!"

She was halfway up when the bedroom door swung open. Mr. Fillmore hurried out of the bedroom looking nothing like his executive self. With his hair tousled and a pillow clutched to his chest, he looked vulnerable, like a little boy.

Birgit recognized the designer pajama pants she laundered and ironed every week, but the shirt was missing. The light from the bedroom shone on Mr. Fillmore's muscular shoulders. Without a word, they passed on the stairs. Birgit had a definite feeling that he hadn't really seen her—his usually tan face seemed to have lost all color.

This time, sleep did not come so easy to Birgit. When in the early morning hours it finally came, it was fitful and her dream unpleasant…

She was back on the Empire State Building and had fallen over the ledge. As she slid farther and farther down, the man from Kansas spoke in a strange monotone. "Tick, tock, tick, tock…eight and counting."

Hands grabbed for her. A face she thought was Bengt's stared down at her, but she was mistaken. It was Mr. Fillmore. He reached for her hand but she couldn't hold on, and she was falling...

14

A morning person, Birgit was almost always the first one in the kitchen. Zoe was usually the first to join her. The basset hound, too old to hurry, would lumber in at the first sound of footsteps, gingerly plop herself down on the floor, and wait for Birgit to feed her. She enjoyed the early mornings most—mainly because Lindsey wasn't up yet. When she was around, the mood in the house instantly changed from peaceful to tense.

At seven o'clock on the dot, Brad Fillmore entered the kitchen, business-like in shirt and tie, smelling good from a cool, crisp aftershave and looking every bit the successful CEO of a prosperous brokerage firm. He hung his coat on a chair, removed a hair from the collar, placed his briefcase on the seat, and picked up the paper Birgit had brought in from outside. They exchanged pleasant greetings, but there was no follow-up conversation. It wasn't part of her work assignment, but since Birgit was an early riser, she didn't mind fixing Mr. Fillmore's breakfast before he left for work.

The morning after the big blow-up, she'd pretended to oversleep, not wanting to face him in the kitchen. But she needn't have worried. When she poured Mr. Fillmore his cup of tea, he flashed his charming, trademark smile.

If he felt any discomfort about that night on the stairs, he certainly hadn't shown it. *Had the incident when the two of them almost collided on top of the stairs been swept away? Was it possible that he hadn't even seen her?*

While Mr. Fillmore ate, Birgit rinsed some glasses left in the sink from the night before and loaded them into the dishwasher. The only sounds came from the rustling of the newspaper, the ticking of the wall clock, and Zoë slobbering in her bowl. The lack of conversation didn't bother her—she found the quiet comforting.

Mr. Fillmore was easy to please. For breakfast, he only wanted orange juice, toast, one egg—soft boiled for exactly three minutes, and a cup of tea. His preference for tea was something Birgit found mildly disappointing. How could anyone start the day without a strong cup of coffee?

Birgit kept a jar of coffee in her room. She brought it down in the morning and whisked it upstairs before Lindsey, who liked to sleep late, showed up in the kitchen. That way she didn't have to explain. Her friend Hilde shared her dislike for the weaker American coffee. Together they had shopped around on their day off and managed to find a German delicatessen selling strong, full-bodied European coffee. It had been ridiculously overpriced, but both of them thought it was well worth the money.

At 7:30, Mr. Fillmore stood up, folded the paper and stuck it in his briefcase to read in more detail on the commuter train to New York City. He opened the door to let Zoë out, put on his coat, thanked Birgit—or "Brigitte," as he insisted on calling her—and muttered, "There is no need for you to be up so early. I can very well fix my own breakfast."

It was his standard phrase every morning. And Birgit's answer was always the same as well. "It's no bother. I'm up anyway."

§

Elizabeth bounced into the kitchen, talking a mile a minute in her usual breathless way. "Morning! Where is Zoë? I'm going out to the garden!" Dressed in her garden clothes—a ratty tee shirt, overalls, and the straw hat that her mother had picked up at Bloomingdale's—she was raring to go. Lindsey had no interest in gardening but had found her daughter's newfound hobby "charming."

Elizabeth liked her hat but not the newness of it. To give it a worn look, she'd rolled the brim back and forth and purposely left it outside in the rain. After a few weeks, it was sufficiently broken in, the luster lost, and its bright red ribbon soiled and discolored.

§

Birgit was not alone in disappearing from Lindsey's radar—Elizabeth had too. Painting, cooking, fundraising, motherhood…it didn't matter. When Lindsey Fillmore focused, her intensity burned like a hot flame, had the lifespan of a moth, subsided, flickered and fizzled out. Her interactions with her daughter were short-lived and followed no pattern. Even so, Elizabeth lived for the rare quality time she spent with her Mom.

In the absence of adequate parental attention, Elizabeth used Birgit as a sounding board—throwing out statements or asking questions. If the response wasn't to her liking, she made a little "hmmm" sound, a mannerism not unlike her mother's. Her disclosures were sometimes surprising, even shocking, and her questions generally featured a combative "gotcha" undertone.

"So, tell me, what group do you like the best, the Stones or the Beatles?"

"I like both, but probably the Stones a bit more…"

"Name one of their songs!"

"*She is a Rainbow.* That's my favorite…"

"Okay, sounds like you know your stuff…"

The daily questions were frustrating for Birgit. Every day, she felt she had to pass a test to prove she wasn't a fake. So much so that the first time Elizabeth treated her to a more intimate, personal conversation, Birgit did not know how to react.

Elizabeth sat on the edge of her bed, head down, her dark, long eyelashes fluttering against her cheeks. Her hand smoothed the floral, designer comforter below. "You think Mom is difficult, don't you?" Birgit rummaged her brain for a diplomatic answer, but Elizabeth saved her the trouble. "I know you do…" She paused, her tone turning defensive, "… but she can be great too."

Birgit nodded her head. "I'm sure…"

"Did I tell you about our trip to New York around Christmas?"

"I don't think so."

Elizabeth launched into the story. "It was cold, not much snow on the ground, but enough to make it festive. Lights, decorations everywhere, and Santas on the streets ho-ho-hoing and ringing bells to get money for needy people. Mom told me to give each of them a dollar.

"I had my new boots on, the ones Mom had bought me just for that day. Not the babyish, flat kinds I used to have…these had heels, not high ones, but still. My coat had a fur collar—a fake. Mom says it's a crime to kill animals to fancy up our clothes."

Although Elizabeth told the story using the first person "I," Birgit sensed that it was as if she talked about herself…and yet, at the same time, about someone else. She spoke in wonderment, in a whisper—as if the memory was so sheer, so fragile that it might tear if she didn't. As she listened, Birgit saw a vision of a small rabbit sitting perfectly still before fleeing to safety.

"We went to Rumpelmayer's in the afternoon. You wouldn't know, but that's the fanciest ice cream parlor in the city. It's amazing—inside is all pink and there are teddy bears everywhere. We split an ice cream soda, but since Mom said I could have anything I wanted, I ordered a cup of hot cocoa, too, with a bowl of whipped cream on the side. It tasted like velvet. The dishes they use are white with the Rumpelmayer logo on the side in mustard yellow. Not gaudy but classy looking.

"Everyone there was dressed up and probably going to the ballet too. Did I tell you we were seeing the Nutcracker that evening? Mom knew some of the people, but didn't talk to them, just to me…"

The girl who had shared those private thoughts with Birgit was a far cry from the one who'd come running down into the kitchen this morning. Elizabeth was impatient and ready to go. "Zoë! Where are you girl?"

Birgit glanced her way. "Your Dad just let her out…Do you want some breakfast?"

"Nope." Elizabeth, always in a rush, seldom stopped to eat anything in the morning. Occasionally, she poured some cereal and milk in a bowl and ate it standing up.

"Are you sure?" Birgit held up a skillet in one hand. "The batter is already made."

She had found an authentic cast-iron Scandinavian pancake pan when browsing in a second-hand store. It looked brand new and might have been a gift to someone who couldn't figure out what to do with the round divots in the bottom. Birgit, thrilled with her find, had tried out the pancakes on Elizabeth. The girl was not an adventurous eater, but her Swedish meatballs had been a success. The pancakes had also gone over well. Elizabeth, intrigued by how small and delicate they were, had even let Birgit talk her into spreading lingonberries and whip cream on top, the Swedish way.

"Well…since you've already made the batter…"

Birgit smiled. "Relax, sit down. It will only take a minute."

Elizabeth closed the door, pulled out a chair, and slapped her hat down on the table beside her with a frown. "Nothing is growing yet."

"I told you it would take time."

"How long?"

"Maybe another nine weeks."

"That long?! You didn't tell me that!"

"I did. You just didn't listen."

Elizabeth looked around. "Mom hasn't come down yet?"

"Not yet."

"That means they fooled around last night! Tuesdays and Friday nights are on the schedule unless Dad has an early tee time on Saturday. He's so boring and predictable...but maybe he's good in bed."

"ELIZABETH!" Birgit cast a worried glance toward the kitchen door. She knew Lindsey was likely to appear at any second. "You really shouldn't tell me stuff like that."

Elizabeth handed her soiled plate to Birgit and grinned. "Don't worry...I won't let you in on anything that would gross you out." She was halfway out the door when she turned and stuck her face back in. "Oh, yeah, one more thing I forgot to tell you..."

The sparkle in Elizabeth's eyes had Birgit worried. She braced herself for another intimate revelation. "What's that?"

"Dad and I are going sailing on the sound this weekend. And you know what? Mom is coming with us!" Elizabeth's voice quivered with happiness.

Once the girl was gone, Birgit continued to wash the dishes, but in the back of her mind, she pondered what Elizabeth had said. *Why was it so exciting that Lindsey was going with them?* Then it hit her. Lindsey didn't like to sail, according to Elizabeth, because she didn't know how to swim.

Birgit understood if fear was her reason for not sailing, but if it was so important to her family, why hadn't she learned how to swim? The woman was an expert at everything else, always challenging herself and others. Was she afraid of water?

15

"I thought we were in agreement!" Brad Fillmore's voice, uncharacteristically loud, burst through the kitchen wall. Birgit, her head halfway inside the refrigerator, was busy putting away leftovers from dinner when she heard the Fillmores arguing. The response from Lindsey was too muffled to make out, but there was nothing muffled about her footsteps as she marched into the kitchen carrying a stack of dirty plates from the dining room table. The rapid clicking of her high heels against the tile floor made a loud statement. Not too gently, and with her non-smiling husband following a few steps behind, she unloaded the dishes into the sink.

The moment Birgit heard the Fillmores approach, she dove back inside the refrigerator, moved some plastic containers around, and did her best to blend in with the appliance.

"This is probably the last good weekend for sailing," Mr. Fillmore said, his voice now lowered a few decibels. "You know you hate it when it gets cold."

Lindsey's tone had an irritating, uppity quality, the voice of a grown-up reasoning with an unruly child. "Brad, dahling, how could I have possibly known that my period would come early?"

"How convenient!"

"No need to be sarcastic. What do you need me for, anyway? Elizabeth will be there to help out and keep you company."

Elizabeth joined her parents in the kitchen. "Dad, if Mom doesn't want to go, why don't we ask Birgit?" Her disappointed tone made it clear that this was not her preference.

Birgit sensed an exchange of looks behind her back. An uncomfortable silence lingered before Lindsey spoke. "Why not?" she said, "Sounds like a good idea to me... Birgit, for heaven's sake, get your head out of the fridge!"

Birgit slowly stood up but was not all that pleased at the unwanted attention. Elizabeth stared at her, grim-faced, Her father made an effort to return his facial expression to neutral. "Brigitte—as Elizabeth said—you're certainly welcome to come along."

Every time Brad Fillmore mispronounced her name, Birgit's heart skipped a beat. The way he said it made it sound exciting, less ordinary. But despite his attempt to be polite, it was evident that he too was disappointed.

Lindsey, who'd instigated the trouble, seemed to be the only one unruffled. "I'm sure she'd rather be out on the water than staying home with me."

"Have you totally forgotten our commitment to the Kerrys?" asked Mr. Fillmore.

Who were the Kerrys? Were there more people going on the boat ride? Birgit looked at Elizabeth for a clue.

"The Kerrys are friends of ours," whispered Elizabeth, "filthy rich people, with a humongous house on the water. We are supposed to stop there for lunch."

"I can't see how me not going will affect anything," said Lindsey. "Let's face it, Brad—they're more your friends than mine. Bud, sorry to say, can be a bit much at times..."

"So, now you don't *like* them, either?"

"Either? What's that supposed to mean? I like loads of people…"

"Only if they're Democrats."

Lindsey rolled her eyes and smiled. "Well," she said, "you can't blame a girl for being selective, can you?" She gave Elizabeth a conspiratorial wink, but her attempt to buddy-up failed. Usually, Elizabeth responded hungrily to any attention from her mother, but not this time. She stared in stony silence at the kitchen wall. Let down again, she was not in a forgiving mood.

Birgit had noticed that Lindsey was an equal opportunity insulter. She easily switched from impeccable Emily Post manners to no manners at all. Birgit found a tiny bit of consolation at not being the only one. The "filthy rich" owners of the "humongous" house were targets too.

Elizabeth turned to Birgit. "Don't forget to bring your bathing suit…I'll bet *you* swim like a fish!" Though she was addressing Birgit, it was obvious the remark was aimed at her mother.

Lindsey ignored her daughter's comment. "Well, it's settled then." She'd made her decision, and her tone said to drop the subject and move on.

§

Birgit woke up feeling a variety of emotions. Apprehension painted one picture and anticipation a very different one. Resentment was also a part— the Fillmores had decided for her, and she had had no say in the matter. The previous night in the kitchen, she could just as well have been a bag of potatoes. *What shelf in the pantry do we put her on?*

Still, to sail on Long Island Sound with Brad Fillmore and Elizabeth— sans Lindsey—was not an unpleasant thought. What clothes should I bring? Shorts…sweats, maybe a jacket, in case it gets windy. A bathing suit? But which one? The one piece or the bikini? The latter looked so much better on her, and it wasn't THAT revealing, at least not as bikinis go. The devil made me do it, she giggled to herself, as she slid into the bikini, covering it with a pair of shorts and a sweatshirt.

Sunlight flooded the room and the branches of the large maple tree outside her window rustled softly in the wind. What a perfect day for sailing!

§

The Fillmores' sailboat was impressive, large, stately, but different from what Birgit had expected. It wasn't the newest in technology, not a fiberglass boat, but a classic wooden beauty.

Seeing her face, Mr. Fillmore smiled. "I guess I am a traditionalist." Without realizing it, he scored more points with Birgit. She was one too—at least when it came to boats.

The name "Femme Fatale" was written in bold letters on the stern. "Lindsey's choice, not mine," said Mr. Fillmore, still grinning. "She's convinced the boat seduced me."

Elizabeth skipped on board, her surly mood from the night before seemingly gone. No matter how precocious she is, Birgit thought, the girl was still only eleven and had a child's ability to bounce back.

"Let me show you around." Elizabeth dragged Birgit down in the galley. "What do you think? Not too shabby?" She proudly pointed to the kitchen, the stove, the sink and the refrigerator. "Check out this bathroom—there's a shower too."

Birgit was duly impressed. The boat was equipped like a luxury condo.

Mr. Fillmore climbed down the stairs to join them and continued the tour. "She has a doubled-planked hull," he explained proudly. "Burma teak on the outside. Western red cedar for the interior…" He gave an elaborate description of the boat but Birgit, distracted by his sheer presence, had a hard time focusing—he could be speaking Swahili as far as she was concerned. *Wonder if he knows that, up close, his eyes match the color of the Baltic Sea?*

Elizabeth cleared her throat. She studied Birgit's face, her eyes narrowing in an all-knowing look. "It's time to get going," she said. "The Kerrys are expecting us for lunch."

Mr. Fillmore maneuvered the boat out onto the sound while Birgit and Elizabeth lay on the deck, sunning. After making sure her father was busy, the girl leaned over and whispered to Birgit. "Mom thinks it's hilarious that most of her lady-friends are gaga over Dad. I do too. He's good looking, but so what? To me, he's just this guy who happened to marry my mom." She opened the suntan lotion and rubbed it on her nose and cheeks. There would be no elaboration.

Elizabeth's nonchalant statement caught Birgit off guard. *Was that a warning? Or am I making a big deal out of nothing?*

Perhaps it was Birgit's guilty conscience, but Elizabeth had hit a nerve. If it truly was a warning, who was the girl protecting? Not her father, obviously, and certainly not her mother—neither of them needed protection. The thought seemed silly to her at first, but the more Birgit mulled it over, the more sense it made—the girl was trying to save her from making a fool of herself!

§

Elizabeth had not exaggerated—the Kerry estate was humongous. The sprawling shingle-style home sat in a protected cove, with a panoramic view of Long Island Sound. Nothing was missing—direct waterfront, private beach, swimming pool, and a deep-water dock.

Mr. Fillmore had worried about arriving late, but the wind had picked up and they'd made better time than expected. A man waited on the dock. As the boat came closer, he waved and whooped happily.

Bud Kerry had the smooth, unlined face of someone who'd never found a reason to worry. He was a big man, not fat, but heading in that direction. His tall frame helped hide some extra pounds, but his baggy shorts hung low enough to expose a flabby waistline.

When Mr. Fillmore debarked, the two friends did the male version of an embrace, the shoulder bump. Mr. Kerry tousled Elizabeth's hair before turning to Birgit. "And you are…"? he asked with a broad smile, reaching out his hand.

Mr. Fillmore apologized for his rudeness. "Bud, this is Brigitte … I mean Birgitte." He mangled her name again. "She's our Swedish au pair… Didn't I mention her?"

"Don't think you did…pleasure…" Mr. Kerry shook Birgit's hand and added, "I knew a Swedish girl once…" His sheepish grin implied that the girl had been more than a casual acquaintance.

Birgit had noticed that American males often looked at her with that same expression when she mentioned her nationality. *It was that dumb movie's fault.*

In early 1950, Sweden had come out with a film that shocked the world. A young couple walked nude into the water. "Summer of Happiness," was a sweet romantic movie but that scene had given all Swedish girls a reputation.

Mr. Kerry pointed to the house. "Okay, shall we? I believe Maggie is waiting with lunch."

Maggie Kerry was a Mia Farrow look-alike, a thin child-woman whose clean-scrubbed face showed no hint of make-up. She wore sling-back sandals, a loose fitting blue shirt, and a wrap-around skirt. Her short light hair was damp as if she had just stepped out of the pool.

Maggie introduced herself in a voice just above a whisper and then led her guests to the veranda where two maids scurried around.

Despite her relaxed appearance, Mrs. Kerry had spent both time and effort on the planning, or she'd had excellent help. The setting was summery and light: a white-linen tablecloth, yellow napkins, a terra-cotta plant pot with yellow tulips placed near a silver plate filled with sand, seashells, stones and pillar candles. The table was sturdy and substantial. *Not the least bit wobbly.*

Birgit had a sudden flashback of her parents' veranda table back home. It rocked a bit, and Dad had a habit of placing a magazine under one of the legs. *Why did the memory of such a small imperfection make her feel out of place?*

The weather couldn't have been better. The view from the veranda was movie-set perfect, with whitecaps and sailboats dotting the sound. A lithe woman with a creamy complexion brought food and drinks to the table. She moved like a wood-nymph, her feet barely touching the floor. Her melodic voice brought with it the sound of the Islands and Belafonte.

When she poured Birgit's ice tea, too many ice cubes fell in from the pitcher and made the glass overflow. "It's okay," Birgit whispered. She dabbed the wet spot with her napkin, all the while thinking, I don't belong here anymore than you do.

When finished with lunch, Mr. Fillmore pushed back from the table and complimented the hostess. "Maggie, you outdid yourself this time."

"Thank you." Mia Farrow was not the flirty type but rested her eyes a second too long on her guest's face. Elizabeth was right—Brad Fillmore did have that effect on women.

The food *had* been impressive: a spicy Mexican dish named Shrimp Veracruz followed a chilled avocado soup, and the dessert was blackberry sorbet. Elizabeth might have longed for a peanut butter and jelly sandwich, but Birgit certainly hadn't. Though the Kerrys—and Mr. Fillmore too—had tried to draw her into the conversation, she still felt intimidated. Sitting next to Elizabeth had helped.

The two men kept up an easy banter, reminiscing about their college years and pranks they'd pulled before turning to politics and the upcoming football season. Abruptly, Bud changed the subject.

"So, now, tell me the real reason Lindsey chickened out."

Mr. Kerry's bluntness drew a disapproving look from his wife. While Mr. Fillmore fumbled for an answer, Elizabeth jumped in. "Mom didn't chicken out," she announced. "She has her period."

Everyone laughed, and Mr. Fillmore looked relieved. He threw up his hands. "Out of the mouths of babes…"

Perhaps she was being overly critical again, but Birgit had a hard time fathoming how Mr. Kerry made so much money. Elizabeth, who had developed a knack for reading her mind, mouthed two words. "Inherited wealth."

"So, Sweet Pea," said Mr. Kerry to Elizabeth, "did you bring your bathing suit? You have your choice. You can swim in the pool or jump in the sound."

Elizabeth shuddered at Mr. Kerry's "Sweet Pea" reference but answered politely. "Yes, I brought my bathing suit, and Birgit did too. "Hers is a bikini and we both like to dive from the dock."

"You go right ahead," said Mrs. Kerry. "Bud and I will sit this one out. We took a dip earlier."

"Doesn't mean I can't do it again," responded her husband.

"I thought you only liked to swim in the pool."

"You know me…I'll do whatever the guests wanna do."

Mr. Fillmore smoothly stepped in. "You three go right ahead," he said. "Maggie and I have some catching up to do."

"Mr. Kerry is such a goof," Elizabeth whispered to Birgit. "What he wants is to check you out in the bikini."

§

Unlike her mother, Elizabeth loved the water and was an excellent swimmer. "I'll dive first. Okay?"

She walked past the grown-ups with small, determined steps. At the end of the dock, she stopped, straightened her back, adjusted a strap on her blue bathing suit, curled her toes around the edge, lifted her heels, pushed off, and made a nice dive into the water. As soon as her head popped up from the water, she gestured for Birgit to join her.

Birgit saw Bud Kerry's eyes follow her every move as she removed her clothes. In fairness, he looked more expectant than lecherous, more like a playful Labrador retriever waiting to a have a ball thrown. She suppressed a smile.

Her nervousness from earlier had disappeared. Around water, she always felt confident. Her dive was perfect and Elizabeth, treading water, saluted her with a raised fist. "Let's see how *he* does," she called out to Birgit the second she surfaced. "Betcha, *he* doesn't want to follow your dive!"

She was right. Mr. Kerry looked like he changed his mind, retreating a few steps. But then he made a running start. The dock squeaked under his weight as he came tumbling down. With arms tucked around his legs, he cannon-balled wildly into the water.

Birgit was amused. When his head popped out of the water, they smiled at each other. Just like a kid. Somehow the water, the dive—and her bikini— had leveled the playing field.

§

"We'll be home later than planned," Mr. Fillmore said to no one in particular, "but it was fun, don't you think?"

They'd left the shore and the Kerrys were waving from the dock. Elizabeth waited for the sunset, but as soon as the sun sank into the sound, she left for the cabin with a Nancy Drew mystery in her hand. Mr. Fillmore turned to Birgit. "Bud invited us all back. Especially you!" He grinned. "You made quite an impression."

"I don't know how…we barely said a word to each other."

"With Bud, you don't speak. You listen. I know Lindsey finds him tiresome, but he's a good guy. With old friends, you tend to overlook a few idiosyncrasies." *Idiosyncrasies? Was that the same as habits?* Birgit still spent hours after work checking her dictionary to learn new words.

She wrapped her windbreaker tighter around her. After the sun went down, the air had cooled and had a fall-like feel. "You're shivering," said Mr. Fillmore. "I'll get you a blanket. How does a cup of tea sound?"

Though she much preferred coffee, Birgit thought anything warm would do. Just the fact that he offered to make it for her was enough.

"Take the helm. I'll be just a few minutes," Mr. Fillmore said. "You're familiar with the buoys, red right returning, and that stuff?"

Birgit nodded. Sailing was something she knew well.

It seemed as if no time had passed when Mr. Fillmore came back upstairs with two mugs in his hands and a blanket over the shoulder. "The kid is out like a light. Being on the water does that to her every time."

He put down the cups and draped the blanket around Birgit's shoulders. She caught a glimpse of his hands, strong and tan. A callus near his left thumb, probably from a golf club, was the only imperfection, discounting the wedding ring on that same hand. Birgit shuddered and straightened her back. He reached to tuck the blanket more closely around her and his touch was more intimate than any kiss.

"Brigitte, I know you and Lindsey are on first name basis." He reached for one of the mugs of tea and handed it to her. "We should be, too, don't you think?"

16

Birgit looked out the kitchen window to find that the leaves on the maple tree shimmered in a vibrant gold. "Fall must have happened while I wasn't watching," she said to Elizabeth.

Her no-fail source of information promptly replied. "Most people don't know this, but the chlorophyll is always on the leaves. You see only the green because the other colors are hidden. When it gets cold, the water stops flowing to the leaves," she said, "and that's why they change from green to gold and red. We studied this in class."

Birgit smiled at her walking encyclopedia. "That's very interesting, but I prefer to think of the changing colors as a mystery—and not as a chemical process."

The last couple of months had been hotter than anything Birgit could remember, and for the first time, she looked forward to the end of summer. In her country, autumn meant resignation, followed by a long, stoic wait for spring. Here in Connecticut, it was more like an energy boost.

Elizabeth, too, wanted summer to be over. The Fillmores' property was lovely, but not readily accessible—at least not for kids too young to drive.

The closest road was a highway, meant for cars not bikes. There had been sleepovers at the house and a few friends had visited, but lately, Elizabeth had turned restless, waiting for school to start.

Birgit teased her. "I know. You just want to go back to school so you can see that guy you like. What's his name again?"

"Charles Walker…the third…and for your information, I never said I liked him. I said he was cute! Those are two different things."

"So, you have a crush?"

"Crushes are for little girls."

"You're eleven…"

"I don't…" Elizabeth paused, searching for an expression Birgit would understand. "…see me as a kid."

"Perceive!" exclaimed Birgit. "I don't *perceive* myself as a kid. That is what you planned to say. Right?" She pronounced the new word distinctly and proudly. "Perceive" was one of the new words she'd added to her vocabulary.

Elizabeth was impressed. "You're getting there, girl!" she said.

§

"Hold on a second, please…"

Lindsey tucked the phone between her cheek and shoulder as she furiously chopped onions and shallots on a cutting board in the kitchen. Ever since Birgit's success with the Swedish meatballs, Lindsey had redoubled her efforts to turn her husband and daughter into gourmets. She put her hand over the receiver and whispered to Birgit, "Get Elizabeth for me, please. She's in the garden."

Just waiting for vegetables to grow had not been enough of a challenge. Elizabeth, on her own, had expanded the garden, putting in shrubs and planting saplings she claimed would become beautiful fruit trees someday. She'd followed a self-made schematic with an ambitious idea to make the area around the barn a park.

Birgit called her, but when Elizabeth didn't respond, she headed for the garden herself. The girl sat on the bench, lost in thought, with Zoë at her feet. When she finally became aware of Birgit's footsteps, she turned around and smiled. "So, what do you think?" she asked, waving her hands at the garden.

As far as Birgit could tell, it looked mostly like clumps of dirt spread around, but she forced herself to see the garden through Elizabeth's eyes—not the way it was, but how it was going to be.

"It's coming along great."

"This is my sanctuary," Elizabeth said dreamily. *Sanctuary.* Birgit put the word in her memory bank—she would look it up later.

"I came to tell you that your mom wants you…"

As soon as Elizabeth heard the words, she changed. The dreaminess was gone. She leaped off the bench and rushed like a hopeful puppy past Birgit toward the house. Birgit followed close behind.

When Elizabeth reached the house, Lindsey blocked her entrance into the kitchen. "Honey, leave those dirty boots outside. And rinse your hands and face in the sink. Birgit, please bring down a clean shirt for her. She's a mess!"

After Elizabeth had cleaned up, Lindsey inspected her daughter. "You've grown over summer. We must buy you some new clothes for school."

Elizabeth was thrilled. "Great! When are we going shopping?"

"Birgit will have to take you. I'm swamped with stuff to do for the Symphony Guild."

Poof! The light in Elizabeth's eyes disappeared. Insensitive witch, Birgit thought. Couldn't you just for once spend a few hours with your daughter?

Lindsey ignored the disappointment on her daughter's face and pressed some bills into Birgit's hand. "Elizabeth likes Bloomingdale's," she said. "Why don't you take her there tomorrow and buy her what she needs? You girls can make a day of it. Go for lunch or whatever…"

Birgit looked down at the stack of fifty- and twenty-dollar bills. "How much of this can I spend?"

"That's up to you. All of it…if that what it takes. I want you to have fun!"

§

The mall was busy, filled with mothers shopping for school with their children. Elizabeth had not spoken since they left the house, and Birgit tried to fill the silence with idle comments. Although they fell flat, she heard herself babble on, unable to stop.

Birgit held up two jumpers, one in navy blue with a tieback and one in a khaki color with pleats. "Try this one. It would be cute on you…or this one… and here are some blouses to go with them."

Elizabeth obediently took the pile of clothes Birgit had picked out and went into the dressing room. She was back in just a few minutes, too quickly to have tried on all the clothes. "Everything fit," she said, handing Birgit the clothes. "Can we go now?"

Birgit disliked the fake cheerfulness in her voice. "How about some lunch before we drive home?"

Elizabeth shrugged. Birgit took the gesture as a yes and headed to the checkout counter. What a shame, she thought. Here, they were in the pre-teen section of Bloomingdale's junior department, and Elizabeth could buy anything she wanted. Still, that hadn't made her happy. Only having her mom with her would have.

The girl had taken one bite of her hamburger and then pushed it aside, and Birgit tried not to make a big deal of it. "Not hungry?"

Elizabeth shook her head in response to the question, and turned to her chocolate milkshake instead. Where she might normally have giggled at the gurgling sound when she sucked on the straw, her face was blank. Birgit felt like an actress, using tired old lines in front of an unresponsive audience.

The girl was neither rude nor impolite, just dejected, and Birgit finally decided that involving her in a conversation was pointless. She checked the bags and receipts before finishing her lunch in silence.

After a bit, Elizabeth finally spoke. "Did your mom go shopping with you for school clothes?" The sentence was the first full one she had spoken since they'd left home.

Birgit nodded. "She did, but she argued with me a lot."

Elizabeth looked up. "At least she was interested." Birgit had not thought about it that way. *Had her mother nagged her because she cared?*

Elizabeth continued the questions. "Did your mom drive you to school?"

"No, I walked or rode my bike. It wasn't that far, and Mom didn't like to drive Dad's truck." The truth was that Vera did not know how to drive, but Birgit did not feel like sharing.

"Didn't she have her own car?"

Birgit shook her head. "No…we didn't live the way you do."

"A different socio-economic level?"

Birgit understood the expression. It resembled the Swedish one. The remark stung a little, but she knew that Elizabeth didn't mean it as a putdown. She had just made her typical blunt observation.

"Something like that, yes."

Elizabeth moved on, unaware. "My au pairs have always taken me to school. Maybe Mom will this year."

§

The girl's excitement over the first day of school overshadowed her disappointment in her mother. She fussed over what to wear and changed outfits back and forth before settling on a navy-blue jumper, a white blouse with a rounded Peter Pan collar and small dainty ruffles, and a short pink jacket. Birgit brushed her dark hair until it shone.

"Before we go, don't you want to show your mother what you look like?" she asked.

Elizabeth was busy putting on her new shoes. The small heels pleased her. They made her look taller and more grown-up. She circled in front of the full-length mirror, critically studying herself. "Not really," she said coolly, glancing at her new watch with the bubble-gum-pink band. "I can't be late. Let's go."

In the car, Elizabeth shared a new grievance against her parents. "They are going on a trip together," she said. "I could go too, but I'll probably have more fun staying home."

Birgit frowned. "No one told me about a trip. Are you sure?"

"Yeah. Dad doesn't want to go, but he will."

"How so?"

"Because he's a wimp. He does what Mom tells him to do."

Birgit didn't know the meaning of the word "wimp," but judging from Elizabeth's tone, she assumed it was negative. "You shouldn't say those things about your dad."

"Sorry," replied Elizabeth. "I forgot you have the hots for him."

Birgit's cheeks burned. "Oh, Elizabeth!" A sudden flashback came to her of Mr. Fillmore draping a blanket over her shoulders, his fingers touching her back. Him saying, "Call me Brad." She never would have, of course. Only in her mind did she sometimes call him by his first name.

Mercifully, the school building appeared, saving her from further embarrassment. Elizabeth looked out the window and exclaimed, "This is it! Turn left here. That'll take us to the parking lot."

The school was a large complex on many acres of land. The middle-school building, the one Elizabeth went to, was a stately old colonial with a white clapboard front. It sat by itself, away from the rest, protected by towering pines and surrounded by green meadows and playing fields. Boys dressed in shirts, ties, and blazers, and girls in outfits similar to Elizabeth's had gathered outside.

Birgit parked, turned off the engine and opened the door to get out. "What do you think you're doing!?" said Elizabeth, her voice suddenly tense. "You can't go with me. I am a big girl now." Birgit followed her eyes and found the source of her anxiety.

Birgit nodded in the direction of a group of boys laughing and talking on the walkway not far from the car. "The blond, cute one to the left," she whispered, "that's him, isn't it? THE THIRD?"

Elizabeth hissed under her breath. "Yes…but don't stare! And don't call him THE THIRD…It's not his fault that his parents put numerals after his name!"

Birgit pulled her legs back into the car. She was about to close the door when Elizabeth stopped her.

"Wait…please! What do I do now? Should I say something to him or just walk by and ignore him? And, please don't stare…"

Birgit pretended to search for something in her purse. "Act normal," she said. "Smile, but not too wide…or nod, the way you do to a friend. Don't skip or run, just walk!"

"I'll do that. Thanks! Sorry for being a pain. You're picking me up, right?"

"I am," said Birgit, "and I will require details."

Elizabeth chuckled and then took a deep breath and slowly walked in the direction of the boy she had claimed she didn't like. He appeared to ignore her completely, but just when she passed, he grabbed the boy standing next to him and wrestled him to the ground.

Good! thought Birgit. He is showing off. That means he likes her. She watched Elizabeth walk across the parking lot. She carried herself well, not looking exactly confident, but not uptight either. As she neared the school, a group of girls her age waved to her. Elizabeth waved back—and Birgit saw her shoulders relax as she hurried to join them.

Birgit let out a sigh of relief. *She would be all right.*

She smiled to herself as she drove away. I act like her mom. But, then again, somebody has to.

17

"Lindsey!"

"In the kitchen, dahling!

Brad, just home from work, walked through the kitchen door. He nodded as he passed Birgit at the stove, but his eyes were solely on his wife.

"Hi," he said, nuzzling Lindsey's ear. "You look and smell delicious."

She had spent a good part of the afternoon soaking in the bathtub with no distractions, no phone calls or art projects, just leisurely working on her already stunning perfection. Now, with her make-up in place, her jet-black hair brushed back into a twist, she was luminous—a rare, exotic bird in a midnight blue kimono with silver threads, high-heeled sandals, and earrings so huge they would look ludicrous on someone less spectacular.

After the meatball incident, Lindsey had made it clear that she was the cook in the house. For Birgit to even be allowed to help was a rarity. Tonight, though, Lindsey had asked Birgit to stir rice, steam asparagus, and help with other menial tasks.

Brad put his briefcase on the seat of the kitchen chair, hung his coat on the back, and loosened his tie. "I'm bushed."

Lindsey's voice dripped with sexual innuendo. "*Too* bushed?"

"Never!" mumbled her husband. He pulled her close and whispered something in her ear that brought on a breathless laugh.

§

Lindsey had spent all afternoon with one purpose in mind. The lights were dimmed, and there were candles on the table. That meant only one thing. Birgit remembered Elizabeth's comments. Tuesdays and Fridays were her parents' "romantic" nights.

"At times, she plays geisha. Kinky, if you ask me…" Elizabeth didn't mince words. "Those two make my skin crawl."

The atmosphere was definitely charged. Birgit cleared her throat, in case no one had noticed she was still in the kitchen. Lindsey, she knew, had no inhibitions. To her, an employee's presence mattered no more than the kitchen table.

Brad at least had the good sense to look uncomfortable. "Oh, sorry, I thought you left," he said. "Are you making dinner tonight?"

Lindsey quickly set him straight. "Birgit is just here to give me a hand. We're having something light. A simple pasta dish with mussels and scallops… Okay with you?"

"Sounds good," Brad said, without conviction. He was not a seafood lover. He pointed to the counter where travel brochures were spread. "What's all this?"

His wife glanced at the counter and back at the scallops. "You know how we've talked about getting away."

"WE?" Brad's tone was light but he gave his wife a subtle glance. "Not sure about that."

Lindsey pursed her lips in a little-girl pout, but the sound of her voice was not that of a little girl's—it had a tempting undertone.

Birgit cringed. The poor guy didn't stand a chance. She desperately hoped that she would be asked to leave. "The food is ready. Should I turn it off?"

Ignoring Birgit's question, Lindsey opened the doors to the cabinets in her usual impatient way. "Where's the colander?" she said sharply. "It would be helpful if things were put back in the same place."

Birgit wanted to say, "They are. Right in front of your nose," but to argue with Lindsey was pointless. She clenched her teeth, bent down, pulled out the strainer from the cabinet, and handed it over without a word.

Brad watched the whole exchange with amusement. Birgit thought she saw him wink at her behind his wife's back and found herself responding with a reflexive surge of happiness. *Like Pavlov's dog*, she thought.

"Why don't we hold off dinner for a while?" he said to Lindsey. "I'd like to unwind with a drink first."

Lindsey lowered her eyes in true Geisha fashion. Not ready for an aggressive full court press just yet, but not ready to let go either. She picked up one of the glossy travel magazines and put it in front of her husband on the kitchen table.

He glanced at it and quietly pushed it aside. "I can't take a lengthy trip now. Too much going on at work. Maybe a few days in the Caribbean?"

Lindsey whirled around. "I hate the islands! They are filled with poor, resentful people! Let's do Europe instead."

"Well, I might be able to swing a week in Scotland later in the month…"

"Not Scotland—then you'd find an excuse to bring your golf clubs. Italy! That's it! Tuscany…no, Florence. We have never been there. I could totally immerse myself in the arts!"

Brad looked at his wife and sighed. "To hang around museums and art galleries sounds like work to me…but I'm open to suggestions. Let's negotiate over a drink, shall we?"

"Let's! On the veranda?"

Lindsey knew she had gained the advantage. The final push would come later. She turned to Birgit. "You've done enough," she said, suddenly saccharin-sweet. "Just leave the food on warm, please. I'll handle the rest."

While Birgit cleaned off the counters, the sultry voice of Dinah Washington, a Fillmore favorite, wafted from the family room. "I wanna be loved with inspiration…"

They like to dance first, Elizabeth had said with disgust. *I assume that's what's called foreplay.*

Birgit had no problem visualizing them on the veranda. Brad would set his drink down and pull Lindsey close. In her high heels, she was almost as tall as her husband—the perfect height for dancing cheek to cheek. He would close his eyes and put both hands on the small of her back.

Dinah's phrasing was crisp and left little to the imagination. *"I wanna be thrilled to desperation…starting tonight…"*

The lyric followed Birgit upstairs.

§

Brad's footsteps were light and bouncy the next morning as he headed downstairs for breakfast. His whistling capped off the whole happiness thing, and Birgit sunk deeper into bed and buried her head in the pillow. No way was she getting up to fix his breakfast. After his night of passion with Lindsey, the thought of asking, "Would you like your egg scrambled or sunny-side up?" was more than she could handle.

Why was she mad at him for? For making love to his wife? Or for being so easily manipulated? Either way, this had nothing to do with her. She was pitiful and in serious need of therapy. Even Hilde, who wasn't the sharpest knife in the drawer, had nosed herself to the truth.

"You don't seem to want to date at all. You said you're over that guy in Sweden, so who…"

"Don't you go there!" Birgit interrupted, using a Lindsey expression.

Hilde dropped the subject, but a flash went off in her eyes.

§

The bell from the master bedroom had an insistent ring. Lindsey had slept even longer than usual. Birgit knocked lightly on the door and stepped inside. "You wanted me?"

Lindsey was in bed with the curtains drawn. Her face was flushed and glowing. "I feel lazy today. Why don't you fix some eggs and bring them up here?" Her negligee lay on top of some bedclothes on the floor—a sheer, rose-colored proof of her victory. She stretched and yawned. Before she pulled up the sheets, Birgit caught a glimpse of an exposed, milky-white breast.

A feeling of jealousy hit Birgit with force—irrational, but undeniably real. She swallowed hard and then answered. "I'll bring it right up. Would you like me to pull the drapes?"

"No, leave them. I'd like to stay in the mood a little bit longer." Her green eyes, the same color as Elizabeth's, but without their innocence, bore into Birgit, challenging her, waiting for a reaction.

She knows! Birgit felt exposed, humiliated. *To send me on the boat trip with her husband had been part of the plan. She had never been worried—Birgit was not in her league, never had been, and never would be.*

119

The silence that followed was palpable, but in no time, the strange glitter in Lindsey's eyes subsided and she was back to looking bored. "You have no problem being home alone with Elizabeth, do you? You two appear to get along. I'm pleased with how well you fit in with the family." She pulled the sheet up higher. "We're going to Italy, but just for a measly ten days," she said.

§

Surprisingly, Elizabeth didn't seem bothered by her parents leaving. First, Birgit thought the girl's air of indifference was an act, but that wasn't the case at all. The unexpected had happened—David Walker III had called. Only to ask about a homework assignment, but Elizabeth's whole focus had changed. No more pouting about, no concern about her missed trip to Europe. The burning question became instead: Will he, or won't he call again? Had he phoned because he liked her? Or because he needed her help? Overcome with doubts, she had apparently convinced herself of the latter. Any attempt from Birgit to tell her otherwise fell on deaf ears.

"Why wouldn't he like you?" coaxed Birgit. "You're both cute and smart!"

"You don't get it! Guys like David don't look for brains. They want airheads—stupid, pretty airheads."

Birgit made another attempt. "Did he say anything at all encouraging?"

"Nope. All he said was, 'See you around.' Even *you* can't read anything memorable into that."

§

Birgit and the Fillmores stood in the entry hall. Brad looked at his wife's bulging suitcases stacked at the front door. "I thought we were vacationing, not emigrating."

Lindsey had packed and repacked and agonized up to the very last minute on what to bring. "Europe might not be chilly at all. Why didn't I pack a few sleeveless dresses?"

Although pleasant, Brad's tone had a touch of impatience. "Beats me, but..." he said, opening the door, "...the limo is here. Stop fretting! If you feel you must have another dress, I'll buy you one in Italy."

The driver came to the door, ready to help with the luggage, and Lindsey stomped her foot. "Darn it! I knew I'd forget something. My black evening dress is at the cleaners. Birgit, please pick it up for me later. The ticket is next to the phone in the kitchen."

Brad gave Birgit an impersonal employer kind of smile and then pinched Elizabeth's cheek. "Take care of my girl, okay?" He looked back at Birgit—there was no wink, no connection at all this time. "If anything comes up, you know how to reach Mrs. Hirschberg, right?" Birgit was suddenly relieved that they'd decided to take the limousine and not have her drive them to the airport.

She and Elizabeth stood watching as the car pulled away. Lindsey lowered her window and stuck her head out. "One last thing...while we are away, why don't you take Elizabeth on some educational trips? This state has some interesting covered bridges. I'd suggest West Cornwall. It has the historical significance Elizabeth loves." She blew a kiss in the direction of her daughter, and they were off.

Amazing how little Lindsey knows of what's going on under her roof. She has no idea that Elizabeth is going through her first serious crush and that visiting historical sites is currently low on her agenda.

Elizabeth sighed. "Finally! I'm glad to see them leave. Aren't you?"

Only one of them, thought Birgit.

§

Elizabeth thought she had made some progress in the relationship arena—David had stopped her in school to thank her for helping him out.

"He smiled," she told Birgit. "I never noticed it before, but he has the cutest dimple in his right cheek."

"So how did you act when he thanked you?"

"Real cool. Anytime, I said." She made a face. "But then I messed it all up by grinning like an idiot."

§

Elizabeth's new habit after school was to come home, go straight to her room, study, and wait for the phone to ring. Any "educational" trips were put on indefinite hold. The gardening, too, was neglected. "I know all I need to know about how to make compost, how to plant, and harvest. Time to take a break," she explained.

Birgit, on the other hand, was not one to slack off. Without Lindsey around, she found new inspiration to clean and make changes. The only area out of bounds was the art studio. In the rest of the house, she had full reign.

She stayed with Elizabeth, except for the two nights a week she spent on adult education English classes. Hilde, who had no interest in joining her, offered to babysit those nights.

"Don't you want to brush up on your English?" Birgit had asked her, astonished.

Hilde had looked equally astonished. "What for? I make myself understood, don't I?"

"But don't you at least want to get rid of your...accent?" Birgit stopped short of inserting "heavy," in front of "accent."

"Of course not. I am who I am."

On the way to class that evening, Birgit stopped to pick up some groceries and Lindsey's dress at the dry-cleaner. She would put it away when she got home.

§

When she opened the master bedroom closet, Birgit felt like an intruder. She had been in the Fillmores' bedroom many times before but never in the wardrobe. The closet was larger even than her room and filled with drawers, shelves, and loads of storage. Birgit glanced around it, marveling. Everything was "state of the art."

Brad's side of the closet was perfectly organized. Birgit looked at the neatly lined-up row of shoes. She instinctively reached out to touch one of his shirts and held the sleeve to her face. There was a hint of his aftershave. The smell made her close the eyes, and she told herself for the hundredth time to get over her crazy, hopeless fixation.

Lindsey's side of the closet was also neat, but larger and brimming over with garments. To make room, Birgit pushed some of the hangers apart. She hung the dress in the open space...and then gasped. *There it was! The same green mini-dress she had so admired at Saks!*

With her heart pounding, Birgit lifted it off the hanger and held it against her. *What would it hurt to try it on?* She kicked off her shoes, removed her clothes and stepped into the dress. She watched her reflection in the full-length mirror, took a couple of steps back, circled slowly, tossed her hair back, and smiled.

Elizabeth appeared out of nowhere. "He called!" she said, exultantly. Then she saw Brigit and stood in stunned silence. The triumphant gleam in her eyes died out.

"WHY," she screamed, "ARE YOU IN MY MOTHER'S DRESS?"

18

Why are you in my mother's dress? The moment following the question had been uncomfortably long. Elizabeth had stared her down, eyes cold, lips set taut. Birgit's feeble attempt to explain herself was cut short—the girl hadn't give her a chance to finish and had left the room with a chilly, "Never mind." Under other circumstances, the snub—a perfect Lindsey imitation—might have been amusing, but this time it wasn't. What Birgit felt was humiliation and guilt. *She doesn't trust me anymore.*

After the dress incident, the relaxed relationship that had developed between them—the easy banter, the teasing, the sharing of confidences—was gone, and Birgit missed it more than she cared to admit. The girl, in a very short time, had become a confidante and friend, almost like a younger sister. They had both grown up with distant mothers, but Birgit, at least, had had the support of her father. Brad, she had to admit, couldn't or wouldn't make up for Lindsey's shortcomings as a parent. He was pleased that his daughter was cute, smart, and witty, but seemed clueless about her needs.

This was all complicated by the fact that the couple's Italian vacation was not the success Lindsey had envisioned. Since they'd returned home, she'd been essentially mum about the vacation. "Pleasant," was all she said when Birgit asked about the trip—hardly a ringing endorsement.

Weeks later, Lindsey finally touched on the subject. She'd searched the house to find a home for the small Madonna painting she'd bought in Italy. The search went on for days before she settled for a place on the hallway wall.

"I felt so at home in Florence," she said wistfully, talking more to herself than to Birgit. "It should've been an enriching experience, but…" Her green eyes stared out into space. "It's a mistake to travel with someone who doesn't share your interests."

She took a step back to study the effect of the artwork against the wall, shook her head, and with an impatient motion removed it, tucking it behind some books in the bookcase. How is it possible, Birgit wondered, to be married to the most attractive man on earth and still feel let down?

§

"Get a life," Hilde told Birgit. "Start going out! Have some fun!"

Brigit thought it was time to take her advice, to stop moping around and get rid of the lingering but hopeless fixation with Brad. Perhaps the deteriorated relationship with Elizabeth was a blessing in disguise—it would help get her out of the house, at least.

She threw herself into studying, did well in her English classes, and became more familiar with the language. These days, she found herself relying less and less often on the dictionary.

Hilde had nagged her about a dance at the International Club in Stamford, a place they were both familiar with, and Birgit had finally given in. But, she'd had second thoughts the moment she'd stepped inside. Maybe her mood played a part, but it seemed to her to be even darker and seedier than she remembered. The second coming of Brad Fillmore would never show up at a place like this, but it was better than sitting at home feeling sorry for herself.

Birgit watched as men of all ages lingered near the entrance, smoking and keeping tabs on the girls coming through the door.

"They're all married," she told Hilde.

"How do you know that?"

"I can tell."

"Party-pooper!" Hilde rolled her eyes and headed for the bar.

Birgit, in enough trouble already because of one married man, had no plans to start a collection, but when a clean-cut young man claiming to be single asked her to dance, she accepted. Looks can deceive, she thought, but he looks harmless enough.

The glow from the fluorescent lights lit teeth and light-colored shirts to a surreal whiteness. Coupled with the purple haze from a strobe light, it created a confused, slightly drug induced feel.

"An LSD atmosphere, *nicht wahr?*" Hilde whispered excitedly.

On stage, the face of the bleached-blonde vocalist flickered in and out of the light as she gave what Birgit thought was a decent rendition of "Strangers in the Night." She shut her eyes and did what she knew better than to do—visualize Brad's face. She scolded herself. *Stop dreaming and focus on the positives.* The guy she was dancing with didn't smell of smoke or too much cologne and he wasn't humming in her ear. Best of all, he was single!

He leaned in so Birgit could hear him. "I'm Patrick Carlini."

She raised an eyebrow and he chuckled. "Yeah, I know that's an unusual combo. I'm a mixed puppy—Mom is Irish, Dad Italian."

Birgit began to relax—Patrick looked to be about her age, and the absence of spark between them didn't bother her. A no-drama evening would be just fine.

About that time, Birgit heard a familiar laugh and Hilde swept by, blond braid bobbing, arms around her newest conquest. Birgit groaned to herself. It was going to be a long night. She kicked herself for agreeing to let Hilde drive.

Patrick interrupted her thoughts. "Where are you from? Scandinavia?"

Birgit nodded, and he looked pleased to have guessed right. Luckily, he didn't mess up a good thing by saying something lame like," It must be cold over there," or even worse, like "Is it true that you girls lie topless on the beaches?"

To Hilde's delight, the night went well enough that Birgit accepted a date with Patrick, who *was* single, didn't smoke, and worked as a salesman for Xerox. Nothing about him was exciting except for the car he drove—a '62 red Plymouth Fury with ridiculously large fins. He'd corrected her when she'd mentioned them. "Not fins," he'd said. "Those babies are *stabilizers*."

With his sandy hair and pale eyes, he was so nondescript that Birgit almost forgot what he looked like between dates. His conversation was uninspiring, mostly stuck on mundane things—the Plymouth's suspension and the newest in copy machines. He was reliable, content, and *dull*. To kiss him was as thrilling to Birgit as licking an envelope.

An unexpected side benefit, though, was the positive impact her time with him had on her broken relationship with Elizabeth. She'd never imagined that her new boyfriend would be the one to repair the break, but unwittingly he had.

"So you're dating!" Elizabeth's response was the first sound of approval Birgit had heard from her in weeks. The girl's eyes—bright and inquisitive—had relief written all over them.

Birgit learned an important lesson. Even though Lindsey was selfish and often uncaring, her daughter would never allow someone else to take her place.

Why hadn't she thought of this before? Simply by seeing someone, Birgit had climbed back into Elizabeth's good graces. She would happily continue dating if it meant saving her relationship with the girl.

But, despite her best intentions, the fling with Patrick was short-lived. Their relationship sputtered and was over by early November. Neither one of them had been invested emotionally in the other, so the breakup was painless and unconfrontational.

Only three things stood out from her time with him: cha-cha tunes, the smell of popcorn, and movies…lots of movies. *Barefoot in the Park, Bonnie and Clyde, The Graduate.* She listened to Richard Burton and a foul-mouthed Liz Taylor, who Birgit thought of as a Lindsey clone, hurl horrible insults at each other in *Who's Afraid of Virginia Woolf?* She sobbed at *Doctor Zhivago* and loved *The Sound of Music* so much that they went to see it twice.

At the end of what proved to be their last date, Patrick muttered something about calling when a blockbuster movie came around, but both knew that was unlikely to happen. Birgit hoped that her general lack of interest in dating had nothing to do with Brad, but she knew better. To block him out was hard, but she worked on it every day. She'd stopped using his first name when referring to him, and in face-to-face meetings with him, she avoided using his name altogether.

No longer did she get up early to fix his food, but she still felt guilty seeing his dishes in the sink in the morning. A cup, a plate with breadcrumbs, and the residue of some orange stickiness all indicated that his breakfast had been tea and toast with marmalade. *No eggs!* To force him out of her mind during the day was possible, but the nights were out of her control. He came to her in her dreams, and in the mornings, she woke up warm and unsettled.

At the same time, dating meant trouble. Most men don't generally leave on such friendly terms as Patrick Carlini had. But if she didn't date, would

Elizabeth question her again? *Could she invent someone? A fictional character who'd be absent a lot? A foreign diplomat? Someone, eventually sent home suspected of espionage—a cultural attaché with the Egyptian embassy? She could name him Omar something,* she decided. *Elizabeth would love the drama.*

Birgit's talent for fibbing surprised her. Effortlessly, she provided details about her mysterious boyfriend and Elizabeth ate it all up. The best part was that the girl was again confiding in her. "Omar" opened up a whole new venue, and Elizabeth—who'd been holding on to a big secret—was ready to share her news.

She'd broken up with David Walker III and become famous in the process. Who dumps the cutest boys in the sixth grade? Well, Elizabeth had, because he was—in her estimation—shallow and cheap. He wouldn't even share a stick of gum, she said. The girls in her class, bewildered at first, were now in awe. The boys too had been impressed, though likely somewhat threatened.

Birgit wasn't really sure Elizabeth believed the tales about her Egyptian suitor, but the girl certainly seemed to enjoy them. After a time, the stories became so tangled that Birgit could no longer keep them straight, so she decided Omar had to be "sent packing." She invented an extradition after an international scandal, based mainly on rumors and unsubstantiated accusations. The issue was settled—the U.S. was sending him back to Egypt.

Elizabeth was infuriated. "It stinks!" she told her mother. "And I'll bet it's because he is an Arab. You should talk to Dad—he has contacts."

"I doubt there is anything we can do on our end," said Lindsey. She shot Birgit a glance that said, "Aren't you a bit old to have an imaginary friend?"

In any case, after Omar left and was no longer a topic of conversation, Birgit was relieved to discover that she'd earned back Elizabeth's trust. No new boyfriends, real or fictional, were needed.

Elizabeth also claimed to be tired of boys. "I'm too young to date," she admitted. "But at least I know I'm not a lesbian. Not to say that's wrong," she quickly added—Elizabeth had inhaled political correctness from Lindsey—"but it's important to know who you are."

The girl is right, thought Birgit. It is important to know who you are… and where you're headed.

19

"I want to sit next to Birgit at dinner tomorrow!"

Lindsey seemed caught off guard. "Well, Elizabeth...I'm not so sure..." Her hesitance made Birgit, against her better judgment, jump in.

"Thanksgiving is for family," she said to Elizabeth. She said it not to rescue Lindsey, but to protect herself from hurt. She could live with not being included, but to hear it spelled out would be a harder pill to swallow. She reminded Elizabeth that Thanksgiving Day wasn't celebrated in Europe. "Besides, I'm perfectly fine sitting in the kitchen. That way I can serve first and then eat and clean up later."

Birgit had no problem reading Lindsey's mind. *Good...one less person to worry about.* Not that her employer had been at all concerned about her—before Elizabeth had brought the whole idea of sitting beside her, Birgit hadn't even been considered.

"Aunt Ethel and Uncle Milton will sit over here..." Unperturbed, Lindsey continued planning the seating arrangements. Elizabeth gave her mother an accusing look, but left it at that. To keep her mom on an even keel was important. If she stayed that way, the holiday would be a success.

Since Lindsey's lone sibling, Ethel Hirschberg, and her husband Milton, were childless, Elizabeth was the only grandchild and she loved the attention she was shown by her relatives.

Boring tasks like cleaning up would fall to Birgit, but the planning, food, and decorations were all handled by Lindsey. Despite their differences, the two worked surprisingly well together, and by Thanksgiving, the house was sparkling clean and decorated to the hilt.

Lindsey looked pleased as she examined the end result. "I absolutely love this house," she sighed. "It called to me the first time I laid eyes on it." Birgit too loved the house, and even though she had only helped with menial things, she was proud of the way it looked. The Fillmore home looked "lived in." It had warmth and character, and the nicks and dents only added to its charm.

Birgit's father flashed into her mind. *Dad used to call me an old soul, and he's right. I much prefer an old house with history to something new and glossy.*

Entertaining inspired Lindsey. Her mind, so often scattered, became focused and razor sharp—nothing was left to chance. What could be prepared ahead had already been taken care of. The two refrigerators—the one in the kitchen and a second in the garage—were brimming over with food.

"Fire-and-Ice," a dramatic, frozen centerpiece was one of her last-minute creations. Tea lights floated on top of a container filled with water, pine cones, silver balls and beads. Tomorrow, the decoration would be removed from the freezer, put on a gold rimmed glass plate surrounded by handpicked greenery and expected to draw admiring "oohs and ahs."

Lindsey's mother and father were flying in from Chicago later in the evening but had refused to be picked up. "We'll rent a car at the airport," her father said, "and we're staying at a hotel, not at the house…end of discussion!"

Their daughter was disappointed, but she shrugged it off. "They can't stand being fussed over," she said. "I should have learned that by now."

Birgit had not met Lindsey's parents and was surprised to learn that her maiden name was Sorensen. Lindsey hardly looked Scandinavian, but the mystery was solved once they arrived. Her father, it seemed, was of Norwegian descent. Mrs. Sorensen, formerly Charlene Dubois from Louisiana, was a delicate-looking woman, shorter than Lindsey, but with the same elegant features, and coloring that hinted to a different, more exotic origin. "Part Creole," Elizabeth told Birgit. "At least that's what Grandpa says. He thinks it's charming, but of course 'Miss Scarlett' totally denies it."

Whereas that was the nickname Elizabeth had given her mother's mother, she'd pinned "Jack the Knife" on Brad's mother. Helen Fillmore, according to Elizabeth, was cool, distant and status conscious. She would arrive Thanksgiving morning accompanied by her son Charles, with whom she shared a penthouse on Manhattan's Upper West Side. Charles, 32, was Brad's younger brother, a part-time writer who Elizabeth said was working on a Ph.D. in a "complex" and "unusual" field.

"My parents think it won't take him anywhere, but that's okay. Uncle Charles is too intellectual to work anyway," she explained, "and Grandma adores him." She imitated her grandmother's high-pitched voice with perfection. "*I love my boys equally*, she says. But everyone knows who her favorite is."

Helen Fillmore was widowed and Brad's father had left her supremely well off. His share of the ownership in the brokerage firm he'd co-founded had been left to Brad, who had a business degree from M.I.T. Charles, a liberal arts major, had no interest in the business world and had been left with a comfortable allowance to pursue other interests.

Birgit had met Brad's mother twice before. Her visits were still infrequent—she was much too busy with her bridge groups, luncheons, trips to museums, and meetings with financial advisers—but wherever she arrived at her elder son's house, Charles was in tow.

Like Brad, Charles was blond and good-looking, but his build was less athletic. To Birgit, he seemed a bit effeminate. Elizabeth again shared the family secrets.

"Everyone knows he is gay, including Grandma. Mom says it would be fine with her if he brought a boyfriend, but Dad and Grandma want to keep him in the closet. They are alike that way...always sweeping things under the rug."

The only similarity Lindsey had with her father was the same loud, belly laugh. Ethel, on the other hand, had the same swagger in her walk, the same openness, the same easy way with people. Ethel was already one of Birgit's favorites, and after she met Mr. Sorensen, she knew he'd be another one.

"What's up, Betty Boop?" he said, teasing his granddaughter.

Elizabeth, who never was called anything other than her given name, grinned from ear to ear as Mr. Sorenson lifted her off the floor. "Grandpa, are we going to play chess again, like we always do?"

Mr. Sorensen laughed and then narrowed his eyes in fake seriousness. "Anytime, but I'll warn you...Nobody beats the old Iron Duke!"

Elizabeth giggled and looked at Birgit. "He beats the crap out of me every time!" she said.

"Young lady," her grandmother said with an indulgent smile. "Watch your language!"

Elizabeth pulled Birgit closer. "This is Birgit. She is Swedish."

Leif Sorensen exploded in a booming laugh. "Too bad! Have you heard the old saying? Ten thousand Swedes came chasing through the weeds after one Norwegian..."

Birgit grinned. "I think you have that wrong...it's the other way around." Mr. Sorensen only laughed that much harder.

§

Birgit was still smiling as she walked back to the kitchen. The voices from the rest of the house reminded her of family gatherings back home. The sense of completeness, of being together. Though that was always the sentiment in the beginning, more often than not, it wouldn't last. Someone would do or say something and the bubble of happiness would burst. Still, year after year came the same anticipation, the same yearning for a perfect event. Birgit could tell that Elizabeth felt the way she once had. She was happy for her and a bit envious too. She missed the feeling of belonging.

"Okay, Cinderella," she said under her breath, trying to shake off a sudden sense of gloom. "Don't feel sorry for yourself!"

Also, just like back home, the kitchen was the place to be. The guests returned over and over for refills of the champagne punch and for seconds of the hors d'oeuvres. They lingered, and Lindsey's coaxing them to move on to the dining room fell on deaf ears. Everyone had such a good time that she finally gave up, poured another glass of punch, and announced that the plan for an early dinner would be put on hold indefinitely.

Elizabeth and her grandfather ducked out of the kitchen for a game of chess. When they returned a while later, Mr. Sorensen smiled broadly. "Miss Scarlett" glanced at her husband's face. "You didn't!"

Mr. Sorensen spun around and punched his fists in the air. "I most certainly did...nobody beats the Iron Duke!"

Elizabeth hissed, trying to sound menacing, but not succeeding. "Old man," she said. "You better watch out...your time will come!"

Birgit carefully maneuvered between guests as she carried plates into the dining room. Brad's voice stopped her in her tracks. "You're working too hard." He took the plates from her, walked to the dining room, and set them down on the side table. He nodded to the gleaming brass candlesticks on the tables and the polished silverware. "I know you had a big part in everything looking so nice. I want to thank you on behalf of the whole family. Please, take a break for a moment and let me pour you some punch."

As he guided her back to the kitchen, his hand touched her arm and created a spark. Birgit jumped and apologized. "Sorry!" Her heart beat like a jackhammer, and the resolve she'd built up over several weeks was instantly gone.

He handed her a small pewter cup with punch in it and she scrambled for something to say. She pointed to the cup. "This looks Scandinavian."

Brad nodded. "It is. From the Sorensen side, of course." He watched as Birgit sipped from the cup. "Be careful. This stuff will go to your head…" His alcohol consumption was, like everything else about him, measured and controlled—he seldom drank more than one cocktail after work and never more than two. This time though, he had made an exception. His eyes were shiny, and a strand of his blond hair, never out of order, dangled loosely on his forehead.

Birgit took a sip of the punch, painfully aware that her face was on fire. She commanded her body to move, but the impulses from her brain didn't register. Afraid someone would see them, she glanced around the room. Fortunately, everyone around her seemed engaged in conversation. In a corner, Lindsey was gesticulating, explaining something to her father and to Milton, her bookish-looking brother-in-law. Elizabeth, who enjoyed adult company, chatted with "Miss Scarlett" and her Aunt Ethel. Only Charles was missing. He was probably in a quieter part of the house catching up on some reading.

Relieved, Birgit looked up, only to find Brad's mother Helen staring at her with a cool, knowing smile on her face.

§

The phone rang just as Elizabeth danced into the kitchen. "Birgit… Mom says they're ready for coffee and dessert!"

Birgit picked up the coffee pot. "Will you get the phone, please?"

Elizabeth nodded. "Hold on…wait…" She covered the mouthpiece with her hand. "It's for you… from Sweden. She says she is your aunt…"

Birgit stopped cold. *Aunt Lola? Why on earth would she call?* Calling family and friends on holidays was standard for her family, but Thanksgiving isn't a holiday in Sweden. Besides, Lola never called—she wrote letters. Not because of cost. Lola was far from a cheapskate—just embarrassed over her limited English and worried that someone other than Birgit would answer the phone.

Birgit set down the coffee and took the phone from Elizabeth. "Aunt Lola?"

"Sorry to be calling you like this…"

Birgit heard strain in her aunt's voice and a cold shiver ran down her spine. The phone felt heavy in her hand.

"I hate to be the bearer of bad news," said Lola. "I took it upon myself to call since no one else is in any condition to do it."

Don't let it be Dad! Anyone but him!

The pure callousness with which Birgit threw the rest of the family under the bus shocked her, but the thought was too instinctive and powerful to be filtered. She listened to the news she didn't want to accept and moved the receiver away from her ear as if distance would lessen the impact. With a sigh that was more of a groan, she sank down on the chair behind her, numbly staring down at her hand. Her knuckles were white.

The kitchen started to spin as she searched for something to hang on to. There was nothing. The only thing real was Elizabeth's small hand stroking her back.

20

Birgit's image of her father had always been that of a sturdy tree, the strongest, most massive, one in the forest. In a storm, smaller and weaker trees would sway and rustle, but the tallest tree never wavered. It stood majestic and mighty—impossible to topple, impossible to fell.

There had been no forewarning. Despite frequent bouts with rheumatism, Torsten Svenson had never missed a day's work in his life.

Then again, there had been Mom's last letter. *Dad is tired,* she had written. *The fishing in the Baltic is drying up, and more often than not he returns home empty-handed.* As Birgit had read those lines, a flicker of concern had come and gone. After all, fishing was cyclical—bad years would follow good ones. Dad knew that better than anybody. It wouldn't get him down.

But, she'd been wrong. Now he was gone, and she wanted answers. It wouldn't bring him back, but she desperately needed to put the pieces together.

In that same letter, Mom had made reference to Arne and his drinking. Ruth, she had written, had begged their father to have a talk with her husband.

Birgit had crumpled the letter in disgust. Her sister's marriage had been a disaster from day one. Ruth should have gotten rid of her deadbeat husband years ago. Why drag Dad into her mess? At the same time, Birgit knew that her father was the only one who could get through to Arne.

Arne had little respect for people in general and, for himself, perhaps even less, but Torsten Svenson was someone he held in grudging esteem. Not that it changed his behavior in any way. He still sulked and argued that he was just a social drinker. Arne's tone, always defensive at first, would later turn agitated. Birgit could hear him say it, just as she had countless times before. "*What the hell is the big fuss about?*"

§

They had met on the island, Lola said. Dad, who didn't want Mom involved, had walked outside the moment Arne's Saab came up on the driveway. A cold wind had blown in from the bay that morning, but Dad had left the house with just his windbreaker.

According to Aunt Lola, her mother had cried inconsolably. "He wasn't wearing the warm down jacket that I asked him to wear," she had said, over and over. "The last thing I did was nag him."

In her mind's eye, Birgit could see the men heading to the dock. Dad, leading the way, walking briskly the way he always did, not bothering with small talk. Arne, the shorter of the two, reluctantly following, hunched over, and pissed off.

Mom had kept her promise not to intervene, but the moment Dad left the house, she'd opened the front door a crack. This last piece of information about her mother didn't come as a surprise. Mom had never been able to stand being shut out. Her last-minute suggestions were a family joke. As the

141

door closed behind you, it swung open again. It never failed—Mom was only pausing to reload. Had she put extra stress on Dad that morning? And even if so, what difference did it make now?

Lola interrupted her thoughts at that point. "Arne was loud and angry, that much I could tell, but the wind was blowing, and the neighbor's son ran his power boat in circles near the dock…joyriding…using the wake… Something was said that I couldn't hear and Arne stepped forward like he wanted to take a swing. Torsten just held him off, firmly but gently, the way you handle a child. His back was as straight as always…and then…well…he just crumbled…"

Birgit stood up, the phone still in her hand. She mechanically walked over to hang it up before reaching for the coffee pot. Although the conversation had been in Swedish, Elizabeth didn't need an interpreter to know that something terrible had happened. All she needed to do was look at Birgit's stricken face.

"What's wrong?"

Birgit stared off into space. "Min pappa…" she said. "My dad…"

Elizabeth tried to guide her back to the chair. "Sit! I'll get Mom!"

Birgit resisted. "No, they are waiting for coffee." Even in this situation, especially now, Birgit's reluctance to draw attention to herself surfaced. Just make it through the evening, she thought.

"Forget the freaking coffee!" screamed Elizabeth. Before Birgit had time to object, the girl was out the door.

Birgit's world had collapsed, had come to a standstill, while life around her continued unchanged. From the living room, she heard the ebb and flow of conversation interrupted by occasional laughter, and then abrupt silence— Elizabeth had entered the room. Mumbling started, followed by the sound of chairs being pushed back.

Seconds later, Lindsey and Brad appeared in the kitchen, Elizabeth right behind them. Their eyes, Birgit observed in a clinical, detached sort of way, still had the shine of high spirits—laughter, good food, and a few too many drinks. Brad, more quickly than his wife, rearranged his facial muscles to fit the situation. "I'm so terribly sorry," he said.

Lindsey smoothly stepped in front of her husband. "So am I." Her eyes quickly surveyed the counters. Birgit, always efficient, had already cleaned up—there was nothing left to do. "Don't worry about a thing. Please...go upstairs. I'm sure you need time to yourself. "

"No, she doesn't!" Elizabeth's voice was determined. "I'll go with her. She shouldn't be alone right now."

The two of them huddled on the bed. "Talk about your dad if it helps... or do you prefer I just sit here quietly?" Her friend's silence scared her.

Birgit opened a drawer in her nightstand and pulled out a photograph. Still saying nothing, she handed it to Elizabeth.

"Your dad?"

Birgit nodded.

"He looks kind." She gazed at the photo. "Where was this taken?"

"Outside Västervik, my hometown. We had left the bay and were heading out to sea. I tried hard to make him smile for the camera." Birgit pointed to her dad's face. "He resisted, but if you look closely you can see that his eyes are smiling."

She sighed. "Dad loved the open waters more than the bay. 'Nothing but sea and sky and you and me, girl,' he used to say."

Elizabeth continued to look at the picture. "You're going home for the..." She seemed hesitant to say the word.

"I am."

"But you *are* coming back, right?"

"Of course."

The girl put her arm around Birgit's shoulders. "It's okay to cry."

Birgit reached up to squeeze Elizabeth's hand.

"I will…later," she said. "But first, I want to tell you a story about the tallest tree in the forest…"

21

Västervik had a different feel than when she had left it. Gusty winds and drizzle met her as she stepped off the train. A fall dreariness had replaced the leisurely summer season.

The newsstand, a hangout for teens, was deserted. In the empty parking lot, leaves and candy wrappers performed a tortured tango—twitching and lifting before the weight of moisture forced them to the ground.

Birgit had chosen to take the train instead of the bus. The changeover in Linköping would not be a nuisance this time because her luggage was light. The train ride was prettier and slower, but none of that mattered today.

The overseas flight, the rush to the inner city, and the bustle of the train station had taken its toll on Birgit. Exhaustion was setting in, and the gossip magazine she'd bought in Stockholm lay unopened in her lap. In the hum of the rails, she heard a refrain of cruel insistence: *Dad is dead, Dad is dead.*

§

"I'll cry later," she'd told Elizabeth, but the tears still hadn't come. To cry meant admitting the reality, and she wasn't ready for that yet. At each stop of the train, anonymous faces stared from the platforms, but the names of the stations began to be familiar: Storsjö, Överum, Gamleby...

Further south, the landscape gradually changed and became more countrified. Red farmhouses dotted the coastline, surrounded by evergreens and white birch trees. On the water's edge, vacation homes were boarded up—no blue and yellow flags were waving. Their occupants would not return until spring.

Birgit had called her sister from Stockholm to communicate her arrival time. Their father's death had not improved their communication—the conversation was awkward as usual. Ruth suggested they meet at the station, but when Birgit answered, "Don't worry, I'll take a cab," Ruth hadn't pursued it further. How Birgit felt about her brother-in-law was no secret. There was no suggestion of Arne picking her up.

On the phone, neither sister mentioned their father. Ruth discussed the funeral in a detached way, as if the arrangements had been made for a stranger. Her manner didn't fool Birgit—Ruth might not have been her father's favorite, but she'd worshiped him just the same. This was just her way of coping.

Ruth answered Birgit's questions in her typically dutiful way. "Yes, Mom is staying with us through the funeral. She is holding up as well as can be expected. It was all so sudden. The doctor prescribed Valium, and it seems to work. Yes, Aunt Lola arrived a few days ago. She's been a big help."

As always, Birgit felt a need to defend herself. She felt her throat tighten, and her voice rose a couple of octaves. "I came as soon as could."

"Of course, you did," said Ruth in her patient, older-sister voice. "Mom is staying in the guest room, but you're welcome to Gunnar's room. He can sleep with Arne and me."

"Where is Lola staying?"

"At Stadtshotellet... If you rather room with her, I can arrange it."

Ruth radiated hurt at the suggestion that Birgit might rather stay with their aunt, but Birgit knew her sister too well. Ruth hated having her routine interrupted—to have Birgit stay with Lola would make her life easier.

§

A young girl occupied the pay phone inside the station and apparently had no plan to give it up anytime soon. Birgit's attempt to stare her down backfired—the girl turned around and possessively put both hands on the receiver. After minutes of staring at the back of a red ski parka, Birgit gave up. She could just as well walk—the hotel was only fifteen minutes away and Aunt Lola would meet her there. She'd reserved a room with two double beds just in case.

Aunt Lola, always good in a crisis, had taken care of all the planning for Birgit's flights, and Lindsey, with unexpected kindness, had rummaged through her closet for appropriate clothes. "You can't go looking like that," she'd said, critically studying Birgit's dark blue coat bought on sale at Caldor's Department Store. In Lindsey's closet were clothes for every occasion, even funerals. Birgit watched numbly as one outfit after the other was brought out.

Lånta fjädrar. "Borrowed feathers," she said to herself as she walked down the street. The coat, as well as the high leather boots, both loans from Lindsey, fit perfectly, but didn't feel right.

With the weather the way it was, the likelihood of running into someone she knew was slim. Was that a good thing? People would be kind, of course, their sympathy sincere. Dad had been both well-liked and respected, but she couldn't handle the thought of having to discuss his passing right now. A kind word, a compassionate look, and she might snap.

"My condolences…sorry for your loss." Wasn't that what people said in English? What was the Swedish equivalent? She tried out a couple of phrases, but none seemed to fit.

§

Walking quickly, Birgit passed St.Petri, one of the town's two prominent churches. Old by American standards, it was considerably newer than St. Gertrud, and dated from the early 1400s. All brick with tall spires, it looked more like a castle than a house of worship.

To know that Dad's burial would take place at St Gertrud was a relief. She and her father had talked about everything under the sun, but never about death, except once, when it had hit close to home.

Birgit had been eight years old when she'd lost her grandmother. "Mormor," Mom's and Aunt Lola's mother, had lived in Stockholm and seldom visited. Never much of a presence in either of her granddaughters' lives, she was still someone real—someone who phoned, sent birthday presents, loved her poodle, her antiques, and caramel custards. Suddenly this person had no longer been a living, breathing creature.

The funeral had scared Birgit witless: the deep hole, the earth scooped on the casket. She'd kept her real angst a secret. *If this happened to "Mormor," couldn't it happen to Dad as well?* She had finally asked him, and his answer had stayed with her.

"When you die, let's say in a million years, where do you want to be buried?"
"Right here in the Baltic Sea."
"We can't just dump you in the water!"

"I was thinking more of a Viking funeral. Put me in a boat, not just any old boat- it has to be a sailing ship. Push it out to sea, shoot flaming arrows at the sails, and watch it burn until it sinks."

"Where do I get the ship and the arrows?"

"Up to you. You'll make the arrangements."

At the time, the thought of a water burial had been oddly comforting. Much better than thinking of him in the ground. Dad had smiled at the idea of a Viking funeral. Surprising, since a big send-off had not been his style.

That had changed now. Mom, sedated, and crazy with grief, would have it no other way. Ruth had prattled on about all the people who'd show up at church, local politicians, union members, any old acquaintances Mom had managed to dig up. Birgit had listened silently, all the time feeling helpless.

This was not what Dad wanted!

In her first call to Ruth from Stockholm, her sister had also said something startling, something that sent Birgit searching for another krona to put in the coin slot. She'd been too late and the line had gone dead, but Birgit had heard enough.

"I hope you won't find it awkward," Ruth had said, *"but Mom asked Bengt to be one of the pallbearers. You know how fond they both were of him."*

22

Birgit's father had believed in God, but he had always been vehemently opposed to organized religion. Mom and Ruth were the churchgoers in the family.

Dad had always protested when Mom pressured him to get ready for Sunday service. "God rested on the seventh day. Why can't I?"

If it had been up to him, he might never have put his foot inside a church, but, of course, this time he didn't have a choice.

"We need to be with respectable people," Mom explained. She was a "Stockholmer," and to her, "city folks," even in a small town like Västervik, were an upgrade from Händelöp. Due to her insistence, the family worshiped in town and not on the island. Birgit didn't think her mother's belief was very Christian but to Vera Svenson, it made perfect sense. To dress up, go to church, surrounded by the right kind of people: That's what you were supposed to do on Sundays.

Though not a regular church-goer, Torsten Svenson had been no stranger to the *Bible*. He'd known it inside and out and had always enjoyed debating it, especially with Rev. Törnwall, his lifelong friend and fishing companion.

Birgit remembered a time when two Jehovah's Witnesses had shown up on the island. Mom had called out the moment she'd caught sight of the two young men in dark suits and ties, walking up the driveway "Don't let those people inside. We'll never get them out!"

Dad, who never liked to see a good debate go to waste, had ignored her. "Please fix us a pot of coffee, Vera," he'd said.

The men had left with more questions than when they'd arrived.

§

Birgit's family huddled outside the entry to the church. The rain had stopped, but the day was still bleak and chilly.

She felt like an outsider, but everyone else played their appropriate roles: Mom, the grieving widow had dressed as if she had rehearsed for this moment. Her coat was the right length—short, but not improper—with enough room to show off her shapely calves and ankles. A flowing veil covered part of her face, but the lipstick, plum-colored, would not last long the way she bit her lips. Her outfit was flawless, but she looked drugged and moved like a zombie.

Ruth, the attentive daughter, held her arm protectively around Mom. Birgit had overheard her sister whisper to Aunt Lola, "I advised against it, but she doubled up on the Valium, said she didn't want to make a spectacle of herself."

Arne held his son in a firm grip, but he didn't need to. Gunnar stood straight and still like a little soldier, his face pale and pinched. Without protests, he had endured Aunt Lola's fussing with his hair. His jacket was clearly a last-minute purchase—the sleeves were a tad too long and it fit poorly over the shoulders. There had been no time for alterations.

"Are you staying?" Gunnar asked Birgit, hopefully. When she shook her head, his eyes darkened with disappointment. She wondered if the boy's parents understood how hard this was for him. Dad had been more than a grandfather to Gunnar—he had also been a safety net when Arne's drinking got out of hand.

Since she'd arrived, Birgit and her brother-in-law had hardly exchanged a word. That she held him responsible for Dad's death wouldn't cross Arne's mind, but he kept his distance, which was just as well.

The wait was long and torturous, but the church bells finally began to ring. "My condolences," Pastor Törnwall whispered to Birgit as he opened the door to lead them in. His round face showed more than the pastor's appropriate somber expression. Birgit thought he looked stricken, and for good reason. His relationship with Dad stretched back to childhood.

Birgit's last visit to the church had been on *Julottan*, the early service on Christmas morning. That day her whole family had come, even Dad. The parishioners who showed up only on special occasions had been given a lighthearted scolding by the reverend. He and Dad, she remembered, had exchanged smiles. For someone who seldom, if ever, went to church, he seemed to know the words to the songs by heart and sang in his booming voice without help from the hymnal.

St Gertrud's Church, Roman Catholic in its early days, was now permanently evangelical Lutheran. It had suffered through fires and wars, and parts had been repaired and rebuilt over and over since the Middle Ages. In 1450, the church had been too large for the small town, but a big church was a status symbol. Now more than five centuries later, the town had caught up with the church. The original granite valves with its uneven texture, the carved door to the sanctuary, the beautiful pulpit and the graceful steeple from the 1700s blended with ease.

As they walked in, the organist played a hymn Birgit recognized. "Teach me, my forest to wither contented." It was one of Mom's favorites.

Birgit looked straight ahead as people respectfully rose from their seats. Out of the corner of her eye, she caught a glimpse of Bengt, for once in suit and tie, which didn't make him look older, but more like a boy playing dress-up. *Did she feel happiness, sadness, regret?* Her feelings on seeing him again were too jumbled to identify. As she passed him, he bowed his head in an old-fashioned, almost courtly manner. His reddish hair—darker, she thought, than last summer—could still not be tamed by a comb. An unruly strand stuck out and Birgit resisted the impulse to reach over and smooth it down.

§

Birgit watched as the white, flower-decked casket was wheeled in. She leaned over to Ruth. "I thought Dad would be cremated!"

"Shh!" Ruth whispered back. "Mom preferred it this way."

Only Birgit knew how her father had wanted to be buried—on a burning ship with sails aflame. She fumed for a moment and then let it go. In all fairness to Mom, a Viking funeral would have been hard to arrange with such short notice.

She sat dry-eyed, through the funeral oration—even through the singing of *her* favorite hymn, "*Blott en dag*, Day by Day." The body in the casket didn't seem to have a connection to her. She had loved her father deeply, yet here she sat, not even crying. Her sister next to her in the pew balled a handkerchief in her hand, sobbing quietly.

Not until Rev. Törnwall gave his personal tribute to Torsten Svenson, a moving, sometimes funny recollection of a lifelong friendship, did something inside Birgit begin to loosen.

She had come to accept that she and Ruth would never be close and might not even like each other, but they shared all the memories. At one particular part, both smiled in recognition and turned to face each other. Birgit saw her sister close her eyes, making a strangled sound somewhere between a cry and a laugh, and blindly reach out her hand.

Birgit took it and squeezed it. And the tears came.

§

The supper afterward was held in a private room at Hjortenbaden's Tavern, a small restaurant on the water several miles from town. The place was pricey, but Mom had wanted privacy. Here she would be less likely to run into anyone they knew. "Arne paid for it," said her mom. She knew her son-in-law's standing with Birgit and tried to give him some credit.

At the few funerals Birgit had attended, there had been a sense of relief when it was over. People had loosened up, exchanged stories about the deceased, even laughed. That didn't happen here. Instead, Vera Svenson sat between her two daughters with a dazed look on her face. For a woman who all through her marriage fiercely protected her independence, she seemed lost without her husband at her side.

Ruth had stopped hovering over Mom and sat quietly, deep in thought. Gunnar, pursing his lips, stared at the candle on the table, and when he thought nobody noticed, moved his finger back and forth through the flame. Aunt Lola gently took his hand and moved it to his side.

Arne, perhaps bothered by the silence, ordered a bottle of wine, which got everyone's attention. Red dots showed up on his wife's cheeks, and Gunnar stopped looking at the candle and stared at his father with a half-open mouth. "It's not for me," said Arne defensively. "I know I'm driving."

Mom leaned over and whispered in Birgit's ear. "He hasn't had a drop since the incident," she said. Birgit had noticed that her mother now referred to Dad's passing as "the incident." The expression annoyed her—why she wasn't sure—but then she and Mom always rubbed each other the wrong way. Keeping in touch by letters had worked so much better—face to face again, the old unease had returned.

Birgit watched as Mom poured herself a glass of the wine. "Should *you* drink?"

"Don't patronize me, please. It's been hours since I took my pills."

For a moment, Mom had become her combative self. Instead of being upset by it, Birgit smiled. Maybe she would heal after all.

§

"How are you holding up?"

The familiar voice caught her off-guard. Bengt stood beside her at the gravesite, his tone kind but impersonal. They had not been in touch since she'd left, and the situation was uncomfortable for both. He looked formal and insulated in a dark-gray, wool coat.

Suddenly, Birgit flashed back to that day on the island—his wet body moving against hers, his eyes never leaving her face. She hadn't cried at all until that moment in church, but now she felt like she couldn't stop. All her strength was gone and she wept soundlessly. She reached out for him and he took a step back, as if touching her sickened him. "Your Dad was a special man," he said. "I'm sorry."

He was polite as usual—doing the right thing. Just talking to her must have taken some effort, but in this small town, everyone knew each other, and people were looking, some openly curious, others more discreetly. If his plan had been to humiliate her, he had succeeded. Birgit pulled her coat tighter around her and walked past him. There would be no more crying, not in front of him, or anyone else.

§

The busy season was over, and the restaurants were adjusting to the reduction in business. Some of the waiters had been let go, and the service was slower than normal. When the food finally came, it was cold.

Nobody seemed to care. Arne, usually mouthy, said nothing and when the waitress came around with the wine, he put his hand over the glass, shaking his head.

Ruth walked with Birgit from the restaurant to the cars. "Mom is moving. She'll stay with us until she finds a place of her own. Where it will be, I'm... no one knows. Aunt Lola wants her to move to Stockholm, and she might, or might not." Ruth lowered her voice. "You know how those two get along."

Birgit stopped and looked at her. "Mom is leaving the island? What about our house?"

Ruth took a deep breath. "Well, it's not official yet, but Bengt is talking about buying it. You know how he always dreamed of a place on the water."

Something was wrong. Mom doesn't make rash decisions. How could she just pick up and leave her—their—house? The place she had lived in all her married life? And sell it to Bengt, of all people! How could he possibly afford it?

Ruth read her thoughts. "Nobody told you? Bengt and his brother have opened another hardware store in Gunnebo and it's going great. He has enough for the down payment."

Was this a plan to humiliate her further? Cozying up to Mom, talking her into selling the house to him?

Birgit scolded herself. *I'm being totally unfair. Except for Dad, have I ever known anyone as decent as Bengt?*

She chuckled to herself. *If Dad were here, he would have chuckled, too. He so enjoyed the absurdity of life.*

Arne pulled Brigit over in the parking lot. The move was brusque and unexpected, but his breath didn't smell of liquor the way it often had, and his eyes were pleading. "I just wanted you to know that it happened fast," he said haltingly. "Torsten…your dad…never suffered."

"Thanks." Suddenly, Birgit's anger was gone. She knew Arne had not caused her father's death, and it was time to forgive and let go. "Gunnar needs you, Arne. They both do," she blurted out.

Arne nodded as he opened the car door for her. "I know," he said.

§

For a moment in the church, there had been a pull, a sense of belonging, but it was gone now. The local politicians and fair-weather friends her mother had assembled didn't matter, but Dad's people—the fishermen—did. She had looked for familiar faces and found them. During the service, they had all looked uncomfortable in their suits and had stood, flexing arthritic fingers, not used to their hands being idle. After the service, they'd paid their respects, shaken her hand, and bowed stiffly, eyes not betraying their feelings. Yet, even with their reserve, they moved her. These men were a part of Dad and her old life.

Her new life was in America. To them, America was more a concept than a country. A bewildering free-flowing mass of contrasts—a plump, tempting fruit with a hard pit in the middle.

23

Tomorrow is another day.

Birgit had adopted Scarlett O'Hara's philosophy. Like the heroine from *Gone with the Wind*, she put off what she couldn't face today to the next day or the next. She'd used this defense mechanism since childhood and had perfected it as a grown-up. Shutting down emotions came easy to her now— it was almost as simple as tightening a screw.

She had tucked her father away in a secret chamber in her heart, and that chamber was now walled off. The future of her mother was another worry, but locking her away was not as hard. She mattered, but not nearly as much as Dad. Dad was the glue that had held the family together; without him, her ties to family and country would never be the same.

Her nephew Gunnar, she had discovered, had a method of coping not so different from hers. "I just pretend that Grandpa left on a long trip and had so much fun he doesn't want to come back," he said. The boy had perked up after the funeral. Maybe because Arne, trying to be a better father, had promised him a visit to the ice rink.

"Bengt is coming too," Gunnar told her. "They're going to teach me how to play hockey. Bengt played for Västervik High, you know."

Birgit smiled at the awe in his voice. To Gunnar, playing on the high school team was huge, almost like playing for the New York Rangers. She had a sudden vision of Bengt gliding down the rink, raising his stick high after a goal. *It was just a few years ago. Why did it feel like a lifetime?*

"I know. I saw him play," she said.

Gunnar squinted his eyes. "You two dated?"

Birgit nodded. "We did."

"But it didn't work out?

"No."

"Because you wanted to go to America?"

"That's right."

Gunnar sighed, the crease in his forehead deepening as he tried to understand the strange world of grown-ups. "I guess that's the way it goes." Bengt was his hero, and Birgit hoped that one day he'd feel the same about his father. Maybe it would happen. Only time would tell. Since Dad's death, Arne, according to Mom, was a changed man.

This time, Gunnar didn't ask if she was coming back. Maybe he didn't want the answer.

§

As her plane descended to JFK, Birgit was determined to shake off both jetlag and the weight of the old country. America was waiting for her, ready to sweep her back up in its largeness and anonymity. The Fillmores, she suspected, would expect her to come back subdued but ready to move on. She would not be surprised.

"Nice to have you back," said Brad. "I missed you...especially in the mornings." His tone struck the right balance between correctness and kidding, and Birgit warned herself not to read anything more into it. The trip away had toughened her resolve not to let her infatuation with him prevent her from doing things like making him breakfast. Their earlier routine was reinstated. He had never asked why it had been interrupted in the first place—he just seemed happy to have her back in the kitchen.

Elizabeth was different from both of her parents. She had a gift for empathy that had nothing to do with age, and Birgit didn't have to hide her feelings from her. The girl had met her with a quick hug and no questions. She looked as she was brimming over with things to tell, but held back, not sure if the time was right.

A couple of nights had passed when Birgit looked up to see her waiting in the doorway to Birgit's room. Birgit waved her in and Elizabeth tiptoed to the bed and sat down. "You don't have to act like everything is all right when it isn't," she said, studying Birgit's face. "You can talk to me. I'm a big girl."

Neither of the Fillmores had asked questions about the funeral, for which Birgit was grateful, but with Elizabeth next to her, she was ready to talk—needed to talk. Maybe there was a limit to what she should have shared with a someone that age, but she couldn't help herself—all she'd kept inside came pouring out. Elizabeth didn't seem to mind. She listened and didn't speak until Birgit finished talking. As with most girls her age, romance—not funerals—was the more interesting topic.

"How did it feel to see Bengt again? Is it totally over between you?" Birgit gave what she thought was an incoherent answer, but to Elizabeth, it seemed to make perfect sense. "Well, since it's over with Bengt and your dad is gone, there's no reason to go back to Sweden...right? You can stay here now," she said, with a child's simple logic.

Squeezing Birgit's hand, she continued, "I've millions of things to tell you…Is it all right to talk about something else now?"

Birgit squeezed her hand back.

"Sure it is! Shoot!"

§

Lindsey, Birgit noticed, had changed in a subtle way while she was gone. She had always been erratic and short-tempered, but now there was an added twist to her behavior—she'd become secretive. Making private conversation in front of Birgit had never been an issue before. Now when the phone rang, she went into her studio to talk. "When I'm home," she said, "I'll take all calls from now on," she said. "Don't pick up."

She had also begun to leave the house suddenly without saying where she was going. *Could she be having an affair?* To Birgit, the thought was absurd, almost laughable. *Any woman married to Brad Fillmore would never dream of cheating.*

Elizabeth had noticed the change as well but didn't dwell on it. "Mom is just in one of her moods," she said. "This is how she gets when she isn't productive. It will pass."

But Birgit had noticed that Lindsey had begun to eat less, often skipping breakfast and lunch. And she was spending more and more time by herself.

When Birgit entered the studio with a cup of tea for her, she could tell that Elizabeth was right about one thing—Lindsey had clearly not been productive. The place was in chaos and discarded art projects filled the bin in the corner.

Out of the blue, Lindsey had ordered a large plate glass window to be installed on the wall facing north. "Northern light is what an artist craves," she told her husband when he fought the idea, pointing out that the large window didn't go with the style of the house.

"This is an old historic house," he argued. "That type window doesn't go with the structure."

Lindsey had pressed on, not giving up until she won the battle.

The studio smelled, too, of stale cigarette smoke. Lindsey had been known to steal an occasional cigarette when Brad—dead set against her smoking—wasn't around, but this was not a matter of one or two. The ashtray on the workbench was overflowing with cigarette butts.

Lindsey impatiently pointed to a place, while pushing brushes and paint tubes to the side. "Put the cup here, please." She noticed Birgit looking at the walls. "I had them painted in a grayish green," she said. "A darker shade will stop the light from bouncing around."

As Birgit set the tea down on the table beside her, Lindsey focused on her face. "Interesting lines…elegant. Not what you'd expect," she mumbled. "Your dad was a fisherman, was he not?" She ground out a half-smoked cigarette into the ashtray.

Was she being condescending? Birgit paused for a moment, not wanting her face to betray the defensiveness she felt about her father's profession. "Yes, he was." She paused again until she was sure she could control her voice. "Is there anything else you'd like me to do?"

Lindsey had obviously gotten the response she'd been looking for. She leaned forward in anticipation. She thrived on conflict—a life without tension bored her. "I haven't done portraits for a while," she said, "but something about *your* face inspires me."

Birgit swallowed hard. "I'm sure you've better things to do…"

"Oh, ple-e-ease!" Lindsey's laugh was interrupted by a coughing fit. "Don't give me your 'I'm just a simple country girl' routine."

She reached for her sketchbook and a pencil. "Stop right there! That expression…keep it…that's perfect!"

A strange smile played on her lips, and she had a feverish look in her eyes. Birgit shifted from angry to anxious and thoughts raced through her mind. *Has the woman gone mad? Isn't this what sometimes happened to artistic types? Didn't Van Gogh lose his mind and cut off his ear?*

Lindsey seemed thrilled by what she saw and she picked up a brush. "Those blazing eyes, that untamed defiance! Believe me, I'm not underestimating *you*, not for a second. Country girl or not, you'd be a formidable adversary."

24

"They're popping up everywhere." Lindsey looked clueless, but Birgit instantly knew that Elizabeth was referring to her garden. As always, she was struck by how uninvolved Lindsey was in her daughter's life. Her lack of interest was nothing new, but in the past, it had come and gone. It was more of a constant now.

Elizabeth's usual response to her mother's vanishing interest had been to try harder and when that didn't work, give up. But Birgit had noticed a change recently. Instead of retreating into sullen silence, the girl was refusing to let Lindsey influence her mood.

Birgit had taught Elizabeth what she'd learned from her father. The girl had used it but had taken it to a whole new level. They'd gotten off to a late start—planting at the end of August—but Elizabeth had thrown herself into garden books and had studied up on what would thrive in New England, with its short growing season, wet springs, and cold nights.

She didn't want her gardening season to end with the first frost, so she had learned how to build cold frames—bottomless boxes made from planks and covered with glass frames to take advantage of winter sun.

As Elizabeth had not proven to be an adventurous eater, Birgit had expected to see her plant only the most common vegetables, but the girl had surprised her. More exotic seeds followed the basic carrots, and, little by little, she had added more variety to her garden. Birgit wondered if she had discovered that eating what she'd grown was different from eating produce bought in the supermarket or farm stands—the girl was now munching on endive, leeks, and scallions.

Birgit also suspected that Elizabeth had changed her eating habits because of her mother, but she was wrong. The girl was growing up, and, whether she was aware of it or not, had begun sharing some of her mother's tastes. Finally, they'll have something in common, Birgit thought.

The first time Elizabeth had brought home a batch of vegetables for her mother to inspect, Lindsey had practically fawned over her. "Absolutely lovely!" she exclaimed. Then, as usual, she'd seemed to instantly lose interest. "I don't feel much like cooking," she said. "Why don't the two of you put together something interesting?"

"Yes, why don't we," said Elizabeth, demonstratively turning her back on her mother to look at Birgit. "Teach me. Both Dad and I like your cooking." The not-so-veiled comment at the end didn't seem to register with her mother, who gestured toward a shelf in the kitchen. "I have various cookbooks—several about preparing vegetables in different ways. Have at it, girls."

Lindsey's attitude clearly hurt her daughter's feelings, but didn't crush Elizabeth as Birgit feared. Instead, it seemed to spur her on. The girl seemed inspired, determined to try every recipe available. In a short time, she learned how to sauté, grill, steam blanch, and puree. Her specialty was a side dish of broccoli that she steamed, sautéed with chopped garlic and olive oil, and sprinkled with lemon juice.

Out of Elizabeth's earshot, Brad asked Birgit, "How much longer is this going on? Where are all those weird side dishes coming from?"

"From your daughter's garden," she said. "Elizabeth's doing the cooking now and isn't likely to give it up soon." Once again, he had been oblivious to everything going on around him. She wondered if he'd even noticed that his wife hardly touched the food on her plate.

He still made Birgit weak-kneed, though, and was, in her mind, the embodiment of perfect, except for this one flaw—he was a boring eater, a "meat and potatoes" man with no interest in experimentation. And now his daughter, once a reliable ally in the food department, had joined her mother's camp.

§

Elizabeth peeked into Birgit's room. "Can we talk?"

Birgit put aside the letter she was writing and cleared a space for the girl on the bed. "Sure."

Elizabeth stayed in the doorway and didn't move. Birgit patted the spot on the bed. "Come on in and sit down."

"I don't want to sit down. I can't." Elizabeth's voice trembled. She stood with legs pressed together, arms hugging her chest.

"What's wrong? Why are you twisted up like a pretzel?"

Elizabeth burst into tears and Birgit instantly knew what was up. "Oh, honey...you got your period." Elizabeth nodded, her face ghostly pale.

Birgit stood up as she watched the girl walk toward her—not with her usual coltish gait, but with small, careful steps. "Stop!" said Elizabeth, between sobs. "Don't touch me, okay? This is so gross. Let me just go into your bathroom to find what I need."

"In the drawer under the sink. Left-hand side. Call me if you want help."

Naturally, thought Birgit, *Lindsey hasn't talked to her daughter about menstruation. Not because it it's an uncomfortable subject but because it was low on her list of priorities.* Birgit was mostly angry, but she was also a little bit pleased. The girl had turned to her and not to her mother!

"Life will never be the same again," said Elizabeth with grim certainty. Birgit suppressed a smile as she headed for the bathroom. There were rustling sounds—drawers pulled out, toilet flushing, water running. After a lengthy silence, the door opened a crack, and a shaky voice came from inside. "Are you still there? I'm not sure how to use this stuff. Will you show me?"

"Of course, honey."

Birgit decided to give Lindsey the benefit of the doubt. Perhaps Lindsey hadn't thought it would happen this soon. After all, Elizabeth had only just turned twelve.

Her attempt to be fair was short-lived. The truth was that the woman who was involved with everything under the sun had, as usual, forgotten she had a daughter.

§

Ethel Hirschberg's cream-colored Cadillac Imperial was parked in the driveway when Birgit returned from grocery shopping. Her visit was unexpected as the two sisters had not been on speaking terms lately. Lindsey and Mrs. Hirschberg, or "Big E" as the family called her, were close, but they'd taken time away from each other to cool off.

"She is so damn bossy!" Lindsey had told Birgit, who had remained quiet because she didn't agree. She would happily trade sisters and work for Mrs. Hirschberg instead. It was true that "Big E" had no problem voicing her opinion, but her nature was caring and warm, so different from that of her younger sister.

The door to the living room was ajar, and when Birgit put away the groceries, she heard the two of them talking. Big E's voice was easy to make out.

"You must tell him!"

Tell him what? It was clear she was talking about Brad. Birgit took a few steps out into the hallway. Listening in was not something she normally did, but this she had to hear.

Lindsey's reply was drowned out by sobs.

Silence first and then footsteps. Birgit quickly retreated to the kitchen.

Big E's voice boomed out again. "I'll be back whether you want me or not. Remember what I said. Tell him! I know he's shallow, but he can't be *that* shallow!"

Mrs. Hirschberg walked rapidly past the kitchen, then changed her mind and turned back and stuck her head in the door. Her eyes glistened with tears.

"Birgit," she said, her voice firm. "Promise me that you will be there for my niece. Elizabeth will need you more than ever in the coming days."

25

Lindsey had been diagnosed with breast cancer shortly after Christmas but told no one, except for her sister, who was sworn to secrecy. Later, when it was all out in the open, Birgit was mystified. Why tell your sister and not your husband? In a case like this, shouldn't you talk to him first?

She couldn't imagine her mom ever having kept a secret of this magnitude from her father, and the explanation that Brad didn't deal well with bad news rang hollow. As always, Lindsey's behavior had followed no pattern and made little sense.

To confide in Big E might have been the right choice, though. Ethel Hirschberg was unsentimental and practical and, of all, knew how to deal with her sister. She urged her to tell the rest of the family, and eventually Lindsey had. "She said, 'If you don't tell, you prove to be both selfish and immature,'" said Lindsey, imitating her sister's barking voice.

The family did their best to be supportive, but since Lindsey was so clearly in denial, they didn't know how to handle the situation. "We're talking about a small lump…just a nuisance really," she said. "Why dwell on it?"

She postponed a visit by her concerned parents in Chicago. "Let's wait until I'm well…I'll promise you it won't be long," she assured them.

But as the cancer made no signs of leaving, Lindsey reluctantly conceded that she was in a fight against a formidable foe. It seemed neither to depress nor frighten her—if anything, it perked her up. Defeating cancer gave her a singular purpose. "Amazing how it sharpens your senses," she said, "I've never felt more alive."

Birgit thought that the days leading into that summer were the best she had had since going to work for the Fillmores. Lindsey was more upbeat than ever and pleasant to everyone, even to Birgit. "I'll beat this thing, you'll wait and see," she promised the family, who by now had turned into believers.

Mrs. Hirschberg was the only one who retained her skepticism. "Brace yourself," she warned Birgit. "This phase won't last. She's fragile…anything may tip her over." Big E would turn out to be right.

§

The cancer that ravaged Lindsey's body had not reduced her interest in the presidential election and, on the evening of June 5, she was determined to stay up all night "if that was what it took" to watch her favorite Bobby Kennedy in the California Democratic primary.

"You might have to do just that," said her husband. "We're talking west coast time here. I'd suggest that you stay upstairs and watch with me from the bed. Then if you get tired, you can just go to sleep."

Predictably, Lindsey refused. "I might be ill, but I'm not an invalid," she said. "I will sit on the sofa downstairs and watch on the console."

Birgit met Brad at the doorway out of the den. "Will you stay with her? I promise it won't be long. She will fade quickly."

Birgit nodded. She didn't mind, really. Politics in America was high-stakes theater, much more entertaining than in Sweden. She went into the den and sat down in a chair beside the sofa. "Why isn't your husband watching with you?" she asked Lindsey.

Lindsey rolled her eyes. "As you might have noticed," she said lightly, "our political views don't exactly coincide." Birgit propped her up with some pillows and brought her a cup of tea. She fought valiantly to stay awake, but dozed on and off, waking up intermittently to ask if Kennedy was in the lead.

Each time, Birgit's answer was, "Too early to call." She was proud to have learned the right phrase.

"This could go on way past midnight," the television announcer said several times and Birgit glanced at Lindsey on the sofa. She was fast asleep. Birgit decided it was time to call for Brad. He came down immediately.

When he woke her, Lindsey responded in weak protest. "I just want to know the result!"

"You will in the morning."

"He will win this one and go on to be President," she said, drowsily slurring her speech.

"That's not a given," said her husband.

His statement would come back to haunt them all.

The frightening sound from downstairs the next morning was more a wail than a scream. Birgit jumped out of bed, threw on her robe, and hurried to find out what had happened. Was it Elizabeth? Brad? Had Lindsey fallen?

"They shot him!" cried Lindsey, sobbing and pointing to the television. "They shot Bobby! First Doctor King and now this...What has happened to my country?"

Big E had worried that any one incident could push her sister over the edge and Bobby Kennedy's death would be it. Lindsey was inconsolable. She stopped focusing on beating the breast cancer and began fighting everyone else instead. Whatever energy she had was used to battle anyone in her path: doctors, nurses, family, friends, and most of all…Birgit.

Hospital visits, drugs, negative readings, and chemotherapy all took their toll, and Lindsey's behavior became increasingly erratic. One day she would be fine, the next impossible. Only her sister still had some influence over her.

Subtle changes began to happen in the household. For the second time, Birgit was asked to join the family at dinner. "We insist," Lindsey said, making clear that this time it wasn't open for discussion.

Why was this again an issue? Birgit was puzzled, but after sharing evening meals with the Fillmores, it became clear. She was the lightning rod! With an outsider in the room, the atmosphere around the dinner table was less charged, less stressful.

Who had asked for her to be there? Was it Brad or Elizabeth? It certainly couldn't have been Lindsey's idea, or could it? Did they think that with her around the conversation would flow easier?

Whatever the plan, it backfired. Cancer lay heavy on everybody's mind, and Lindsey made no effort to make things easier. "Why so morose?" she asked sarcastically. "Someone dying?" The uncomfortable silence that followed seemed to amuse her, and egg her on.

In time, her reactions became more and more unpredictable. She was coughing more, but smoked openly even in front of Brad, daring him to say something. The family had worried about how the hair loss after chemo might affect her, but to their surprise, Lindsey wasn't the least bit bothered. She who had always taken such pride in her glossy dark hair seemed strangely nonchalant about losing it.

Big E finally coaxed her into buying a wig. "How about a trip to Manhattan tomorrow? Make a day of it…find a wig, have lunch at the Four Seasons…We can ask Helen to join us…" Including her mother-in-law was flat-out rejected, but otherwise, Lindsey seemed amenable to the idea.

Big E winked at Birgit when leaving, knowing she had won a small victory. Earlier in the week, in her no-nonsense way, she had said to Birgit, "She's difficult, isn't she?" and Birgit had silently nodded.

"But mostly to you." Birgit nodded again.

"You know it's not really personal, don't you?"

This time, Birgit shook her head. "Then why does she do it?"

"I would think it obvious," said Big E. "It's because you're young, you're beautiful, and you're very much alive."

§

Lindsey returned from the day in New York in an unusually good frame of mind. Big E came in with several shopping bags…and a wig. She held it up for Birgit to admire.

"Finest European hair…exactly my color, quite natural looking, and of course," she added with a smile, "outrageously expensive."

At dinner, the clock seemed to have been turned back to the days before cancer. Lindsey looked gorgeous although she was thinner and her face was somewhat more pale. This only emphasized her eyes, making them appear even larger and more luminous. Like a green-eyed Liz Taylor, Birgit thought. Brad seemed to feel the same—he watched his wife as if mesmerized. Birgit felt a stab in her heart.

The conversation was, for once, light and relaxed—uncontroversial. Elizabeth told some funny stories from school and everyone laughed. She, too, had been withdrawn lately—her garden almost forgotten. Her vegetable fetish was gone, and lately, she ate very little. She seldom laughed, but when she did, it was sometimes too long and too hard.

Then suddenly something changed. Birgit tried later to remember the sequence but couldn't. It was something small, something Brad said. Lindsey, without warning, suddenly slammed her fist on the table, tore off her wig, and threw it across the room.

Her bald head appeared obscenely white and naked, and Elizabeth let out a wounded gasp. "Oh, Mom…"

Brad, hating scenes, looked away quickly, and then stared down at the plate in front of him. Birgit caught a glimpse of distaste in his eyes, and Lindsey had obviously seen it too.

"What's the matter, dahling? Not a pretty sight?"

Elizabeth stood up so violently that her chair tipped over, her eyes deep pools of despair. When she ran from the table, Birgit excused herself and tried to catch her, but she wasn't able to. The girl shook her off and locked herself in her bedroom.

§

Why am I staying?

Birgit asked herself the question many times. "I can leave anytime I want. Get another job or go back home for that matter…I'm not a slave!" And then she would think, but who would take care of Elizabeth?"

"Don't lie to yourself," Dad used to say. "If you do, you'll never figure things out." And she was lying to herself right now. The truth was—yes—she loved Elizabeth and wanted to protect her, but the real reason she had stayed was Brad. Because of him, she hadn't dated anyone after Patrick. How could she when the bar had been set so high that every other man fell short?

Her feelings about him had become an obsession—no doubt about it—an unhealthy, suffocating obsession that she was unable to shake. The nights were the worst because her dreams were unfiltered, and she often woke up aroused and confused and…hopeless.

Perhaps, if Lindsey had been a different woman, the decision to stay or go would've been simpler. If she'd been the kind of wife Brad deserved, the situation might've been easier to accept. But it wasn't.

I hate her, thought Birgit, *and I want to see her dead!*

26

Not even Lindsey was able to cope with constant turmoil, so a tenuous calm followed the episode with the wig.

This must be what battle fatigue feels like, Birgit thought—*exhaustion, resignation, powerlessness*. She hoped the worst was over but didn't believe it—she suspected Lindsey was just reloading.

Elizabeth was the one Birgit worried about most. Her scores on tests had slipped during the spring, but luckily, since the school year had been about to end, they had done little damage to her final grades.

Summer vacation offered little relief. She regularly had dark circles under her eyes, wanted no friends over, and had stopped riding her bike and spending time every day in the garden.

Birgit was at a loss. How could she help? Elizabeth wasn't a small child—you couldn't make things right by kissing her boo-boos or handing out coins for the ice cream truck.

Birgit had also noticed that Zoë, the old basset hound, was slowing down. Now and then, she'd found a small puddle in a corner and quickly cleaned it up, not mentioning it to anyone. The dog had always been low maintenance, had not been a picky eater, and wasn't one to crave attention—her behavior and disposition had always been predictable, at least, until now. Her barks had changed into drawn-out, mournful howls, which sounded both pitiful and sad. "Maybe she wants to remind us that she's still here," said Elizabeth. Birgit agreed.

There was no doubt that Zoë was loved. Despite her advancing age, her lack of puppyish charm, her bad breath, and her rheumy old eyes, she was still a valued member of the family. When she knelt down to rub the dog's scruffy neck, Elizabeth always teased her.

"Silly ol' dog. What good are you?" Zoë always responded to the girl with a contented thank-you growl and a look of devotion. The dog never left the house without company anymore, not even if the door was open. She could no longer climb the stairs, but when Elizabeth put on her garden clothes, Zoë was ready, eagerly waiting at the front door.

Elizabeth rubbed the hound's head. "Are you sure you're up for this?" Zoë swished her tail a few times against the floor and let out an affirmative "woof."

"Okay, then," Elizabeth said and opened the door. "Off we go!"

Zoë squeezed by her, and gingerly lumbered ahead to the garden.

And then, a week later, Zoe was nowhere to be found.

Elizabeth ran around searching for her to no avail. She stopped in the kitchen and when her eyes met Birgit's, they both had the same thought— *old dogs who know their time is up wander off, looking for a place to die.*

In answer to the unspoken question, Elizabeth snapped. "No! She's here!" She whistled frantically. "Bad dog...come out right now!"

Birgit wasn't sure how she knew, but she was certain.

"She's in the garden."

Elizabeth stomped her feet, tears springing to her eyes. "No, she's here! She's just playing games."

"Sh-h-h," whispered Birgit softly, wrapping her arm around the girl's shoulders. "Let's go together and find her. She needs us."

Birgit's intuition had been correct. The old basset hound had dragged herself out to the garden. She lay in her favorite spot under the bench in the shade of the apple tree.

When she saw her, Elizabeth took off running. All Birgit could do was watch and pray that her premonition would prove to be wrong, that a miracle would happen, that the dog would raise up and wag her tail.

"Get up, baby!" Elizabeth screamed. "Oh, why don't you get up?" She buried her face in the dog's fur and cried her heart out as she cradled Zoë's lifeless body. Birgit knew instinctively to let the girl be—Elizabeth's grief was too deep, too private, to be disturbed. Finally, the sobbing stopped, and Elizabeth let go of the dog and stood up. "I should've been with her," she said bitterly. "She was always there for me."

Elizabeth retrieved a shovel from the shed and began digging fiercely. Birgit brought out another and joined her. They worked side-by-side without speaking until the hole was large enough.

They laid Zoë's body in the ground and covered the grave with dirt. To mark the site, Elizabeth arranged a collection of shells and smooth stones she'd gathered at the beach. Afterward, she whispered a few words. Birgit didn't try to listen—this was a private moment between two friends who'd grown up together and shared their short lives.

§

In the weeks to come, Birgit found herself listening for the sound of paws against the tile floor in the kitchen. Lindsey too showed rare emotion. "Strange," she said, "I didn't know her time was up. I was certain she'd outlast..." She left out the "me," but it was obvious what she was thinking.

Although Birgit had hoped otherwise, after Zoë's death, Elizabeth continued to be distant. When she'd tried to console her, the girl had simply said, "You can't make me feel better, no matter how hard you try. I know you mean well, but please leave me alone."

§

Although Lindsey spent much of the time in her room, her presence was everywhere, affecting the mood in the house. Birgit wasn't sure exactly when the family had begun speaking in hushed tones, but Big E, never one to modulate her voice, was quick to bring it up. "Why does it feel like a morgue in here?" she boomed, and then swiftly corrected herself. "Library," she said. "I meant library."

The only time the gloom lifted was when Big E showed up. Ethel Hirschberg could still make her sister laugh, which nobody else could manage. She treated her sister no different now than before and argued and teased her like always. "Get off your butt, and stop feeling sorry for yourself!" she barked.

Brad was spending more and more time at work, often returning home late in the evening. On weekends, he stayed around the house but seemed unsure of what to do with himself. His discomfort irritated his wife. "For heaven's sake, leave! I can't have you moping around watching me. Get your golf clubs, or go sailing. Do something!" Brad hesitated, but relief was all over his face. He *looks like a little boy*, Birgit thought, *who's been told his time-out is up*.

"If it's all the same to you," he said," I might take the boat out for a couple of hours." Lindsey just waved her hand at him.

Birgit knew he couldn't possibly ask her to join him—that would have been, to use her Aunt Lola's word, "unseemly." But why didn't he ask his daughter to come along?

She quickly excused him, silencing her disapproval. Men sometimes aren't good in situations like this, she thought. But a little voice persisted, "Dad...and Bengt...would've handled this better."

§

Big E pushed open the front door, carrying an armful of lilacs from her garden. The fragrance filled the hallway. "Hello...Anybody home?"

"For Lindsey?" Birgit asked, instantly regretting her question. Who else? "I'll find a vase in the kitchen."

Big E smiled and shook her head. "No, not for Lindsey, for *you*. For putting up with her." Tears welled in Birgit's eyes and she buried her head in the flowers. The familiar smell brought back memories.

Third grade and the last day of school, the beginning of summer vacation; the little schoolhouse, adorned with flowers Lilacs were her favorite. None of the others smelled like that. The scent would forever signify freedom with an endless summer ahead.

Big E interrupted Birgit's reverie. "Are you all right? I meant to make you happy, not make you cry."

"Sorry, I'm just emotional."

"I understand. These are trying times."

Birgit wiped her eyes and smiled. "Thank you for being so kind." She doesn't understand, she thought. She thinks I'm sad because of Lindsey.

When the visit with her sister was over and Mrs. Hirschberg said good-bye, Birgit noticed that her eyes were red-rimmed. "She didn't have a good day," she said.

Birgit was conflicted, her feelings jumbled. She couldn't stand Lindsey and secretly wanted her gone, but for Big E's sake, she hoped her sister would live.

27

Judging by Ruth's last letter, it appeared that Bengt had fulfilled his dream of owning a place on the water by buying Birgit's childhood home on Händelöp Island. At her father's funeral, there had been talk that the house would go on the market, but she had thought it just a rumor initiated by Ruth. Now, it was a done deal.

Birgit tried to ease her own pain. *Better Bengt than some stranger. After all, he loves the place.* Still, someone else would be living in the house where she had grown up, and that was hard to accept.

Ruth had seemed more relieved than upset. As usual, she looked at the sale of the house from a practical point of view and prattled on about the benefits for Mom.

"We both know she's is a city girl at heart," she wrote. "For her to leave the island and move to Västervik is the right choice. There is a newly-renovated two-bedroom apartment in the center of town that she might be interested in. Anyway, until she decides, she's welcome to stay with us.

"Another option would be Stockholm. Aunt Lola, as you remember, has all those extra bedrooms, but you know how those two get along..."

But how could Mom just pick up and leave…discard all the memories, and just walk away from the place where she'd raised a family and lived all of her married life?

Birgit scolded herself. The island might be a summer paradise, but it was cold and isolated during the winter months. She'd left for America and happily waved goodbye to the family. How could she be resentful of Mom for wanting to move on with her life?

Lecturing herself did no good—inside, she was still steaming mad, more at Ruth than Mom for being so darned practical and not the least bit broken up. Most of all, she was angry at Bengt for taking something that was hers and making it his. And for—this was the most troubling thought—perhaps bringing another woman to live in what had once been her home.

Birgit knew that her roiling emotions were irrational, pathetic, and selfish, but she was confused. *Why do I feel like I'm suddenly orphaned when I am the one who chose to move thousands of miles away?*

She tried to shake her gloomy mood, but without success. Her friend Hilde had gone back to Austria when her contract expired. Although they hadn't shared many interests, Hilde had been a good listener and Birgit was in need of a sounding board. Elizabeth had disappeared into a shell and was spending more and more time at the only place she seemed to feel safe—with the Hirschbergs. Besides, to burden a 12-year-old girl with her own petty concerns would not be right—the girl had enough problems watching her mom wither away.

Uneasiness continued to occupy all corners of the house. Birgit heard different medical terms and treatments discussed in whispers on and off the phone, all of them alarming. Lindsey seldom left her room, and when Birgit brought her food she was always sitting alone, absent her wig, looking pale. Birgit tried to feel sympathy for her, but the illness hadn't made

Lindsey any more bearable to be around. She clearly didn't plan to go gently into the night.

Birgit had been left in the dark as to what was going on, so the morning when Brad took a feeble Lindsey to the hospital, she understood the seriousness of the situation, but not the extent.

"I'll take Elizabeth for a couple of days," Big E said. "She needs a change of scenery right now. I assume Brad has informed you of the situation."

Birgit shook her head. "No, he hasn't. Please tell me!"

Even Big E's voice was strained. "Lindsey is having a double mastectomy, and is, of course, devastated. The doctors seem to think it's the right choice. Perhaps the only one…" She paused. "So, Birgit, please, for now, keep on doing what you usually do."

§

It was late when Brad returned from the hospital. He didn't speak, and Birgit didn't ask any questions. The casserole she'd prepared for him was left untouched, and he went to bed early.

Wasn't this her secret dream? She and Brad alone in the house… no Lindsey, no tension or angry outbursts?

Now it had actually happened and Birgit felt numb.

It was 2 a.m. and still sleep wouldn't come. Birgit put on her bathrobe and walked downstairs to the kitchen for a snack. The door to the master bedroom was ajar. A dim light shone through the crack. As she passed by, from inside came a muffled, pained sound, and she peered into the room. "Brad," she whispered, "are you all right?"

There was no answer, but instead of going on to the kitchen, she opened the door wider. "Brad?" She saw the outline of his body and heard his sobs.

It happened so easily—to walk over, reach down and stroke his hair seemed like the most natural thing in the world. Natural, but insane—any moment he could turn over and ask, "What do you think you're doing?"

He stirred and she tried to pull her hand away. "Don't, Brigitte," he said, his voice tight and urgent. "Stay!" It might not have happened if he had pronounced her name correctly. *Birgit*, after all, was a girl brought up with simple small-town values. *Brigitte*, however, was a different story—a sophisticated, but an insatiable woman, *probably a Parisian*, the kind who'd laugh in the face of morality.

Birgit had been pushed aside and Brigitte, the other woman, effortlessly took her place. From the day they met, she'd dreamt, fantasized, obsessed about this moment. Nothing could stop her now. When he opened her bathrobe, mumbling the name that wasn't hers, rules no longer applied. There wasn't even a second of hesitation and, as her breasts spilled out of the bathrobe and he buried his face in them, she gasped.

Thoughts raced through Birgit's mind as Brad's hands and mouth moved everywhere. *If this is a dream, I never want to wake up.* She had no illusions that Brad loved her, but it didn't matter. Tonight, she might be used, her body violated, but she would savor every moment. Brigitte had taken control—she knew what to do, how to please him and tempt him with her dark secrets. The night might be a one-night stand, but it would be one he would never forget.

The sound of shattering glass woke Birgit from a sound sleep. She was in her own bed! Her first feeling was one of relief, instantly followed by disappointment. *Had this been another one of her dreams?*

She sat up. No, it was real—every shameful, sordid, delicious detail. Why hadn't she stayed with him? Why had she left the room? Slowly, the answer came back to her. It was the lingering smell of Lindsey, a whiff of her perfume.

But it had definitely happened! Her mind might have needed convincing but not her tender body.

She pulled the covers tighter around her, closed her eyes, and smiled. "Today, I may be fired," she mumbled to herself. "But it was worth it."

She opened her eyes again and glanced at the alarm clock. It was 10 a.m.! She threw back the covers, grabbed her bathrobe, and headed downstairs. When she rounded the corner into the kitchen, she decided the world had gone mad. Brad Fillmore, who never missed a day's work, stood at the kitchen counter in a pair of boxer shorts, surrounded by shards from a broken glass.

"I dropped it," he said.

Birgit reached for the broom, but Brad waved her off. "Don't bother," he said. "It can wait."

"What about work?" As the words came out Birgit realized how stilted and unnatural she sounded. *How do you talk to your employer after a night of wild sex?*

He smiled wickedly. "Not planning on going in today."

Was this the same man who never missed work? The man who'd bought a heavy-duty jeep just so he could get to the train station in any kind of miserable weather? Birgit was stunned. *This couldn't go on. She'd made it too easy. He obviously didn't plan on firing her, but she didn't want to be his new toy!*

She glanced at the kitchen clock and remembered the time. "Oh, my God! Mrs. Hirschberg could be back with Elizabeth any minute…"

Brad's wicked smile returned. "Big E plays bridge every Wednesday morning. They won't be back until this afternoon." He set his teacup down and she backed away. "Brigitte…" he said. "Where were we?"

He untied her bathrobe and pushed it off her shoulders. As it fell to the floor, what was left of Birgit's resolve was gone.

28

Big E stood in the foyer. "Don't ask me why," she said, "but she's adamant about seeing you."

That Lindsey wanted to see her could mean only one thing—somehow, she knew! Had Brad broken down and confessed? So far, he hadn't fired her. Maybe he'd decided to leave that task to his wife.

Birgit managed a weak smile. "Okay. I'll need directions to the hospital." She thought for a moment. "Should I bring Elizabeth?" If Lindsey were going to discuss her indiscretions with Brad, she certainly wouldn't do it in front of their daughter.

Lindsey's sister looked straight into Birgit's eyes and shook her head. "No. She insisted on seeing you alone."

Does she know too? Birgit suddenly felt paranoid, unable to face her. Actually, she'd avoided eye contact with everyone recently—Elizabeth in particular. *After sex, do you give off a scent other females can pick up?*

Her stomach churned. *Was it a hangover from last night…or this morning?* She blushed. The daytime lovemaking had been every bit as memorable as the evening session.

Ethel drew Birgit's focus back to the matter at hand. "So, it's all arranged then?" Birgit took a deep breath and nodded. If Mrs. Hirschberg suspected anything, she hid it well.

§

The corridor had an unmistakable hospital smell and although Birgit wasn't walking briskly, the echo of her footsteps seemed disturbingly loud. The closer she came to Lindsey's room, the more she slowed—the sterile surroundings, the hissing sound when the double door opened and closed, the blank walls, the skating-rink-shiny floors all added to an atmosphere of doom. *There was no place to hide.*

A nurse in the hallway followed Birgit to Lindsey's room. "So, *you* are the young woman taking care of Mrs. Fillmore's daughter and husband," she said pleasantly.

Am I ever, Birgit thought.

"We must not get her excited," the nurse warned. "She's quite weak after the operation."

We? Why do hospital personnel insist on using the plural pronoun? Birgit sighed. The nurse with her round face and professional smile didn't look as if she would cause trouble. *That* role belonged to Birgit.

The two of them entered the room together. After checking her patient's vital signs, the nurse lingered at the door. The voice was slurred and weak, but the dismissive tone was vintage Lindsey. "Thank you, Arlene."

She turned her attention to Birgit. "Come closer," she said, sounding as if she had pebbles in her mouth.

Birgit closed the door and took a few tentative steps toward the bed. Lindsey gestured to where her breasts had been. "For heaven's sake, this is not contagious!"

Birgit stared at her nemesis. Her most dominant feature had always been her eyes but never like now. In her thin, drawn face they looked like two huge saucers.

Lindsey stared at a spot on Birgit's cheek where makeup hadn't quite concealed the rash from Brad's beard. "You look like hell!" she said. "Everything okay at home?"

Another long stare followed the question. Birgit looked away, pretending to admire the flower bouquets on the nightstand. "It's fine."

"Elizabeth? She spent some nights at my sister's?"

"She did." Birgit felt her face turn crimson.

Lindsey didn't say, "How convenient!" but she might as well have. She continued to stare at Birgit and then finally opened her mouth and said it.

"You *fucked* him! You fucked my husband!"

Birgit wasn't sure what shocked her the most—the raw obscenity or the terrifying calm in Lindsey's voice. There was no outrage, no explosive anger, no sign of disappointment. She spoke as if merely stating a fact.

Birgit figured there was no point in denying it. Besides, her face, as usual, betrayed her.

"Yes."

"Was it good?" The look in Lindsey's eyes was strange, probing.

When she'd come into the room, Birgit had felt like a sacrificial lamb waiting to be lashed and ready to plead for mercy. That was no longer the case. She had discovered that the woman in the bed with her mutilated body wasn't able to intimidate her anymore.

"Very!"

"Of course!" A bitter laugh covered the wistfulness in Lindsey's voice. "Brad does have certain undeniable talents." A sudden spasm of coughing shook her body, and she grimaced in pain.

Birgit poured her a glass of water and was struck by the absurdity of "the other woman" aiding her fallen enemy.

Lindsey closed her eyes for so long that Birgit began edging away from the bed, thinking she had fallen asleep, but not so. "Maybe because of his Presbyterian righteousness, I never dreamt he'd cheat on me," she said, eyes still closed. "Undoubtedly, I underestimated you…again."

She lay still for a moment and then opened her eyes and pointed to a chair in the room. "Bring it over here," she said slowly. Birgit complied.

"This is probably the only real discussion you and I will ever have, so sit down and listen." Birgit nodded.

"As we both know, there is no love lost between us, but we need each other. You need me dead…and I need you to take care of Elizabeth."

Birgit thought for a moment. "What about Mrs. Hirschberg?"

Lindsey shook her head. "No, Ethel is too set in her ways. Elizabeth needs someone younger. Someone more like you."

Birgit was shocked. *Had illness made her softer?*

Lindsey read her thoughts. "I had this operation for Elizabeth. I thought that I might get a second chance, but that's not going to happen."

"How can you be certain? You've only just had the operation."

"Regardless of what they told me, I know my body. Believe me when I say it didn't work." She took a sip of water and set down the glass.

"Elizabeth deserved better than what she got. I was a lousy mother and Brad never wanted children in the first place."

Birgit was stunned. She agreed that Elizabeth deserved better, but was the woman delirious? Of course, Brad wanted children!

Lindsey's voice dropped to a whisper. "You know what the most painful thing in life is? It's to have it all and not enjoy it."

The same nurse who had shown Birgit in returned carrying a small medicine tray. After one look at Lindsey's wan face, she nodded to Birgit. "Sorry, but it's time for you to leave."

Lindsey, who almost always objected when someone made decisions for her, didn't argue with the nurse. She sank back into the pillow and reached out her hand, waving Birgit closer. Her voice was barely audible, so Birgit had to bend down to catch her words.

"If this hadn't happened," she whispered, pointing to her chest, "you wouldn't stand a chance."

29

Lindsey died in the fall just as the trees started to turn. "Your body knows when your time is up," she'd said. "You don't need doctors to tell you."

Birgit had tried to temper her animosity toward her rival—a decent person, she thought, doesn't wish for someone else to die. She hadn't exactly wanted her dead—*gone* was really what she'd meant. In theory, the words mean the same, but "gone" has a gentler sound—a romantic connotation, a flock of birds vanishing in the sky, the sun gently sinking into the ocean.

It had not been a fair fight—she'd won by default. Still, Brad had made love to her and Lindsey's vulgar characterization of their affair hadn't changed anything. Birgit refused to have her experience with Brad cheapened. Dead or gone, Lindsey was no more...and it was up to her to seize the opportunity.

It wouldn't be easy. Lindsey was, in many ways still as present as when she was alive. Reminders of her were everywhere—her paintings on the walls, an unfinished portrait in the studio. Butts from her Virginia Slim cigarettes overflowing a forgotten ashtray on the railing. The Le Creuset pots, her favorite cookware, in the kitchen cabinet. A novel, dog-eared, with passages underlined. An impressive collection of clothes and shoes in the bedroom closet.

Someday soon, her things would have to be organized and sorted, saved or given away. Birgit hoped that task wouldn't fall on her. Despite the bad blood between them, she didn't want to be the one "erasing" Lindsey.

Her now dead employer, though brutal, had been honest. She'd once said to Birgit, "You're a capable young woman. Why on earth don't you make more of yourself?" A back-handed compliment, it had hit a nerve, because the words echoed Birgit's feelings. She didn't know what to make of herself, but what she *wanted* had become crystal clear.

She thought about her attraction to Brad. *When had the first "what if" entered her mind? Was it when fixing Brad's breakfast in the early morning hours, or the day she tried on Lindsey's dress in the master bedroom closet? Had it popped up during time spent with Elizabeth?* What she knew was that it had started long before she and Brad had made love, but that magical night had brought it all within reach.

§

Arranging for Lindsey's funeral saw Big E and Brad's mother lock horns. Brad stayed out of the conflict and let the two women battle it out.

He's in a daze, Birgit told herself, as usual explaining away any possible flaws. Yet, at the same time, his seeming nonchalance bothered her.

Big E, who knew that her sister hadn't cared one iota about organized religion, voted for a small, family-only, non-denominational ceremony, but Brad's mother was adamant about a big to-do in a huge Presbyterian Church.

Brad, a lapsed Presbyterian, finally had to take a stand and sided with his mother, so a compromise of sorts took place. The church remained

Presbyterian, but went from massive to quaint and wooden-white, with room for just the family and a select group of close friends.

Big E had put together a loving montage of her sister's life to be displayed in the sanctuary. One of the photos, a personal favorite of Lindsey's, showed her at a fundraiser with Bobby Kennedy at her side. Her mother-in-law, a staunch Republican, objected strongly. "A funeral shouldn't be a place to display one's political affiliations."

"Boohoo!" muttered Big E. "Believe me, if we had a photo of Nixon crawling all over Lindsey, this discussion wouldn't be taking place."

The elder Mrs. Fillmore eventually caved, but at the funeral, pinned to the lapel of her Chanel suit, was a diamond-studded elephant broach.

During the service, Elizabeth sat between her father and her maternal grandparents, the Sorensens. Birgit sat directly behind her, one row back. Elizabeth suppressed her weeping throughout the ceremony, but Birgit saw her shoulders begin to shake. *Which mom did she miss? The flawed one or the one who only existed in her dreams?*

Lost opportunities, she thought. I won't make Lindsey's mistake. I'll always be there for her. Those thoughts would be smashed that very evening.

After the well-received, almost Lindsey-like dinner she'd put together for the immediate family, Helen Fillmore cornered her in the kitchen. First, a compliment—Helen, like her son, was a stickler for etiquette. "Lovely," she said. "We can't thank you enough," and then it came.

"I assume with your many talents you'll be looking for other opportunities soon. I'm afraid that you and Bradford under the same roof will have tongues wagging. Of course, I know my son's character, but people like to gossip, and we wouldn't want Elizabeth subjected to rumors, would we?"

Birgit was too dumbstruck to answer, so she continued. "With Lindsey gone, I'm afraid my son will be a highly-sought-after commodity."

Birgit could almost hear the wheels turning. Helen had just lost her daughter-in-law but already had possible replacements in mind. Lindsey may have been too much of a free spirit to suit her mother-in-law, but she'd belonged in the right "stable." Birgit was totally unacceptable. She had been useful, the family was grateful, but now it was time for her to move on. The Brad Fillmore Sweepstakes would begin soon.

Helen's icy blue eyes didn't blink even once. "Jack the Knife," Elizabeth's nickname for her, had always been something Lindsey found hysterically funny. Now having been expertly sliced and diced, Birgit had to agree. The name fit.

She knew she could make the woman's smile instantly disappear. All she had to say was, "You needn't worry, Mrs. Fillmore. Your precious son thrashed around in bed with his little Swedish au pair just a few nights ago!"

But she resisted. Brad's mother might influence her son to a degree, but not in the way Lindsey had. Birgit had learned from the master manipulator herself. *This* woman, with her millions in the bank, her expensive clothes and haircuts, didn't scare her. *I'll take you on too*, she thought, and almost heard Lindsey laugh.

Birgit simply nodded respectfully and said, "You've certainly given me food for thought."

Big E didn't seem to share Mrs. Fillmore's apprehension about Birgit. If she had any misgivings about Birgit's staying on, she didn't raise them. In fact, she'd been supportive of the idea. "Elizabeth needs you right now," she had told her. "She can't go through any more upheavals. I hope you'll be there for her."

Elizabeth needed her, Helen Fillmore wanted her gone, Big E thought she should stay. The question was, *What does Brad want?* Since Lindsey's death, he'd avoided her. He'd been polite but reserved.

He felt guilt, Birgit surmised, but their lovemaking gnawed at her. *Had she simply been a diversion? Someone to use in a moment of weakness?*

She had none of the mysterious qualities that seemed to both fascinate and repel Brad. Lindsey had driven him crazy, but she had never failed to intrigue him. That would have to change.

In a montage of photographs Big E put together was a picture of Lindsey and Brad on their honeymoon. Brad, a young man who had fulfilled his dreams, looked squarely at the camera. There was no doubt, no reservation in his eyes, just blissful happiness. Lindsey, breathtakingly beautiful as always, leaned against her husband's shoulder. Her smile might have fooled the average viewer, but Birgit recognized that faraway look in her eyes—the search for something more, something no one could give her.

I wouldn't be like that, she thought. *I'd cherish every moment.*

30

Birgit decided to leave Lindsey's things alone at least for a while, avoiding touching anything in her closet or studio. Brad, on the other hand, quietly cleared out what was his from the master bedroom and moved into the guest quarters. *Was the bed he'd shared with his wife too lonely or did it become an uncomfortable reminder of his infidelity?*

Whatever the reason, his attitude toward Birgit had changed and she didn't know what to make of it. Their one passionate night and morning seemed now as if it had never happened.

When Birgit asked him about what to do with Lindsey's belongings, he was noncommittal. "Do what you think is best," he said.

Her question was just a formality. Since Lindsey's death, Brad had left all decisions involving the house to Birgit. But one thing was clear. Her being gone had not opened the doors Birgit had expected. Her only hope was to make herself indispensable.

§

The dress incident with Elizabeth was still vivid in her mind and the thought of touching Lindsey's clothes again was almost nauseating. Her rescue came from the unlikely team of Big E and Brad's mother, Helen. When both ladies called and offered to help, Birgit gratefully accepted.

That Big E, an ally of hers, would show up, was not a surprise, but the support from Helen was. Brad's mother was, after all, the one who'd made it clear she wanted to get rid of her. Her grandmother's plan to interfere made Elizabeth furious. "Why doesn't Gram mind her own business?"

But, Helen acknowledged that she'd changed her mind. She confessed that she would not have given in so easily had it not been for Charles, who had sided with Big E. Mrs. Fillmore quoted him, imitating his high-pitched voice: "Mother, this is the sixties, not the turn of the century."

§

Where the clothes presented a problem, Birgit needed no help with clearing the studio. She stored Lindsey's art supplies in boxes and her canvases in bins against the walls for easy access. She hardly glanced at the art as she worked, but stopped in her tracks when she came across a familiar face—her own. Birgit assumed that Lindsey had drawn it from memory—when her health had begun to decline, her talk of using Birgit as a model had been forgotten.

The charcoal sketch looked unfinished and yet somehow complete. Birgit's first impression was that the sketch was too attractive to be her, but the likeness was uncanny. *Was this how Lindsey saw her? Her chin lifted, lips compressed, eyes blazing? What had caused that defiant look?*

Then she remembered. She'd been standing right on that very spot when Lindsey had commented on her classic facial structure, insinuating that the

198

fact that her father had been a fisherman made it a surprise. To have this spoiled, self-centered woman even hint that her beloved father was something *less* evoked the anger that Lindsey had so perfectly captured.

As she stared at the sketch, she realized that she had played right into Lindsey's hands that day, that her nemesis had gotten exactly the expression she'd wanted—suppressed anger and fury.

Birgit was tempted to throw it away. No one would ever know, but how could she? Disposing of the work of someone this talented, no matter how she felt about her personally, went against her nature. She was no art expert, but the drawing was excellent. Besides, could it be called stealing when you are the subject?

In the end, her Capricorn practicality won out. She rolled up the sketch, placed it at the bottom of her underwear drawer, and promptly forgot about it.

§

The clearing of Lindsey's closet was to have happened while Elizabeth was at school, but Helen Fillmore's morning bridge game had lasted longer than she'd planned. When they'd all heard the door open and close, Helen whispered from the kitchen into the hallway. "I don't think Elizabeth should be present when we do this."

The girl, who'd slipped into the kitchen behind her grandmother, dropped her schoolbooks on the counter. "I can handle it. Let's have it over with!" she said, teeth clenched.

"I'm only looking out for you." Helen tried to explain, but Elizabeth was already out the door and up the stairs. Of the three of them, Big E took the lead. Helen and Birgit followed behind. When they reached the bedroom, Elizabeth was standing, arms on hips, legs spread apart in a combative stance.

Big E tried to smooth things over. "Honey, let's calm down. I take full responsibility for not involving you. I was wrong—you should have a say in what to do with your mom's clothes."

Elizabeth responded with a shocking coldness. "I couldn't care less! Just get rid of it—all of it! Salvation Army, Red Cross, or whatever, but not to any organizations in this area. I don't want to see any of Mom's friends parading around in her clothes."

Helen shook her head. "Dear, I seriously doubt that anyone in your mother's circle frequents second-hand stores." Birgit was sure it was an attempt to reassure Elizabeth, but the comment seemed to aggravate her granddaughter further.

"THEY DO SO." All heard the rising anger in Elizabeth's voice. "They followed her like sheep and copied everything she did. Granny, the red dress you're holding onto was bought second-hand and worn at a Christmas party. Mom said she got loads of compliments."

Helen removed her hand from the dress as if stung by a bee. "Amazing," she said nervously. "I seem to be learning new things every day."

It was too cramped for all four of them to be in the closet, so Birgit backed out, and Elizabeth followed—meekly this time, her fighting spirit gone. Helen and Ethel silently gathered up the rest of the clothes and put them into bags. Birgit heard Ethel clear her throat several times, and when she glanced her way, she saw her caress the fabric of one of the dresses and wipe tears from her eyes. Helen, conscious of etiquette but not so emotionally invested in her daughter-in-law's death, made appropriate noises of approval, praising the quality and style of Lindsey's wardrobe.

Birgit watched as Elizabeth's face went blank again. When she followed the girl's eyes, she saw that the last dress on a hanger was the green one—the one that had caused the problem between them. Still, Birgit knew that nothing had ever looked better on her, and she swallowed hard when Big E removed it from the hanger.

"Hang on a second," said Elizabeth in a clear, authoritative voice. "Mom never wore this, not once. See, the price tag is still there. She told me that this shade of green wasn't hers and that it would look much better on Birgit."

Birgit froze. Of course, what the girl said had no truth to it. Lindsey wouldn't have dreamed of giving away this dress—or any other—to her.

Big E shrugged and looked to Birgit. "In that case, it's yours." She graciously handed the dress to her.

Helen opened her mouth as if to say something, but then paused. "Such a lovely memento," she finally said.

Birgit clasped the dress to her chest, suppressing her joy. The dream dress was hers! "Thank you," she mumbled. Elizabeth's lips curled into small, knowing smile.

Helen, completely oblivious to the exchange, looked to her granddaughter. "I'm sure that you want a memento of your mother's as well."

Big E watched Elizabeth with an almost pleading look. She had argued and disagreed with her sister for most of her life, but the love had always been there. Birgit too watched the girl closely. *Please, don't turn it down. Don't do it for Helen. Do it for Ethel.*

After a long moment, Elizabeth pointed to a lonely cardigan on a shelf, an unattractive reject, a gift to Lindsey from a relative years before. "I'll take that one." It was shapeless and drab, but near the end, when fashion no longer mattered, Lindsey had worn it because she needed the warmth.

Once in hand, Elizabeth pressed it to her cheek. It wasn't the scent of her once glamorous mother that made her do it. It was the memory of the fragile, frightened one—the one who had been so much easier to feel close to. Tears came cascading down and the young girl sobbed into the sweater.

Big E's voice broke. "Oh, honey…"

Blinded by tears, Elizabeth stumbled into her aunt's outstretched arms.

31

What would it take to make him notice her again?

To have a sister to confide in would've been nice, but Ruth wasn't that kind of sister, and besides, she was too far away. Distance had not made their hearts fonder and when Ruth had asked questions about her position, Birgit had been evasive, wary of her motives.

Discussing Brad was out of the question. Even from a continent away she could hear Ruth's mocking laugh. *Why waste your time on a dream?* Except for the one reckless moment that had produced Gunnar, her sister had always kept her feet firmly on the ground. *Had she ever even dreamt of Prince Charming coming along?* Probably not, since she ended up with Arne!

On the other hand, Birgit's dogged persistence had always amused the members of her family. "You get something in your head and that's it," Mom had always said.

How could two sisters be so different? Ruth's life was meticulously mapped out. Her working hours were 9 to 5 in the beauty parlor. Her weekends consisted of boat trips or drives in the country, depending on the season and the weather.

The only change in the schedule came on the second Saturday afternoon of every month. That day was set aside for visits to the in-laws. Arne's folks, the Berglunds, were friendly, hospitable people who often included Birgit and her parents in their monthly get-togethers. During her teenage years, Birgit dreaded the visits for many reasons—two, in particular: being forced to go (Mom and Dad insisted) and being told to put on a happy face no matter what.

It was the same thing over and over—the same dull conversations every time, void of any subject that might cause friction. Ruth bringing her gooey Princess Torte. Arne telling dumb jokes, forgetting the punch line.

How could they stand it? Ruth and Mom she could understand, but Dad? Why on earth did he go along?

"There are things in life you'll do for peace," he patiently explained. "Especially when it comes to family." Birgit knew better than to argue.

The horseshoe hedge, called a *berså*, hid the Berglund's outdoor furniture from the outside world. After years of tending and trimming, the hedge had become what Mrs. Berglund envisioned—a sweet-smelling oasis, a place to unwind, relax, and entertain family and friends.

After coffee and cake, Birgit generally retreated to the hammock at the other end of the lawn. From there she could hear chatter and laughing from the street—children playing soccer, the thump of the ball against the pavement. She sometimes hoped a ball would fly over the fence and break the monotony.

But it seldom happened, so she had always brought a book with her. Reading her mother approved of but not sitting around sulking. "The girl is 'bookish,'" Mom proudly explained to Mrs. Berglund, who mumbled something vague in response. Arne, her son, had never shown such an inclination.

The Svensons might have been better read, but the Berglunds were the ones with the money. Their car dealership had done well and their villa, located in the upscale part of town, was a spacious contemporary with the newest in appliances and a small but manicured lawn.

"It looks like a postage stamp," Mom commented after their first visit, but her light tone didn't mask the envy in her voice. Birgit sighed. The Svenson home was surrounded by water, craggy cliffs, wild and untamed vegetation that *did* need work…but how could Mom even compare the two?

Mrs. Berglund always served Ruth's Princess Torte, the coffee, and a variety of home-baked cookies in the *berså*. To spill coffee on the starkly white, perfectly-ironed tablecloth was unthinkable. Afterward, Mr. Berglund always brought out a flask of aquavit after the coffee. "The best part of the day," Dad would say.

Arne's parents, despite their son's obvious drinking problem, served liquor freely. According to Mom, they were in denial. "You should have refused," she scolded Dad on the way home, "if for no other reason than to make a point!"

"Vera…" said Dad, using that tolerant tone that made Mom crazy, "you don't tell another man what to serve in his own home. Besides, I like my schnapps!"

§

Lately, Birgit had begun to look back at those days with both fondness and remorse. They had treated her so well, and she'd been a brat!

Why did she suddenly remember every little detail? The silly way mom sipped the coffee with her little finger pointing out. Ruth's worried look as Dad lifted the dainty blue cups with his big callused hands. *Was she afraid he might spill and embarrass her?* Birgit, who'd seen how gently he held a hurt baby bird, had no such concerns.

Was to follow convention the safe, acceptable way to live? Should she have stayed, married Bengt and, who knows, lived happily ever after? With Dad gone, why did Mom stay in a place where she never quite fit in, instead of returning to her beloved Stockholm? *Was she the only one brave or dumb enough to follow her dream?*

§

"I know tomorrow is your day off," Brad said in the flat, impersonal way he talked to her lately, "but I have an art dealer…an acquaintance of my mother's coming in from New York to take a look at some of Lindsey's paintings. I'd hoped you might whip up something for us to eat. Of course, I'll make it up to you later. This man is a serious buyer or I wouldn't ask."

Birgit willed herself to sound calm and professional. "I'll be happy to help out."

Brad smiled a distant smile. "I'm sure this is not on top of your list of things to do, but thank you."

Birgit was thrilled that Brad asked her to help him entertain their guest, but the conventional part of her made her wonder why Brad had chosen to get rid of his wife's artwork so soon after her death. Perhaps it was just the abstracts—the pieces he hated—that he was willing to part with so quickly.

Birgit had not dealt with art dealers before but had developed a preconceived notion that they were hippie-like, pretentious. Adam Grayson would prove her wrong. When he appeared, he was dressed conservatively—in a suit, a starched white shirt, and a narrow navy-blue tie. Tall and serious-looking, his speech was clipped and measured and his deep-set blue eyes seemed to evaluate everything around him. Although there were sprinkles of gray in his short dark hair, he looked younger than Brad. The gray, Birgit decided, was premature.

§

Salmon was the only seafood Brad liked and Birgit had chosen to serve it with a cold dill sauce and a side dish of steamed artichokes. She'd been pleased with her menu until the moment they had all sat down to eat. Then the doubts crept in. *What if their guest didn't care for seafood?*

Grayson immediately put her at ease. "Miss Swenson," he said politely, Americanizing her name by pronouncing a "w" instead of the Swedish "v." "The food is excellent! How did you know this is my favorite dish?" He put down his fork and took a sip of wine. "Lovely. Pinot Noir?"

Birgit smiled and nodded.

"A perfect complement...salmon's best red-grape partner in my opinion. Most people traditionally serve fish with white wine—a mistake, I think."

Birgit could almost hear Lindsey's voice. *Be daring! Do the unexpected!* For once she felt grateful to her old boss. *She could do this!*

A nudge from Elizabeth said, "I told you so," but more importantly, Brad smiled with approval. "My housekeeper is an excellent cook." Birgit fought a sudden urge to giggle. *Housekeeper? Not just an au pair anymore. When did she get promoted? How about part-time mistress while we're at it?*

When Brad toasted her, Birgit's smile was more intimate than she intended. Their guest, who seemed to observe even the smallest of details, clearly noticed the exchange and a hint of recognition appeared in his eyes.

The two men finished their business dealings before dinner and the transaction went smoothly. Three of Lindsey's watercolors changed hands, which was more than Brad had expected. Grayson expressed an interest in two of her acrylics but said he needed more time to think about it.

"A matter of space and finance," he said, "but if you don't mind, I'd like to return for a second viewing."

Brad seemed pleased. "Certainly! If I'm out when you drop by, I'm sure Ms. Swenson can show you in."

If Elizabeth resented the unloading of her mother's paintings, she didn't show it. The girl acted mature and composed during dinner, asked intelligent questions and showed more of an understanding of art than Birgit had expected. Lindsey's influence was reflected in her comments. Brad, on the other hand, tried to hide his boredom but Birgit could see his eyes glaze over.

She, on the other hand, was thrilled to learn more about the art world, and Adam patiently explained the evolution of techniques, European modernism versus American, how Jason Pollack and Hoffman differed from Picasso and Matisse, and how Pollack dripped paint on canvas, not just to create a picture but an event.

How contagious his passion was, how his eyes lit up, and his voice softened when he talked about the things he loved! Birgit could've listened all night. She realized she was a bit tipsy—not so much to embarrass herself—but enough to float around in a warm glow. *And* the awareness that the evening had been a success.

§

Adam Grayson left with the understanding that he would be back. When the door was closed behind him, Elizabeth's face bore a wicked grin. "I'll bet on it!"

Birgit realized too late she'd fallen into a trap. "Why?"

"He's not coming back for the paintings. He's coming back because he wants to see more of *Ms. Swenson.*"

Birgit blushed. "You're always making things up."

"Go ahead. Pretend you didn't notice he's cute—a bit stuffy, but cute—and that there's no ring on his finger."

"Elizabeth! Stop this right now!"

"Or else what? Are you going to spank me?"

"Crossed my mind." With a grin, Birgit grabbed Elizabeth's arm, but the girl was too quick for her. She slipped out of the grip, stuck out her tongue, and ran giggling up to her room.

When she reached the top of the stairs, she turned and called out dramatically, "Pinot Noir? What an excellent choice, Ms. Swenson!"

32

Nobody had expected Brad's mother to show the restraint she had after the funeral. She'd been supportive and had allowed her son time to regroup. But a three-month grieving period was long enough, she'd decided. Proper etiquette had been observed, and now it was time to move on.

When she finally called, Brad was both annoyed and amused. "For crying out loud, Mother. It's much too early for me to start thinking about seeing someone. Besides, if and when that happens, it will be up to me. I'm a big boy and don't need my mommy to arrange my love life for me." He'd said all the right things, but despite his protests, Birgit was doubtful.

It was clear—matchmaking was Helen Fillmore's specialty. Who's who in New York? Most of them she referred to by first name. To get the line-up set, she scrutinized every attractive single, divorced, or widowed female in the city.

Elizabeth watched it all in amazement. "Granny is a barracuda," she said to Birgit. "Dad doesn't stand a chance." Her observation confirmed what Birgit already knew—the odds were not in her favor. She had met the competition on the streets of Manhattan. A formidable bunch, exuding money! Attractive, intimidating women, thin and toned and often with dogs in tow. Not cuddly, close to the ground animals, but tall, sleek, elegant pets with an attitude of privilege just like their owners.

"I swear," Elizabeth said, "I'll run away rather than hang around with some socialite stepmother."

"I'm sure that's not a choice you'll have to make," said Birgit, sounding more certain than she felt. Elizabeth's statements echoed her own thoughts.

Elizabeth shook her head. "Don't kid yourself. Dad is a WASP. He doesn't do unexpected well."

You can't be more wrong, Birgit thought. *He made love to me, with his wife in the hospital, and skipped work for a repeat performance. Hardly expected behavior.*

Still, a gnawing fear inside told her Elizabeth might be right. Women, all trying to hide their true intentions, were calling for Brad daily with invitations to various events. So far, he'd resisted them, but how long would that last?

§

Birgit, in full force with dinner preparations, slammed pots and pans around a bit noisier than necessary. "A Miss Hamilton called again today," she told Brad. "She wants you to call her back."

"Thanks, I'll do it now so it won't interfere with dinner." He picked up the glass with his Dewars White Label and took it with him into his office.

The Hamilton woman had called a few times before, which meant she felt encouraged. Her voice, Birgit had noticed, was reminiscent of Lindsey's, silky smooth and tempting.

"I've accepted an invitation to Carnegie Hall," Brad told Elizabeth at dinner. "Might do me good—a change of scenery if nothing else."

Elizabeth said nothing. She knew that her dad wasn't a fan of the arts, but a huge fan of women who were.

Brad ignored her silence and looked at Birgit. "You two won't mind being left to yourselves Saturday night, will you?"

"No, not at all," said Birgit. "We'll find something to do." As the words came out, Birgit regretted her answer. She wished that she'd said she was sorry, but that she had a date.

Brad whistled a tune as he left the table. "All set, then."

Elizabeth stared hard at Birgit, as if to say, "SEE, I *told* you!"

§

The abstract paintings Mr. Grayson had shown an interest in were still in Lindsey's studio. A last-minute business trip had interfered with his plans.

"Come whenever it's convenient," Birgit heard Brad tell Adam Grayson over the phone. "Ms. Swenson is always here."

§

Birgit looked critically at herself in the mirror. True, there were things in her favor. She was young, looked okay—better than okay actually—but that was not the point. Lindsey and that Hamilton lady were the type of women men like Brad wanted—sophisticated, intriguing, hard to read, all qualities she didn't possess. She practiced Lindsey's breathless intonation, her "Jacquie Kennedy" voice. At first, Birgit thought she sounded horrible, but with time, she mastered it. Finally, she was ready.

§

The phone rang and Birgit answered it.

"Ms. Swenson?"

Adam Grayson spoke in a husky voice that, in the pre-Brad era, might have raised Birgit's interest. "Sorry, it has taken so long to get back. Would it be all right if I dropped by sometime this week for a second look at the paintings? You set the day and the time."

Remember, calm, collected, in control—this is a practice run. "I have a few things to take care of tomorrow morning but how would early afternoon suit you? Say around one?" Birgit smiled to herself. She liked the way she'd handled herself—she'd been polite and firm, but not overly accommodating.

"I'll make it a point to be there," said Grayson. Birgit was vaguely irritated that he sounded amused.

When Elizabeth heard about it, she yelled triumphantly. "Didn't I tell you? He wants to see you again!"

"Nonsense…if that was true, he wouldn't have waited this long."

"Don't you get it? It's a tactic to keep you guessing." Elizabeth grinned and then pretended to be confused. "But why did you have to pick a time when I'm in school?" She paused again, and then acted as if she'd had an epiphany. "Ah-h-h…you want to be *alone* with him, don't you?"

Birgit threw up her arms and laughed. "You found me out!" Elizabeth was probably wrong, she thought. Adam Grayson's interest was in the paintings, not her. But, so what? Trying out her new approach on him might be fun, and who knew where it might lead?

33

Birgit had always taken pride in her ability to read people, but Adam Grayson proved to be a challenge. The business transaction went swiftly and without a hitch—there was no small talk or wasted time. Adam picked out the painting he liked, wrote the check for the amount agreed on, handed it to Birgit, thanked her, and headed for the door.

Birgit was disappointed. *So much for Elizabeth's predictions.* She made herself a promise not to listen to the girl again—it was clear that Grayson's interest had been Lindsey's art, not her. She put her ego in check as she walked him to the door. *So be it. Accept it.*

He stopped at the doorstep, fiddling with his car keys. "Mr. Fillmore calls you Brigitte...but that's not your real name, is it?"

"No, it isn't. It's Birgit."

"Bir-git." He tasted the word slowly. "Vigorous, hard...Swedish steel and granite." He smiled and nodded. "It suits you."

"Thanks. You are kind, but I think my name is drab."

"I disagree. As a matter of fact, I prefer it. Brigitte sounds too much like a French sex kitten, which I'm sure you're not."

A smile crept into his blue eyes and Birgit blushed violently. *Damn him...he knows or suspects, at least.*

The businessman seemed to enjoy her discomfort. Suddenly, he wasn't in a hurry to leave and Birgit was impatient.

"This tap dance is entertaining," she said, "but a bit juvenile, don't you think?"

Grayson rested his hand on the door handle. "You're right, so let's get to the point. Ms. Swenson...Birgit...I like you, and unless you find me objectionable, I would like to see you again. And please, call me Adam."

Birgit's obvious surprise was genuine and he waited before continuing.

"You've made a big impression on me. Why else would I spend four hundred dollars on a painting I needed like a hole in the head except for a chance to see you again?"

He walked away grinning, not waiting for an answer.

"I'll be in touch."

§

SoHo, with Adam Grayson as guide, turned out to be an experience. He seemed familiar with every nook and cranny and enthusiastically described the old cast-iron buildings, the lofts, bars, theaters, bookshops—even the red-light district. Birgit received a true history lesson—how the area south of Houston St. had gone from prosperity to disrepair and back again to become a home for photographers, designers and gallery owners. The buildings left behind after the textile industries had moved southward in the 1950s, he explained, had been taken over by artists. The rent was cheap, and the unoccupied lofts with their tall ceilings and plenty of light had become a haven for people with a creative touch.

Most galleries were on the buildings' second floors with living spaces underneath, but the entrance to Adam's place was at street level. Once inside in the hallway, Birgit realized she had expected to see mostly abstract art displayed there, but Lindsey's art was one of only a few.

"A tortured soul," Adam said, standing in front of the painting. "I bought it against my better judgment, but it grows on you. Agree?"

In Birgit's view, the painting was one of Lindsey's worst, just a collection of blobs, lines, and dots. "Perhaps."

Adam apparently caught the reluctance in her tone. "You didn't like her."

"No."

Birgit was grateful that he dropped the subject, as any reference to the Fillmores would bring on thoughts of Brad. He hadn't crossed her mind for hours now and it was a welcome change.

Adam's loft was neat and sparsely decorated. "I'm a proponent of the Japanese way of living," he explained. "The less, the better—no extra clutter."

During their time together, Birgit had considered that they might end up at his loft and what might follow. To see the day ruined, she thought, would be a shame. Until then, it had been thoroughly enjoyable. Adam had no downside that she saw except that…he wasn't Brad.

Birgit's concern was misplaced—within minutes Adam's loft was packed. Creative people of all kinds began streaming in, making themselves at home. They plopped themselves down in lounge chairs, on sofas, on the floor, and the unmistakable aroma of marijuana filled the air. Some known names in art were supposedly there, mixed in with younger less-established artists, but Birgit had never heard of any of them.

Adam disappeared into the crowd, and a young woman dressed in a bandanna, peasant blouse, and a green ankle-long skirt hanging from the hip motioned for Birgit to sit down beside her. She smiled at Birgit and moved closer, whispering, "Do you feel it?" Her breath smelled of something exotic and spicy—Indian food perhaps?

Birgit obediently closed her eyes. *Do I feel it?* FEEL WHAT? "Maybe a little," she said.

The girl nodded happily. Whether drug-induced or not, Birgit thought the wave of love and acceptance felt warm and comforting.

Adam tapped her on the shoulder. "Are you okay? Sorry to leave you alone. Had something that needed my attention."

"Of course, I'm okay, but I am not a pot smoker."

"In this atmosphere, you don't need to be," said Adam, lightly. "It's getting late. You must be starved. Want a bite to eat?"

Birgit nodded to some stragglers who undoubtedly had taken root. "Are you going to just leave them?"

Adam nodded. "They'll be fine. I'll get rid of them later." He looked around and sniffed the air. "Yeah, I definitely have to air out this place."

They ate a late dinner in a restaurant with brown epoxy tables and no tablecloths, but a good and varied menu. Birgit was sure Lindsey Fillmore would've referred to it as "shabby chic." With his white shirt, short haircut, and chiseled features, Adam looked completely out of place.

Birgit gestured at the general area through the angular, not-so-clean restaurant window. "How did you end up here…?"

Adam grinned. "Just say it! In something this seedy."

"You look more like…like a…" She searched for a word. "…Republican."

Adam laughed out loud. She liked the sound—deep and uninhibited.

"I *am* a square peg trying to fit into a round hole."

Adam buttered his slice of Italian whole-wheat bread and looked up briefly to wave to a bald Hare Krishna passing by. The man, dressed in a saffron-colored robe slowed, put the palm of his hands together, and bowed back to Adam in a dignified manner.

Adam lowered his voice. "That guy goes by the name 'Archylta,' which I've been told means the infallible one. Believe it or not, he used to be Bob in a former life." He paused for effect. "*And*, he was once a stockbroker on Wall Street."

"You're putting me on!"

"Well, maybe a little. But only about that last part. Bob, I'm sure, waited his whole life for a group like Hare Krishna to come along. I guess we all need to belong somewhere."

Adam refilled Birgit's glass with Chianti. "Talking about being odd…I guess I am too, especially from my parents' point of view. Ever since I was a kid, I had this fascination with shapes, forms, and colors, but in every other way, I was your typical All-American boy—played sports, was a decent baseball player. Inside, though, was this secret passion.

"When Dad, who'd pushed me toward finance, found out, he wanted to send me to a military school. I think he was afraid I was gay. Fortunately, Mom, for once, stepped in and put a stop to it."

He looked up at Birgit and then back at his plate. "The sad part is I can't draw worth a lick. I have a vision of how it should come out, but it never does. So damn frustrating! Since I sorely lack in artistic talent, I'm doing the second-best thing, surrounding myself with people who do."

Birgit was intrigued. She found herself liking this guy. He brought with him a feeling of ease—something she'd been missing lately.

Adam looked at her empty plate. "You enjoy food, don't you?" He smiled. "I like that. There is nothing more dispiriting than people picking at their food."

Birgit suddenly felt daring, flirty, and blamed it on the drinks. "So, what *don't* you like about me?"

"Only one thing."

Somehow, Birgit knew instantly he was talking about Brad. She wasn't sure how he knew about them, but he obviously did.

"Aren't you going to ask what?"

"No."

"Didn't think so."

Birgit set down her fork. "Will we see each other again?"

Adam nodded. "Yes. Unless it becomes complicated."

"Complicated how?" She looked out the window, avoiding eye contact, but no answer was forthcoming.

Adam signaled the waiter for the check.

The air outside was humid, filled with all of the smells Birgit had come to associate with New York. They were not all pleasant, but they were part of the city. She took a few uncertain steps and realized she was tipsy. Adam automatically stepped across to walk between her and the roadside, gripping her elbow protectively.

How sweet! At least the men she'd known were well-mannered. Dad certainly was, Bengt and Brad, and that guy she dated for a millisecond with the red Plymouth Fury... Strange, she could remember the make of the car, those hilarious fins, but not his name.

The urge to giggle bubbled up inside her. *What was she doing in these sky-high shoes? Didn't cobblestones belong in Europe? Don't ever, ever, drink Chianti again.*

She almost tripped, but Adam steadied his grip on her elbow. She leaned her head against his shoulder. *What would it be like to spend the night with him?*

"I'm in no rush." Adam's matter-of-fact tone grabbed her attention.

"Don't think you can read my mind!"

"What do you mean?" he said, with a sly smile. "I just did."

219

34

Elizabeth chatted happily, blissfully unaware of the tension around the dinner table. Just a few months short of becoming a teenager, her focus was strictly on herself and her peers. Birgit remembered that time of life well. Self-absorption at that age was almost an art form. Grown-ups were suddenly irrelevant—well-meaning perhaps, but a nuisance.

§

The atmosphere in the house had changed. Birgit almost missed the days when she had dined alone in the kitchen. That was long before Brad and I made love, she thought.

She thought again. Making love was not the right term to use. There had been nothing gentle or loving about that night—just torrent coupling. She wondered if she should feel ashamed, but it didn't matter. The memory of that night sustained her.

But why had Brad distanced himself? Regrets? Guilt? A feeling that she didn't belong?

In a futile attempt to win him back, she'd cooked his favorite meal—meatloaf, mashed potatoes, corn, and gravy—which, of course, changed nothing. Their sexual encounter remained the elephant in the room, filling every corner with its constant, oppressive presence.

Elizabeth sat at the table looking expectantly at her father. "So how was the opera...and your date?" Birgit pretended not to listen.

"Fine, I guess." Brad cleared his throat. "That is, if you like listening to obese people profess their love in song."

Elizabeth persisted. "And the date?"

"Aren't we being inquisitive today!" said her father, laughing. "Yes, that too was fine."

"I forgot her name. Are you seeing her again?"

"The name is Gloria...Gloria Hamilton...and the rest is none of your business."

Elizabeth now turned to Birgit. "And how did *your* date with Mr. Grayson go?"

Aware that Brad was listening, she made sure not to look at him. "It was fine. I enjoyed it."

Elizabeth dropped her fork onto her plate. "Something is weird about this. *I'm* the one who should be dating, not you two."

Her father answered without looking up. "Nonsense—you're a child."

"I'm thirteen!"

"Twelve."

"Okay...twelve and three-quarters if you must be picky...but there are countries where girls are married and have babies at my age."

Brad wiped his lips with his napkin. "Hopefully, that's not in your plans."

Ignoring him, Elizabeth turned back to Birgit. "So where did he take you?" At this, Brad settled back in his chair.

"SoHo. I had a very enjoyable time and learned a lot about the area."

For the first time, Brad spoke directly to Birgit. "So you met the avant-garde group and the protesters? The ones with a cure for everything that ails this country? I can see how that must've been interesting!"

Birgit didn't care for his mocking tone. "They were all very nice!"

Elizabeth made no attempt to hide the excitement in her voice. "Did you all sit around and smoke pot?"

Brad shot her a stern, fatherly look. "I think that's enough questions for one day. What Birgit does in her spare time is none of our business."

Birgit stared down at her plate. *Why does he sound so stuffy? Is this the same man who practically tore my nightgown off not long ago?*

She lifted her eyes again and found him looking at her. The thumping in her chest started up again. She looked down again. Despite Adam, nothing had changed—she was hopelessly, terminally, in love with Brad Fillmore.

§

"We're going to do something special this weekend." Birgit smiled at the way Adam assumed control.

"Oh?" She heard herself sound a little like Lindsey—she'd mastered the same teasing, breathless way of speaking. It wasn't right to lead him on, but he was a big boy, and she *did* like his company.

Birgit envisioned different, pleasant scenarios. *Drinks at The Russian Tearoom, perhaps, before a Broadway play?* God knew she needed to get away from the Fillmore house!

"You're in for a treat," he said. "We're going to Shea Stadium to watch the Mets play. You've heard of them, haven't you?"

Of course, she had. They were New York's other baseball team. Why not Yankee

Stadium! It didn't matter, really. Soccer ruled in Sweden and she knew absolutely nothing about baseball.

Adam responded to her silence. "Are you disappointed?"

"I'm just surprised," she said, covering for her disinterest. "I didn't take you for a baseball fan."

"Art and baseball actually have a lot in common. The grace…the symmetry…the movement." Adam enthusiastically listed comparisons, followed by details of something about a diamond—the oldest and most sophisticated piece in sport's history. "To understand America," he continued, you have to understand baseball. I guarantee you'll love it. It's a thinking person's game."

Birgit played it coy. "Why Shea? Isn't Yankee Stadium the home of the best team?"

Adam's silence betrayed that her question had not been well received. "Granted," he said, "the Yankees have the pedigree, the tradition, the mystique, but I like the Mets more."

"You're always pulling for the underdog!"

"Maybe so, but once you see them play you'll understand why I feel the way I do."

§

Elizabeth yelled up the stairs. "Your date's here. Just stepped out of the car. The baseball cap looks cute on him."

Birgit hurried to put on her shoes. The last thing she wanted was for the doorbell to ring and have Brad answer it. As she came down the stairs, she saw Elizabeth standing in the foyer with a backpack.

"You're heading out too?"

"Oh, I'm going to a slumber party…didn't I tell you?"

That's a positive sign, thought Birgit. Elizabeth had said it like such a thing was an everyday event, but since her mother's death, her only visits away from home had been to see Big E.

The girl grinned. "I don't see *you* bringing any overnight stuff?! No slumber party in your plans?"

Birgit suppressed a smile. "Scram!" she hissed to Elizabeth, before opening the door. They were met with the smell of apples and wilted leaves, the aromas of fall. Suddenly Birgit started to look forward to the day. Besides, she thought, Elizabeth was right—Adam *did* look cute in a baseball cap.

§

The game itself she didn't care for, but she loved the trappings surrounding it: the packed stadium, the green grass of the outfield, the banners, streamers, handkerchiefs waving, the overall excitement. Adam bought her a beer, a hotdog, and a souvenir baseball bat. She even sang along with the crowd when "The Old Ballgame" was played and saved the ticket stub as a memento.

The Mets, Birgit learned, were the guys in blue and orange. The player drawing the biggest ovation from the crowd was a young pitcher named Seaver. Batter after batter failed to get a hit off him. The more they missed, the more the crowd cheered.

"Tom is going for a no-hitter," Adam explained.

The Mets had scored a couple of early runs, but after that nothing more had happened. The opponents kept swinging away without success. In the eighth inning, someone finally got a clean base hit, which brought on collective sigh from the crowd.

Birgit, bored, almost clapped—almost. Adam gave her a deadly stare, and she put her hands back in her lap. "Do that," he said, "and you'll never come here again."

On the way home, Adam was mostly silent. "Didn't you enjoy any of it?"

"I loved the hotdogs."

"Contact sports might suit you better. Boxing at Madison Square Garden for our next date—okay with you?"

Next date? She liked his company...*and* how he changed skin like a chameleon—from professional to artsy to a sports fan and back again. But, was that enough? She wasn't sure. *Just let things happen*, she urged herself. *See where it goes.*

It would be a piece of self-advice that would prove impossible to follow.

§

After a few awkward moments in his loft, Adam was subdued. "I'll take you home," he said. "This is obviously not working."

They drove back to Greenwich in silence. As they approached the farmhouse, which at 2:00 a.m. was all lit up, Adam finally spoke, a rare sarcasm in his voice. "It looks like Daddy is waiting up for you."

Adam stopped the car and walked around to open Birgit's door. He nodded in the direction of the house. "For your sake, I hope it works out. I don't want you to be a girl chasing after moonbeams." He planted a brotherly kiss on her cheek, got back in the driver's seat and pulled away.

Birgit stood in the dark and watched as Adam's car turned onto the highway. When the tail lights disappeared from her sight, she felt a familiar sense of loss. *Had she again let something of possible value slip through her fingers? Had she even given him a chance?*

The door swung open even before she put her key into the lock.

"You're late!"

Brad pulled her inside and kicked the door shut. "I don't want you to see that pseudo-intellectual creep again."

His voice had an intense, tight sound, not Brad-like at all and Birgit, frightened, did not respond.

"I don't know what the hell is happening, but I can't get you out of my head," continued Brad. "God knows, I've tried." He pressed her up against the wall.

Although she was scared, she was excited, too. *This was what she had dreamt of, wasn't it?*

And then he touched her and kissed her and the feeling she'd tried to fight filled her, melted her, traveled to places it shouldn't. She wanted him so much that she could have cried, but she pulled away, just enough so she couldn't feel his erection.

"I want more than this," she said.

"Want more than what?" he said, breathing heavily.

"I want it all." She searched his eyes, but saw only lust. He pinned her harder to the wall.

Birgit willed her voice to be steady. "Brad, I mean it."

"Whatever you want," he said. "Just stop talking."

35

"Does that mean you'll be my new mother now?"

Birgit wondered if Elizabeth was being flippant, but she was frankly too happy, too wildly excited to be terribly concerned. She pinched herself to make sure she wasn't dreaming. Brad had asked her to marry him!

She had dreamed of this moment from that very first day when he'd picked her up at JFK. In the beginning, she had only worshiped him from afar—a young girl's innocent crush on someone out of reach.

When had her moral compass begun to fail and give way to this hungry, shameless obsession? If Lindsey had been a kinder, sweeter person, would it have changed anything?

Sadly, the answer was no. It had no bearing whatsoever!

Despite her happiness, Birgit was still a realist. It was clear that Brad didn't love her the way she loved him. So why had he agreed and asked her to marry him? Was it simply lust? Fascination with her youthful body? Convenience? Familiarity? Or was it something more mundane?

Birgit realized that in spite of her uncertainty, his reasons didn't matter. She would now be Mrs. Brad Fillmore the second. She lacked Lindsey's exotic beauty, elegance, and artistic talent, but she was attractive, young, and determined. It might take time for Brad to love her, but in the end, she would make it happen.

"No need for a big wedding," Brad said. "Just us. Why involve a bunch of people?" Since he was conventional by nature in all other aspects of his life, Birgit knew he must have struggled with the decision. Perhaps it was his way to avoid those relatives and friends who would question if he'd lost his mind. On the other hand, to unceremoniously get married by a justice of the peace had not been part of Birgit's dream, but it was what it was.

It was clear that patience would be of the essence. Lindsey always managed to get Brad where she wanted him—not by driving a hard bargain, but by keeping him guessing, intrigued, and sometimes frustrated. Would that work for her too? She could only hope.

When she'd found Brad waiting for her in the doorway that night, it had been oh, so tempting to let go without making any demands. But she hadn't. To be stuck in the role of housekeeper/au pair/mistress was not what she had in mind. Without a challenge, she'd learned, he bored quickly—something the fawning socialites his mother introduced him to were finding out too late. Their objective had been different from hers—regardless of status, money, and pedigree, Birgit wanted to be with him, spend her life with him.

The wedding could not come soon enough.

§

When he told her, Brad's mother refused to acknowledge the impending marriage. "All my efforts on your behalf wasted. It's sheer madness," she said. "We'll talk when you come to your senses."

He had smiled when he'd quoted his mother to Birgit, but there was no doubt that her words had wounded him. Brother Charles, who over the years had perfected an attitude of detachment, hadn't commented at all.

Lindsey's parents, on the other hand, had naturally been shocked that this was happening so soon after their daughter's passing, but they sent their well-wishes and a tasteful gift. Ethel, on the other hand, was pensive and thoughtful. She hesitated before finally calling Birgit.

"Are you sure this is what you want?"

"Well...there *is* Elizabeth to consider," Birgit responded, almost choking on her words. *Had she even once thought of the girl?*

Luckily, Big E didn't probe any further. "Of course," she said, "my sister would've wanted someone full of life like yourself to care for her daughter."

Their conversation was enough to make Birgit stop and think. Elizabeth hadn't seemed pleased when they'd shared the news. But hadn't she said that she rather run away than see one of her grandmother's selections as her step-mother? Had she surmised that this had been Birgit's plan all along?

If so, she hadn't been far from the truth.

§

No matter what, Birgit's heart was singing when she called Sweden with the news. She bubbled over, talking endlessly since she no longer had to concern herself about phone bills. Brad almost seemed bothered by Birgit's inherent frugality. Lindsey had often said that talking about money was so *bourgeois*. Did Brad secretly agree?

Ruth commented on the importance of a traditional ceremony, which Birgit laughed off. Not even her sister would destroy her mood. Her mother was pleased for her but seemed concerned that the affair had been sprung on her without any forewarning. But when promised a visit at no expense to her, she softened. Since her father's death, Birgit knew her mother had struggled financially—she could hear the sudden excitement in Vera's voice. Ruth, on the other hand, was indignant. "If we come, we'll pay for ourselves!" Birgit just smiled.

Meanwhile, Brad acted as if someone else had made the decision for him, as if it had all happened too fast. At night, in bed, was the only time Birgit had no doubt. Although she knew he might not love her, he wanted her with a hunger that equaled her own. This was one area where she had control.

§

Brad set his briefcase down on the counter. "We all need a change. I've been thinking about a move, at least temporarily."

Both Birgit and Elizabeth looked at him in disbelief. Change? Moving? This had all come out of nowhere. Lindsey had often worked herself into tears to get him to even take a vacation. He loved the area, his work, his golf outings, his foursome—the boat rides on Long Island Sound. A Connecticut Yankee through and through, he had never shown any indication of wanting a different life.

Elizabeth spoke first. "You got to be kidding! All my friends are here. This place is home!"

Brad continued in a father-knows-best voice. "Elizabeth, we have all gone through an upheaval this last couple of months. I can take a leave of absence for a while, lease the house until we decide what we want. I've been thinking of Florida, somewhere around Sarasota—"

"Florida! That's the place where old people go to die!"

Brad ignored her. "As I said, my preference would be Sarasota. Lindsey and I spent a week there once. It's a charming spot on the west coast, just the right size. Great beaches, excellent shopping, fine restaurants, and lots of culture..." He turned to Birgit. "What's *your* take, honey?"

Honey? This was the first time he'd used any term of endearment toward her. In that instant, Birgit knew she would happily follow him to Siberia if that's what he wanted. And, the idea of sitting around a pool with drink in hand was not an unpleasant thought.

Before Birgit could even respond to him, Elizabeth jumped back in. "We like gardening!" She looked to Birgit for support but saw none. "Nothing grows in Florida!"

Brad shrugged. "So I guess you would have to get used to palm trees. Worse things can happen." He paused. "Let's drop it for now. It was just an idea."

Birgit knew that confrontations of any kind bothered her new husband, and based on his current demeanor, she had a feeling that moving to Florida was more than a fleeting thought.

Elizabeth appeared to fear the same. As she left the table, she glanced toward Birgit, and her lips silently formed the word "traitor."

36

The blinding brightness, the never-ending sunshine…wasn't it too much of a good thing? *If it weren't for Brad, would she even like Florida?*

Despite its location—as far south as it gets—Florida still lacked a Southern identity. A state unto itself, it's a narrow strip of land populated by people from all walks of life—Hispanics, Jews, European nationals, transplants from the north, beach combers, sun worshipers, multi-millionaires, drifters, homeless people, crooks, seniors looking to finish out their days in the sun.

Elizabeth was more certain about her attitude toward her new home. "If it wasn't for the water, no one would bother to come." The state had become her nemesis, a place she blamed for all her woes. It wasn't just the heat, the bugs, or the flat terrain. Its biggest flaw was that it wasn't Connecticut, which she now idealized.

Birgit too missed the North—the muted colors, the pretty evergreens, the cooler weather—and she agreed with Elizabeth about the palm trees. Certainly, there were attractive ones, primarily found on upscale golf courses and in gated communities, but the rest were like those which framed the Tamiami Trail. Sad…and withered.

Brad, however, didn't share either Birgit's or his daughter's attitude. He'd quickly adapted to a more relaxed lifestyle, and had left his high-powered Wall Street persona behind.

Birgit had mixed feelings about moving there. Elizabeth, on the other hand, showed no such ambiguity. To return home to her friends, relatives and her old life was her goal, and she feverishly hoped that the vacation would turn out to be just that—a vacation.

§

"Honey, let's get you out of those drab clothes and into something a bit brighter." Maybe it shouldn't have bothered her, but Brad's remark rubbed Birgit the wrong way. Was it a veiled hint that she looked frumpy, that she lacked fashion sense?

He apparently saw the expression on her face. "Sorry...that didn't come out right..." His regretful tone smoothed things over, as usual.

Birgit looked at herself in the mirror and sighed. Maybe he was right. A change might be good. Besides, what woman tells her husband "no" when he wants to update her wardrobe? If it was what he wanted, she'd put away her navy blues and her beloved earth tones and any other clothing he thought "drab."

The next morning, Birgit began by going out to Siesta Key for some sun and then having her hair cut short. Next, in a beach-side shop, she bought a turquoise miniskirt and a low-cut evening dress in a coral shade. New shoes and sandals followed—some high-heeled and dressy, others flat and casual. The finishing touch to the shopping spree was some spectacular custom jewelry.

When she returned, Brad was pleased. "Why stop there? Let's keep shopping!" He suggested they go to St. Armand Circle.

The saleswoman in the store turned to Brad. "Doesn't she look sensational in plum? And that charming accent…may I ask where it's from?"

Hello, I'm still here, still present, and can actually speak for myself. Is this woman actually flirting with him? Brad's impact on the opposite sex was something Birgit had come to accept. When he entered a room full of women he owned the place! *Annoying? Yes! Satisfying? Definitely!* She was, after all, the one he left with.

"She is Swedish," Brad said softly. "My Viking princess."

Birgit tasted the phrase. *Terribly corny, but sweet!* She pirouetted slowly around and watched his eyes shamelessly undress her.

Brad suddenly checked his watch. "Damn…it's late…we'll take it all," he said. "Just put everything in shopping bags please…no need to hang it up."

Soon after, they left the store, with Brad carrying all of their purchases in one hand. He put his other arm around her. "How much time until Elizabeth comes home from the beach?"

Birgit shrugged. "Not much! Why?"

The tone of Brad's answer was teasing. "Don't you mean not *enough?*"

The nuzzling of her ear, his urgent, warm breath against her cheek were familiar preludes. Birgit closed her eyes, well aware that the tingling in her body had nothing to do with the outside heat.

"Let's find another spot," he whispered. "There must be a deserted beach somewhere near here."

§

"You guys were sure gone a long time." It was not a surprise that Elizabeth was annoyed. Since they'd left Connecticut, she had been in a perpetual foul mood. Still in her bathing suit, her shoulders, thighs and nose were bright red. The Coppertone lotion Birgit had put in her bag had clearly not been used.

"Lots of shopping to do." Birgit avoided making eye contact with her and heard how timid and evasive she sounded, which bothered her almost more than the girl's attitude.

Elizabeth reached over to pull a tuft of grass from Birgit's hair. "Not just shopping I see…" She examined the strands closely. "Sea oats," she said, "usually found on beaches in Southwest Florida." She dropped them on the ground before turning to go. "Oh, yeah, and just so you know, your t-shirt is inside out." Birgit heard her stepdaughter spell the word G-R-O-S-S, each letter distinctly pronounced as she walked away.

At dinner, Elizabeth questioned her father. "We're just renting, right? We're not moving here permanently, are we?"

"Don't know about that," said Brad. "Nothing is etched in stone. Let's just go with the flow and see what happens, okay?"

He thought for a moment. "If nothing else, we might look for a second home," he added, "a place to spend the winter…celebrate Christmas…that kind of thing." Birgit listened quietly. For a bright man, her husband really had a knack for saying the wrong things. Elizabeth was an old soul, a traditionalist…didn't he know that? For her to spend Christmas anywhere other than Connecticut, especially when her mother had been dead for less than a year, was unthinkable.

Nonetheless, Brad went forward with his plans, narrowing his search for a house or condo down in Sarasota area. An energetic realtor showed them around. "This might be a bit further out than what you want, but I just had to show it to you." She'd smartly saved the best for last. The view from where they were parked was spectacular.

Brad let out a whistle. "That's some piece of real estate!"

"Prime!"

The excitement in the realtor's voice accentuated her New York accent.

"Too bad the house is part of it," said Birgit. In the upscale Casey Key neighborhood, the cottage almost qualified as an eyesore, except for where it was. The slightly smudged, pink sorbet of a house sat on a strip of land a few hundred feet wide, facing two of the finest waters imagined—the calm bay on one side, the glittering Gulf on the other.

They all gazed on the water in awe. Even Elizabeth forgot the negatives of the house—the color, the lack of maintenance, and the slight tilt. Nor were the shortcomings of the house enough to dissuade Brad. Birgit recognized the gleam in his eyes. It meant only one thing—unless the inside of the house was a total disaster, overrun by cockroaches, rats and snakes, he wanted it…and badly.

"Location, location, location!" repeated the realtor, eager to bring the focus away from the house, and back to the view. "Casey Key at its finest! In the east, you'll have sunrise over Little Sarasota Bay, and in the west, sunset over the Gulf of Mexico…how could you possibly beat that?"

Elizabeth pointed to the small building at the end of the dock. "Is that a boathouse?"

The realtor nodded. "It most certainly is. I have the keys if you want to see it."

"I think so," said Birgit. She turned to her husband. "What about you?"

"You girls run ahead, I'll check it out later." He brought out a pen and notepad. "Right now, I have some figuring to do."

Birgit followed the agent and Elizabeth down the path. It's not *my* father's boathouse, that's for sure, she thought. Torsten Svenson had built his boathouse himself. It was nothing fancy, just a place to store fishing rods, bait and all things water-related. In her mind's eye, Birgit saw it all—the dank bathing suits hanging from hooks on the wall; Ruth's and her blue life jackets in the corner; boat cushions stacked on a bench, giving off a faint mildew smell that she, for some reason, never found offensive.

It had been a long time, but a sense of nostalgia crept in. The symptoms appeared out of nowhere—heaviness in the chest, throat constricting, tears welling up in her eyes. She swallowed hard and composed herself.

The realtor knocked on the gray wall of the boathouse. "Teak," she said. "The original wood has turned silvery over time. Pretty, isn't it?" She put the key in the lock and they stepped inside.

The builder had taken full advantage of the limited space and created not just a boathouse, but a miniature summer cottage. It contained a nook sufficiently roomy to accommodate a twin bed or sofa, and a small table and chairs and a tiny bathroom with a toilet and shower. The pantry had a stove, a sink, and a small refrigerator.

The realtor looked critically at artwork on the walls and pottery on the window sill. "Sorry," she said, "I was told that this place had been thoroughly cleaned out." She crinkled her nose. "And that smell…I'm not sure where it comes from…"

"I know, said Elizabeth with a hitch in her voice. "My mother was an artist…" Of course, thought Birgit—linseed, oil paint, turpentine. *Lindsey's studio.*

The realtor nodded. "I'll make sure it's taken care of."

Elizabeth's voice was tight. "No. I like it the way it is." She looked pleadingly at Birgit. "Can we go now?"

§

Brad was still scribbling figures as they returned. "And now," he said to the realtor, "comes the scary part, the unveiling of the house."

The house turned out to be far less a problem than they'd first expected, but it needed work—lots of work. Brad grinned. "It's manageable."

"Why don't I take the young lady for a walk?" said the realtor, with a confident smile, "and leave the two of you to talk things over?"

Birgit touched her husband's hand. "Happy?"

Brad beamed. "How could I not be? This is one hell of an investment!"

It wasn't exactly the answer Birgit had hoped for. "But, he's a man," she reminded herself, "and men are different."

37

"Very competitive." That's how friends and relatives had always described her. To argue would be pointless—Birgit knew that they were right.

But to compete with someone who is deceased is not fair game. Dead people have a definite advantage—they've made their mistakes, the past has become fodder for anecdotes, flaws are glossed over, and comments that once hurt have lost their sting and been turned into a smiling, shaking-of-the-head acceptance. *To speak ill of the dead is a no-no.*

Still, Birgit obsessed about Lindsey.

"It's like comparing apples and oranges," Brad patiently explained when she brought it up. "You can't! The two of you are not the least bit alike."

"Different? How?"

"Physically, for one. You're strong. Lindsey was delicate, almost fragile."

Strong? A lumbering ox is strong! To be called "delicate" and "fragile" was so much more appealing to Birgit.

Brad drew his wife closer. "No matter what," he whispered in her ear, "you're my Viking princess."

Birgit pulled away from his embrace." So, what was your nickname for Lindsey?"

Brad shook his head. "I can't remember."

"Yes, you can. Go ahead and tell me!"

"All right, then. It was Scheherazade."

"Scheherazade? From *The Thousand and One Nights*?"

"Yes." Brad looked as if he were surprised that Birgit was familiar with the classics, and she was insulted. What had *he* ever read, other than golf magazines and the *Wall Street Journal*?

"Scheherazade was beautiful, mysterious, captivating and well-read, wasn't she?" said Birgit.

Brad got up from the couch, visibly irritated. "Enough of this!"

Birgit instantly knew she had gone too far. Instead of strong, she'd come across as pathetic and needy. 1-0 to Lindsey.

§

The remodeling of the new house became Birgit's project. Her husband's lack of interest bothered her at first before she realized that it was more than a challenge—it was an opportunity.

Her predecessor had been a woman of many talents, but she'd been indifferent to the upkeep of her house. The few improvements made were always with her art in mind. For instance, the installment of the huge picture windows in the house had been typical Lindsey. They'd improved the light in the studio, but they clashed terribly with the structure of the house. The remodeling project, Birgit decided, was her chance to shine.

§

"Do as you please," Brad said, "but stay within the budget." He then mentioned a figure so large it made Birgit's head spin. *In this situation what would Lindsey do? Probably not jump up and down and clap her hands.*

"I'll do my best," Birgit said coolly, hiding her excitement behind a blasé face. To have free hands to do what you want without financial constraints or interference…how exhilarating was that!

The house, she thought, should be warm and welcoming with soft colors—no white walls and pink flamingos. That might be Florida, but it wasn't her! The money apparently didn't matter to Brad, but Birgit, frugal from childhood, was determined not to overspend. She politely listened to neighbors' recommendations and interviewed several area contractors, but she wasn't sold on any of them. What she was looking for was someone with new ideas who would also be willing to listen to hers.

§

The day Raul drove up the driveway, Birgit was outside inspecting the tilt of the house and trying to figure out what to do about it. He stepped out of his truck, walked up to where she was standing, and parked himself beside her, so he could look from the same vantage point as she.

"Landscaping might be the way to go," he said finally. "You'll never totally hide it, but you might be able to disguise it."

"And *you* know how?" Birgit asked, a hint of sarcasm in her voice. This total stranger had intruded on her property—had just showed up without an appointment.

Plus, he looked nothing like any of the remodeling experts she'd met. His bronzed skin was pulled tightly over sharp features. The black hair under his straw hat long and stringy and he wore a faded olive-green vest over a sweat-soaked shirt. She might have guessed that he was a Latino day-laborer looking for work, but his dark, intelligent eyes, his almost-flawless English—although accented—and the shiny new truck he drove told her differently.

"Yes, I do," he said simply, wiping his sweaty hands with a bandanna. "I'm Raul," he said, reaching out his hand. No last name was offered.

He flicked his cigarette on the ground and stubbed it out with the heel of his shoe. "Anything else you'll need to have fixed? Wanna show me the inside?"

Birgit stared pointedly at the cigarette butt. It was a foreign brand, unfiltered. Raul followed her eyes, bent down and picked up the butt, and added yet another item to his already bulging pockets.

"*Lo siento,*" he said.

Perhaps she was too naïve and trusting—Brad had often accused her of being so—or maybe she was just desperate to find anybody who would listen to her. Whatever the reason was, Birgit allowed Raul to accompany her into the house.

His no-nonsense approach was appealing. Before long, she had walked him from room to room discussing her plans.

"Hold your thoughts… I'll be right back."

Raul, who had listened quietly without interruption, disappeared down the stairs and through the doorway. When he returned, he had a roll of paper under his arm. A pencil appeared from one of his pockets and he began to sketch in concentrated silence. Fluid strokes danced over the papers, and then he was done. "Bueno!" he said to himself. Looking pleased, he handed the drawings to Birgit.

Trying to articulate her plans had been the most exasperating part of the process with the others. At the end of the previous meetings, she had someone else's ideas and not hers. That was not the case this time—Raul's sketches had captured the essence of what she'd wanted to be done. It was right there on paper.

§

Brad smiled when she told him the news and teased her. "So you picked up a Mexican? Do you know his credentials or do I just have to assume he's great?"

Both excited and aggravated, Birgit stumbled over her words. "He's not Mexican. His crew is Mexican and Cuban, but he is from Ecuador. And I promise I'll check his recommendations and make sure he stays within budget."

Brad looked at her, amused. "And what if he doesn't work out?"

"Then I'll fire him!"

Brad laughed. "Yeah, I can just see that happening. Seriously, though, if everything checks out, go ahead. Like I said earlier, this is your baby."

38

The move was a fait accompli—even Elizabeth could see the writing on the wall. If the new house hadn't been proof enough, her enrollment in a new school certainly was. The word "temporary" no longer applied; Florida had become the permanent destination.

"Time to adjust," her father said without much sympathy. Elizabeth just glared in response.

§

The front door opened and Elizabeth stepped inside. "How was school today?" asked Birgit, wondering why her voice sounded so unnaturally cheerful.

The girl brushed by her, avoiding eye contact. "Good," she answered, but the body language said, "Leave me alone."

Birgit waited in the hallway for three familiar sounds—the thud when Elizabeth's backpack dropped to the kitchen floor, then a beep when the refrigerator door opened and closed, and finally the blaring noise when the TV in the family room was turned on.

Birgit marched in and lowered the sound without a comment. There was no protest from her stepdaughter, who lay motionless on the couch, eyes on the ceiling, a picture of victimhood.

§

The remodeling of the house would take several months, and they'd lucked out by finding a short-time rental in the vicinity.

"Why can't I stay in the boathouse instead?" Elizabeth whined.

To call the child's bluff and say, "Go right ahead, honey!" was tempting. But what would that make me? Birgit asked herself. The wicked stepmother from a Grimm Brothers' fairy tale? What if she woke up frightened in the night and needed comforting?

A gift to Elizabeth in the form of a canoe hadn't had the desired effect, either. She had offered a polite "thank you," but had shown no sign of enthusiasm for it. She'd inherited her father's athleticism and love of the water, so she'd quickly learned to keep her weight centered when stepping in and out of the craft. Once perfecting the balance, the paddling technique had come easy to her—before long, she was touring the bay. But she always returned to shore with the same long face.

Birgit vented her frustration to Brad. "How long will this go on?"

He shrugged. "Let's hope it's just a phase."

§

The remodeling was Birgit's responsibility but also her refuge. Before Brad's daily golf game, he took his daughter to school and picked her up on the way back. That helped Birgit get to the site early and stay until mid-afternoon.

The mornings had become a hassle. Elizabeth regularly dragged her feet and picked at her food while her father paced impatiently. Birgit assumed that he was more concerned about being late for his foursome than on getting his daughter to school on time.

No need to feel guilty! It wasn't like she hung around watching soaps, sunning herself on the beach, lunching with the ladies, or sneaking off for an affair; she had a job waiting for her.

After straightening up after breakfast, making the beds, and packing a lunch, Birgit was always eager to go. The distance between the condo and the new house was only minutes away, and despite the heat, Birgit usually rode her bike.

She was not sold on Florida yet, but she had to admit that the coastline made up for the state's other shortcomings. A canopy of trees shaded part of the road until the water came into view and it took one's breath away. Waves nibbled playfully at the sky and shades of emerald and sapphire melted into a teal blur at the horizon.

This first twenty minutes alone at the house was her favorite time of day. There was no hammering, no talking—just the shrieks from gulls circling above the water. She stepped carefully over planks, paint cans, rags, and tools, breathing in the sweet smell of freshly-cut wood as she walked from room to room and visualized the finished product. It was thrilling.

Footsteps and the smell of coffee signaled that Raul had arrived. The two of them had established a comfortable ritual. He would make coffee for both of them. Delicious South American coffee—the best in the world, he claimed. After coffee, the drawings would come out. Minutes later, Raul's crew would arrive.

Although the silence was gone, Birgit was intrigued by the crew's constant chatter, their laughter and singing along to music from a transistor radio.

"How come they're always so happy?" she asked Raul.

"Their lives are simple," he explained. "Their worries are easily understood…no complications."

Raul, on the other hand, did not share his crew's sunny disposition. And he tolerated no familiarity between them and Birgit. When one of the workers attempted to call her by her first name, he barked. "Senora Fillmore para ti!"

Birgit kept any light-hearted bantering with him to a minimum. Even so, Raul seemed to respect her and the ideas she brought forward.

Respect? Was that what she hadn't gotten at home?

Elizabeth's surly manners could be excused—the girl was, after all, a teenager who had lost her mother. But what about Brad? Did he respect her? His smile at times seemed condescending. He did not look at her the way he had at Lindsey.

Would she always come in second?

39

Birgit found herself juggling two very different lives. One took place at the work-site, where she dealt with people who, except for Raul, spoke little or no English. Her other life—the leisurely one—was spent in three locations: the beach, the exclusive boutiques at St. Armand Circle, and the country club, "doing lunch" with the ladies.

Strangely, she found herself more at ease using gestures with her Latino workers than when talking to her newfound acquaintances at the club. The socializing at the club was light and friendly, often gossipy, but seldom touching on anything personal. The banter took some adjustment, but Birgit was a quick study and learned how to use humor and her "foreignness" to her advantage. Her occasional bluntness was excused as a language deficiency.

"You express yourself in such a unique way," said one of the women. "Nothing that we could get away with of course…but it sounds kind of cute coming from you." She was accepted, she realized—even popular—but painfully aware of not fitting in.

One morning over coffee, she shared her concerns with Raul, but she regretted it as soon as the words left her mouth. *Was she so insecure and lonely that she had to discuss her problems with her employee?*

"How to fit in?" responded Raul. "That must be a rich person's worry. Nothing I can relate to. What does your husband say?"

Birgit changed the subject and cut the conversation short. Brad had said nothing because she hadn't told him yet. Lately, her insecurities had ruled her life. To be perceived as vulnerable had become her greatest fear. Brad liked his women strong—his first wife might have looked delicate, but she never showed weakness. She finally tried to bring up the subject to him, but it backfired just like it had with Raul. *Were all men that way, uncomfortable with feelings, their own and others?*

"Fit in?" Brad said. "Why on earth wouldn't you? You fit the perfect criteria: financially well off, young, attractive." He hadn't added "and married to me," but Birgit had no need to be a reminded. She was well aware that her charming, handsome, scratch-golfer of a husband was a major asset—the country club environment was Brad's natural habitat. He floated effortlessly from one venue to the other, making friends while his wife floundered, unsure of herself.

Birgit refused to blame her situation on anyone but herself. The women she spent time with were okay—a bit shallow perhaps, but friendly enough.

"Florida is the perfect playground for well-to-do grownups," Brad explained. "How, when, or where you made your money is irrelevant. To have it—that's what matters." He searched Birgit's face. "Contrary to me, Lindsey hated it here—the sunshine, the beach, and the people. Too many of the nouveau riche, according to her taste. I hope you don't feel that way…"

"Of course not!" she said. She smiled and made a secret vow. No matter what, she would never, ever speak ill of the Sunshine State.

§

Lydia Wellington and "Hunter" Crawley were two of Birgit's new acquaintances. Their husbands, Dave and Jake, were both excellent golfers and fixtures in Brad's daily golf routine.

Dave and Lydia had a beautiful home at the club, while Jake and his wife Hunter were snowbirds from Long Island who owned a lovely condo overlooking Sarasota Bay.

Lydia was proud to be an equity member of the club and secretly felt superior to her friends. To her, Birgit and Hunter with their associate memberships and non-resident status were nothing more than "paying guests." Hunter was part of the inner circle regardless of membership—she was the top tennis player at the club.

Both of them gossiped about people Birgit didn't know and would probably never meet. To feign interest in the conversations, she nodded occasionally, raised her eyebrows at the right times, and made small clucking sounds of approval or disapproval, depending on the subject.

The friendship between Lydia and Hunter was a difficult one for Birgit to figure out. Lydia took pride in being politically correct and never spoke openly about anything. Her sentences often began with, "You didn't hear this from me…it might be a rumor but…" Hunter, on the other hand, was in sore need of a filter and was outspoken to a fault.

She often showed up late for their weekly lunches at the club dripping wet from the court. No apology would be offered—she would just plop herself down at the table, grab a towel from her tennis bag, and dry herself from top to toe. Beginning with her short brown hair, she would work her way down: face, neck, armpits, and end with her muscular thighs. "Thunder thighs," she would say, smiling and patting them affectionately.

Despite her unpolished ways, Birgit preferred Hunter over Lydia. Her "free spirit" act was a bit over the top at times, but she at least appeared genuine. On this particular day, Hunter announced nonchalantly, "Brenda Stanley made an ass of herself on the court today." Lydia sent a quick, apologetic look around before leaning forward, giggling with anticipation. Birgit braced herself for what might come, but was saved by a familiar voice.

"Hope we aren't interrupting…"

Their three husbands walked up to the veranda. Brad, in the lead, looked as fresh as if he'd just stepped out of the shower, a stark contrast to Dave and Jake, who were both dripping wet.

Lydia's pale blue eyes rested on Brad and the distinct tone of her voice changed into a breathless Marilyn Monroe whisper. "Of course not! Won't you please join us?"

Dave shook his head. "Just stopped for a minute. We still have the back nine to play." He was a large, powerful man with broad shoulders—no Brad, but not bad looking either. His weight was well distributed, except for the beginning of a paunch.

Lydia again directed herself to Brad, ignoring the other two, including her husband. "How are you hitting the ball?"

Brad smiled. "So far I've been lucky."

"Lucky, my foot," said Jake, a short, wiry man, known for his powerful drives. He looked to Birgit. "Your hubby is putting on a clinic today." She felt childishly pleased.

Brad bent down and gave his wife a peck on the cheek. "Having a good time, honey?" *And suddenly, magically she was!*

Brad's touch had that effect. The Tequila Sunrise she had carefully nursed was swept down in one swallow and the heat spread wonderfully throughout her body. Her husband's fingers rested lightly on her neck, and she blushed.

Lydia watched with poorly disguised envy, while Hunter made a point out of looking blasé. Aware that she was not considered to be as attractive as her two friends, Hunter did not engage in flirting. She greeted Brad with a curt nod and rocked back in the chair. Her stance was deliberately unfeminine, legs wide apart and hands clasped above the head.

Brad, undeterred, studied her with clinical interest. "Well, Champ, who did you demolish on the court today?" Hunter sat up straight, pulled her feet together and smiled broadly, acknowledging his compliment.

Pleased to have won her over, Brad turned his attention to his wife. "Don't forget the party at the club tonight," he said. He looked expectantly at the two couples. "I assume you'll be there too?"

"Not us," said Dave. "I have a poker game lined up this evening." Lydia gave her husband an icy look. The card game had obviously caused some marital friction. Hunter and Jake both shook their heads: No surprise there—they were known homebodies.

Brad managed to look genuinely disappointed. "Too bad." He looked down at Birgit and smiled. "But I can count on you, right?" Birgit winked at him in response. "I won't stand you up." *Maybe she'd enjoy the evening, after all.*

Birgit's afternoon confidence lasted only so long. By the time Brad escorted her to the entrance of the club, her insecurity had returned. Brad sensed her discomfort.

"You look spectacular tonight." He glanced at her up and down. "Green is very becoming on you. Is the dress new?" It wasn't—it was the dress from Lindsey's closet but Brad knew nothing about it. The story behind the dress had stayed a secret. Elizabeth had never mentioned catching her in the dress.

"Mingle, shall we?" Brad picked up two glasses of white wine from a tray, handed one to his wife and kept the other one for himself. With an encouraging nod, he was gone.

Birgit clung to the wine glass as if it were a life raft. Between sips, she looked up and around and smiled weakly at no one in particular. The wine tray was within reach and, shortly thereafter, she finished a second glass and then a third.

She was no longer intimidated. The women, she noticed, were overdone, too much glitter on their outfits, too much make-up…and their figures were nowhere near as good as hers. Her dress was superior too—elegant without being showy.

"Aren't you too attractive to hide out?" The man beside her was darkly handsome in a Fernando Lamas sort of way.

"My husband seems to have left for a moment."

"Isn't he taking a big risk leaving you all alone?"

Birgit responded in a flirtatious tone. "He's supremely confident."

The music and noise drowned out the man's introduction, but she picked up that his name was Tony. Within minutes she was surrounded, not only by Tony but by his many friends.

Brad spotted his wife and her entourage across the room. His eyes flashed as he approached them.

"So, *there* you are!" He slipped his hand tightly around Birgit's arm. "Gentlemen, thanks for keeping my wife company," he said. "Unfortunately, we'll have to exit early tonight."

"But, I'm having such a good time…"

Brad firmly steered her toward the door. "I can see that."

"You told me to mingle…"

"Mingle means meet new people, not collect strays." He was angry…*and* jealous.

Birgit had never felt surer of herself. "Don't pull my arm. You're walking too fast."

"Well, get rid of those damn heels."

Birgit bent over and took off her shoes and then looked up at her husband, who seemed to tower above her. "You're so tall!" she said with slurred speech.

"And you're so drunk."

Birgit giggled. "Do you want to take advantage of me?"

Brad was clearly annoyed but also aroused. "Hell, why not?" He jerked her through a side door and headed for the golf course.

The light from the ballroom flooded the ninth hole, and on the balcony, the light from a cigarette flickered. "People might see us…" said Birgit.

"Not in the sand trap, they won't."

40

"This Christmas I want to go home to see my family," said Elizabeth. The emphasis was on the words *home* and *my*. She was obviously not talking about her father and Birgit. And "home" was not Florida, but her beloved Connecticut.

Birgit's feelings were hurt. And what about us? Don't we count? Are we just here to feed you, drive you places, clothe you and put a roof over your head? Her inner voice was eerily familiar, indignant and accusatory, vintage Vera Svenson. Does parental influence never cease to exist? Birgit was a million miles away and still echoing her mother. She kept her voice steady. "I assume you mean Big E and your other relatives up north?"

Elizabeth's tone quickly went from demanding to pleading. "I guess so."

She grabbed Birgit by the hand. "Please...pretty please, ask Dad to let me go...I'll stay with Big E, but the rest of them will be there too. Granny and Charles and Grandpa and Grandma Sorensen from Chicago—it will be just like before." Birgit mentally filled in the blanks. *Before I entered the picture.* She was now the dreaded stepmother, a necessary evil, not someone you would want to spend times with on holidays.

Relief shortly replaced her annoyance. Having Elizabeth away and Brad all to herself opened up all sorts of possibilities…

Then her mood changed again. Was their marriage strictly based on sex? It was a question she was asking herself with increasing frequency. Their love-making was immensely satisfactory, but what else did they have in common?

In the past, she'd thought of Elizabeth as someone to protect, to share things with—almost like a younger sister. Why had her feelings changed? In one of their recent clashes, Elizabeth had angrily accused her of being a fake, a person not in touch with her feelings. "Mom might've been a phony sometimes," she'd told Birgit looking her squarely in the eyes. "But she knew she was. It was an act. With you, I'm not so sure."

Birgit had been tempted to slap her, but she had restrained herself. Vera Svenson had claimed it wasn't spanking, but her light slap across the cheek had the same effect. It had been every bit as humiliating as her slapping Elizabeth would have been. Vera's sudden outbursts were legendary, and her daughter had not forgotten.

Elizabeth had studied Birgit's face with interest. "See," she said, "that's what I mean. Nothing about you is real."

Maybe, as Brad had suggested, the girl was going through a phase, a teenage rebellion of sorts. But regardless of the reason, she was increasingly difficult to be around. Birgit thought she'd tried every option—kindness, understanding, anger and threats—but nothing had worked. So many positive things had developed lately and her life would be good except for Elizabeth.

The remodeling of their new home had been a resounding success. Due to Raul's ingenuity, its flaws had been covered up and turned into charming differences. No doubt, his expertise was the main reason that the house had turned out so well, but Birgit had definitely been a major contributor. The house had been her project from beginning to end, and the fact that she'd succeeded with minimal involvement from her husband made it extra special.

However, with the joy of completion had come the realization that it was over. She missed the morning bike rides, the thrill of seeing the house rise in the early morning mist, the daily planning sessions with Raul, the sound of the crew members speaking in a language she couldn't follow, even the tunes from the Spanish music station.

Slowly, but surely, Birgit's attitude toward life in Florida had improved. She was eager to move into "her" house. Tennis and bridge lessons had also added to her confidence—she finally felt she was beginning to fit in. Brad was no longer the only one drawing attention. She too received admiring glances. The "Fillmores from Connecticut" had become a sought-after couple, and the phone rang frequently with invitations to various events.

And Brad was pleased with her increased popularity. His physical attraction to her had never been in doubt, but that was no longer her only trump card—she was also gaining in other areas. Her mimicking his first wife's erratic behavior—one moment passionate, next moment aloof, at times formal, other times shockingly candid—didn't seem to be a turnoff. Rather the opposite. Lindsey could both infuriate and intrigue her husband but always managed to keep his interest alive. Now Birgit could say the same.

Still, though, unless they were preludes to sex, Brad had an aversion to conflict, and to discuss the latest flare-up with Elizabeth would be counter-productive. The messy situation with his daughter was Birgit's to handle as far as he was concerned. When she brought up the idea of Elizabeth's spend-ing Christmas elsewhere, he hadn't reacted with anger. There had been a few perfunctory remarks, but nothing more.

Elizabeth had been delighted at first, but then her eyes had darkened and she had grown silent. Birgit had noticed the mood change, but Brad hadn't.

And strangely, although Brad didn't mind his daughter leaving, he objected to *his* mother being a part of her Christmas. After her son's marriage to "the au pair," Mrs. Fillmore had broken off all relations with him, communicating only via Elizabeth.

In the past, Brad had always loved finding the perfect presents for each of his relatives, and he'd already finished his shopping. This time he'd left his own mother out. "The old battle ax doesn't deserve any consideration," he told Birgit, who secretly agreed, but thought it would be better take the high road.

"Let's not be petty," she said.

Brad grudgingly relented.

§

What would Christmas in Florida be like? Birgit wondered aloud.

"Tacky!" Elizabeth said without hesitation. "I, for one, couldn't stand it."

The truth was that Birgit was leaning that way too—an early look at Christmas decorations in the shops hadn't filled her with confidence. She and her predecessor had that in common—the love of a traditional Christmas with, if not a heavy snowfall, at least a light dusting on the ground and a pleasant chill in the air. To see garlands dangling haplessly from palm trees seemed terribly wrong.

"You get used to it in time," her friend Lydia said. "I felt the same way my first year here, but I promise you that the tree in the foyer at the clubhouse is the real deal, a majestic Vermont white spruce decorated to the hilt. Stunning."

Practical-minded Hunter just shook her head. "You're such a romantic with your white Christmas sentimentality. Was Jesus not born in Bethlehem? No snowing there as far as I know."

§

Brad handed his daughter a small box at the airport. "Not to be opened before Christmas!" The wrapping paper, Birgit recognized, came from one of the more exclusive shops on St. Armand Circle. Earrings? A bracelet? Was he trying to make amends for not fighting harder for her to stay?

Elizabeth parroted the typical adult response. "You shouldn't have…but thank you." With no sense of curiosity, she dropped the gift into in her purse.

"I've shipped the rest," Brad explained, "even one for dear old Mom."

His light tone made no inroads with his daughter. "We'd better say goodbye now," she said. "Time for me to board."

Birgit forced a smile. "Merry Christmas! Please say hello to Big E from me." She attempted a hug but felt the girl stiffen and free herself from the embrace.

"Sure," said Elizabeth, and then she was gone. Birgit watched the girl walk away. Mixed with some relief was a touch of envy. Elizabeth would spend the Christmas holidays surrounded by relatives who loved her.

In the midst of all of the holiday bustle, she hadn't given her own family much thought, but as she and Brad walked through the airport, each of them drifted across her mind.

How would Mom cope her first Christmas without Dad? Would Ruth, the upholder of every conceivable tradition, drive herself and the family batty in the process? Would Arne sneak out to illegally chop down a tree in some godforsaken forest? And Gunnar, her precocious little nephew—would he contemplate Christmas in the same solemn manner he did everything else—waiting, not just for presents, but for the magic surrounding the time of the year?

As they approached the exit to the parking lot, Birgit mused aloud to her husband. "Did Elizabeth look a little peaked?"

He shrugged. "Perhaps a little." Birgit felt his light grip on her elbow as he ushered her out into the blinding sunshine. She glanced up at his handsome face.

He's clueless, she thought. Utterly clueless.

41

Elizabeth came back from her trip to Connecticut a different girl—pleasant, polite and with a much-improved attitude. What triggered the change was unclear, but Birgit suspected that Big E had had a hand in the transformation. The peacemaker in the family, Big E had a knack for staying neutral in conflicts without compromising her integrity. Despite her sister's adverse relationship with Birgit, she had never wavered in her support for the Swedish au pair. Had she had a heart-to-heart conversation with her niece?

Whatever the reason, Birgit was thrilled to have the "old" Elizabeth back. Listening to the girl's breathless account of the Christmas vacation made her realize how much she'd missed her. Elizabeth still had that calming effect on her, which sadly, her husband didn't. With Brad, she was seldom at ease—she was either, excited, aroused, apprehensive or insecure, but never relaxed. Was it his fault or hers? Was she trying too hard to be the perfect partner?

Birgit realized that she'd become so immersed in her new life that she had neglected her friends and family. Big E was an example—Birgit had vowed to stay in touch but hadn't.

The same was the case with her relatives in Sweden. She had invited them to visit but had not followed up. Mom, according to Ruth, had hurried to renew her passport and had even taken an evening course to brush up on her English. Birgit could tell her sister was dying to come too, but was not going to beg. When they'd spoken, she'd had that familiar quiver in her voice. "Only if we're welcome…" A champion in dishing out guilt, Ruth had succeeded this time.

"Don't be silly. Of course, you are," Birgit had answered. "You pick the time." Ruth, knowing she'd won the battle, was suddenly more flexible about when. Gunnar had to finish school first, and Florida in the summer would be unbearably hot, at least for Swedes, so how about the fall?"

"Just give me the dates, and we'll be ready." A burden fell from Birgit's shoulders—now she had only Big E to contact and clear her conscience.

§

Brad had not been as affected by his daughter's mood as Birgit, but since he despised dissension, he too was relieved by her new attitude. "Didn't I tell you it was a phase?"

Despite her new positive outlook, though, Elizabeth's stubborn contempt for the Sunshine State continued. She wasn't as vocal about it as before, but it was clear that her views hadn't changed. Florida, in her mind, was a landing spot for shallow transplants, not for people who treasured their roots! Knowing that their old home was just rented out kept her hopes alive.

The same was true of their beloved sailboat. "Femme Fatale" was at a boatyard on Long Island Sound, still there and waiting. Birgit had convinced herself that Elizabeth would get over it. Unfortunately, she hadn't shared those thoughts with Brad.

Not long after Elizabeth's return, Brad turned to Birgit at the dinner table. "Honey, you remember the Kerrys, don't you?"

She nodded and he continued. "Well, I've been in touch with Bud and Maggie. They've offered to sail our boat down in the spring, spend some time with us, and then fly home. I didn't suggest it—they brought it up, of course. I offered to pick up all expenses, but they didn't want to hear of it—said they just wanted to have some quality time with us."

Quality time? What did that mean? Of course, she remembered the couple and their palatial estate overlooking the Sound. Bud, Brad's exuberant college roommate—the man Lindsey had branded as boorish—and his wife Maggie, who despite her lackadaisical manners had been a coolly efficient hostess. Birgit still remembered Maggie's sudden laugh and furtive little glances when Brad was around. She forced enthusiasm into her voice. "Sounds great!"

Meanwhile, Elizabeth looked as if someone had punched her in the stomach. Birgit had no difficulty reading her thoughts. With the boat gone, the house will follow and Connecticut will never be home again. Leaving her favorite dessert untouched, Elizabeth stood up. "Excuse me, but I have loads of homework to do." Her voice flat, she sounded so unlike herself that even Brad noticed.

"What the hell was that about?" he asked, once she'd left the room. "Did I say something wrong?"

"Teenagers…" said Birgit. Her accompanying smile was ingenuine. For the hundredth time, she wondered why she was hesitant to share her real thoughts. Would she and Brad ever have a real honest to goodness conversation?

"You can't talk to men like you do to women," Hunter said the next day at lunch when Birgit mentioned the interaction. "They're wired differently."

Birgit smiled and nodded in agreement, knowing the statement was a generalization. Hunter had obviously never met a man like Birgit's father. With Torsten Svenson, you could talk about anything!

42

Contact between the Kerrys and Brad had been sporadic during "Femme Fatale's" voyage, but finally, Bud had called ship-to-shore with an approximate arrival time of mid-to late-afternoon the following day.

The sailboat was Brad's favorite toy, and Birgit had never seen him as excited as the day it was scheduled to enter Sarasota Bay. She watched in amazement as her usual calm and composed husband nervously began pacing the dock around lunchtime. Since wind and current can make sailing unpredictable, Brad had a perfect excuse to start scouting the waters early, but as the hours went by with no sighting of the boat, he became more and more anxious.

Birgit was worried too, although her concerns had less to do with the safety of "Femme Fatale" and its passengers and more to do with the dinner plans. Lindsey had been a master entertainer who could put together an elegant meal in the blink of an eye—a talent Birgit didn't share. Improvising was not her strong suit.

§

By late afternoon, the wind died down and the waves that lapped the shore did so almost bashfully. Equipped with a pair of binoculars, Birgit took turns with Brad on the dock, practically willing the boat to appear.

When a dot appeared on the horizon, for a moment, her wishes seemed to be fulfilled. Excitedly, she called out to Brad, who came running.

"That's not her," he said after a long hard look. "The sails aren't right."

How he could tell from that far away was a mystery to Birgit, but she wasn't going to question him—her husband was an experienced sailor and knew his boat like the back of his hand. She sighed, left him to fret by himself, and returned to the kitchen. Maybe this late, a salad and some cold cuts would be acceptable.

Then, long after the sun had dipped into the sea, she heard the call she had been waiting for. "There she is—that's my girl." Brad's voice was filled with such deep affection that Birgit wondered what it might be like to be a boat. How wonderful to be worshiped for nothing other than your sturdy build, sleek look, and ability to whip through the waves!

Elizabeth, not sharing in the excitement, watched in stony silence as the sails grew larger and larger. She had once loved the boat every bit as much as her father, but since "Femme Fatale" would now sail the Gulf of Mexico instead of Long Island Sound, she no longer held the same appeal.

"Is it just me or does the kid seem kind of blah?" asked Brad when Elizabeth was out of earshot. "Hopefully she isn't going into a funk, especially with our guests here. Doesn't she have friends to visit? What about sleepovers and things like that?"

Birgit felt a tad defensive. Maybe she should have made some sort of arrangement for Elizabeth, but how was she to have known that the girl, as Brad put it, "would go into a funk?" Sleepovers? With whom? Where? Elizabeth had befriended no one since they'd been in Sarasota.

Bud hollered from the deck, pounding his chest in gorilla-like fashion. "We made it! Not much wind in the end, but here we are." His jump to the dock was not as agile as he might have hoped, but he recovered from the near stumble and looked to Brad for approval. No embrace was forthcoming from his old friend—he had to settle for a manly shoulder bump and a congratulatory slap on the back. Bud looked down at his clothes and grinned. "I know I look like hell."

Birgit agreed—Bud needed a shave and his Irish complexion, not conducive to tanning, had turned painfully red. His wife, as usual, was his polar opposite. Maggie appeared fresh and unruffled, with a face that showed no sign of wind or sun exposure. As she gracefully stepped out of the cabin, showing off her white, muscular ballerina-like legs, Birgit wondered if she'd spent the entire voyage below deck. An unfair assumption perhaps—according to Brad, Maggie was a skilled sailor who loved the sea!

Elizabeth greeted their guests, not with her usual enthusiasm, but pleasantly enough. Brad kissed Maggie on the cheek before climbing on board to check out his prized possession. Bud followed like a puppy dog, explaining the route he had taken and the obstacles he had conquered on the way. Out came the nautical chart and, based on the lively interaction between the two men, Birgit knew she was in for a long night. To play hostess to Maggie would be a challenge, regardless—the unnerving Mona Lisa smile Birgit remembered from their first meeting was already in place.

"Marriage seems to agree with you," was her guest's first remark. *An innocent comment or not?* It was hard to tell. *Was Maggie referring to their last and only meeting when she was still the Fillmores' au pair? Had she really meant to say, "Little girl, you have come up in the world!"?*

Birgit lectured herself and answered sweetly. "Thank you. You look pretty amazing yourself, especially after such a long trip." She wasn't exaggerating—Maggie did look amazing in a wholesome sort of way. "A cute, unassuming girl," Brad had called her. Looking at Maggie's clean-scrubbed face, Birgit was acutely aware of her own elaborate makeup.

§

One day followed the other in lazy Florida fashion. Brad and Bud played golf most days, and Maggie and Birgit either went shopping, to the club, or to the beach. Fortunately, the Kerrys insisted on eating out most nights and Brad, familiar with Maggie's preference for fish, had studied up on seafood places in the area. He started by introducing the couple to high-end restaurants, but quickly learned that was a mistake. Casual, off-the-beaten-path places were more their taste. On one of their last nights, he found the perfect spot—an old crab shack, rustic enough to meet Maggie's approval.

"So authentic…so quaint," she squealed. "How did you find this place?"

Brad stroked the rough surface of the table. "Oh, I stumbled on it some time back and loved it. It's so old Florida, I think." He avoided eye contact with Birgit, who knew that he didn't much care for seafood and had never put his foot in the place before.

"It isn't just fish," Bud explained. "My wife gobbles down everything from the sea—clams, oysters, sautéed algae, even plankton. Did I tell you about the trip we took to Korea?" He shook his head and looked at Brad and Birgit. "I know what you're thinking. Who vacations in Korea anyway? Well, *we* did, so Maggie could get her fill of crispy seaweed with sea urchin soup. Asians are nuts by the way. They eat anything that swims, floats, or grows on the ocean floor."

That's a slight exaggeration," said Maggie, her fixed smile in place, "but Bud is right. I could live on strictly seafood with an occasional Mai Thai…"

She lifted her glass to the group, gave a fleeting glance to Birgit and Bud, but a longer one to Brad.

Birgit tried to steer the conversation away from things with fins. Her voice seemed shrill when she compared it to Maggie's soft whisper. "How did the two of you meet?"

Bud quieted a burp with his fist. "She's a fucking mermaid who just surfaced on my beach one day…"

"Pardon our language," said the mermaid.

"Not *our* language. *My* language," her husband muttered.

"Whatever you say, darling."

Brad looked around for the waiter. "Well, folks, it's been a long day. Maybe we should call it a night."

"Maybe we'd better," Maggie agreed, looking at her husband. "I'm afraid that some of us had a bit too much to drink."

"Not *some* of us," Bud hiccuped. "Just one. *Moi.*" He motioned for his wife to go ahead while he rose unsteadily from the table.

"Fucking mermaid!" he said.

§

Brad and Birgit lay in their bed. "Overall, I think the evening went well," he said.

"Yeah, but your friend Bud drinks too much."

"At least he doesn't touch the hard stuff anymore."

"But he compensates with beer."

Brad faked a yawn and turned over, facing away from Birgit. "So, he drank a little too much. So, what? He's having a good time. Stop picking on the guy."

Birgit stared at her husband's back before reaching to turn off the lamp. *Clueless,* she thought. Lately, she had begun to associate that word with him more and more.

One thing was for certain: Bud was not enjoying himself and it was not just because of Maggie. Something else was eating him. Lindsey had not been comfortable with the couple either. Maybe she had more in common with her old adversary than she thought.

43

A light breeze was cooling the air, and the temperature was perfect for a cookout. "Since it's your last evening, how about we eat at home tonight and relax," said Brad. "I'll throw some steaks on the grill and a piece of salmon for the little mermaid."

At his reference to her, Maggie blushed and nodded happily. "So domestic," her eyes seemed to say. "I bet you'll look cute in an apron."

§

Both couples were pleased with themselves. The Kerrys had done what they'd set out to do—return "Femme Fatale" to her owner—and the Fillmores had reciprocated by being gracious hosts. Together they enjoyed a Florida sunset so spectacular it almost looked fake.

Bud poured drinks while Maggie fixed the salad. Brad, in an excellent frame of mind, whistled as he fired up the grill. Birgit could tell her husband was happy. The visit had gone well and more importantly, he had his beloved sailboat back.

In the morning, they had made love—slowly, tenderly—and now they exchanged intimate smiles at the table. The disagreement about Bud's drinking was no longer an issue.

Birgit had set the table near the boathouse. Elizabeth liked to think of the area as belonging to her, but since she'd snubbed them for dinner, Birgit couldn't care less about her territorial rights.

The two couples ate quietly together, enjoying the view. Once dinner was over, Bud lifted his glass to Birgit.

"My buddy always gets the beautiful girls," he said.

She smiled and mumbled "thank you," but that whole area of discussion made her uncomfortable. *Was she imagining, or was there a dissonance in his tone?* Brad had often teased her about her habit of reading something into the most innocent remarks. *Was she again looking for trouble where there was none?*

Brad grinned. "As I remember, you didn't do too badly yourself."

"Well," said Bud, "I had my picks of the leftovers…"

Though her face didn't show it, Birgit was mortified. *What a thing to say in front of your wife!* An uncomfortable silence followed, and Brad, always the consummate host, scrambled to make light of the situation.

"You must be going back to our old college days. Maybe I got lucky a few times, but let's face it—you're the one who ended up with a real live mermaid…"

Bud glanced at his wife. Her ever-present smile was gone and her jaw clenched. "Oops! It seems I'm in the doghouse again."

Still trying to change the subject, Brad slapped his taut belly. "Anybody up for a walk? I don't know about you, but I'm stuffed." He looked around for takers.

Maggie nodded, but her husband didn't move. "Not me," Bud said. "You two hop along. Birgit and I will find ways to amuse ourselves."

Birgit looked for Brad to come to her rescue, but he was too busy helping Maggie up from her chair. She wasn't keen about staying with Bud, but to abandon him would be rude—and could potentially end up in disaster. In his condition, he might wander out onto the deck, fall in, and drown.

Brad ignored the scorching look Birgit gave him. "Well, I guess it's settled then. We won't be long." He put a protective hand under Maggie's elbow and, as the two walked away together, Birgit felt a sense of betrayal.

Bud followed them with his eyes. "He sure knows how to operate, doesn't he?" There was unmistakable resentment in his voice.

So, that's it!

Birgit had wondered about the relationship between the men. *Did it go all the way back to their college days?* That they were opposites was clear—her husband, smooth, handsome, confident—and Bud was…

She couldn't find a right word.

Was their relationship a win-win situation? Did Bud supply Brad the adulation that he didn't crave, but was accustomed to? Did Brad's easy popularity help Bud's standing with the in-crowd? Maybe playing second fiddle for so many years had begun to wear thin. Had the visit stirred up ghosts from the past?

Bud cleared his throat and interrupted Birgit's thoughts. "Why so quiet? Trying to figure something out?"

Birgit forced a laugh. "No. Just listening to the sound of the waves."

Bud's eyes returned to the empty ice chest and Birgit pretended she hadn't seen. The fact that there was more alcohol in the house was not something she wanted to share.

"You think I am…in…inebriated," said Bud.

"I don't *think* so, Bud. I *know* so."

"I have great capacity…"

"I'm sure you do."

Birgit searched her brain for another subject to keep the conversation going until Brad and Maggie returned.

"The boathouse is the only place I haven't seen," said Bud. "Are you hiding a body in there?" He giggled at himself.

"That's Elizabeth's place. She often keeps it locked." Birgit hoped against hope that it was true this time.

"Why don't we check?"

Before Bud had a chance to move, Birgit was on her feet. "Okay. I'll take a look." She hurried across the deck and turned the doorknob to the boathouse. She was relieved when it didn't budge. "Yes, it's locked. I guess you'll have to see it another time."

She turned around to discover that Bud had crept up behind her. Swaying slightly, he struggled to keep his balance. The look on his face frightened her.

He shoved her brusquely aside and reached for the doorknob. "Why don't I believe you?" So close that Birgit could smell the beer on his breath, he twisted it hard and grunted in frustration.

Pinned against the wall, Birgit felt the rough planks digging into her back. *What options did she have? Sweet-talk him? Appeal to his better angels?* There was no way to escape—he was a big man, who though not in great shape, exuded strength. She was strong, but not that strong.

His features had dissolved into a mass of seething anger. Though directed more at her husband, they were terrifying. "Bud...stop," she said, hating the pleading sound in her voice.

"Not a chance," he said. "It's me who'll get the pretty girl this time."

Out of nowhere came the sound of another voice. "What are you guys up to?"

Elizabeth sat in her canoe just below them, her eyes fixed on Bud.

Birgit had never loved the sound of her stepdaughter's voice more than she did in this moment. Her knees buckled as relief and gratitude flooded her body.

Bud pulled violently away and made a futile attempt to rearrange his expression to more closely match his usual "good ol' Uncle Buddy" face. "You're a quiet one, Elizabeth," he said as steadily as he could. "I didn't hear you come in."

"So I noticed." One glance at Birgit's face told the girl everything she needed to know. "Where is Dad?" she asked coolly.

Birgit found herself wondering the very same thing.

44

"God, I'm sorry!"

Brad sounded so remorseful that Birgit almost believed him. What he was sorry for was unclear. Was it for leaving her alone with his drunken friend or for returning home after midnight with their female guest?

"I didn't have a choice—Maggie was a mess," he said. "Had no idea how bad things had gotten between them. She sat down on the bench near the water and just started sobbing. What was I supposed to do? Walk away?"

Elizabeth's voice was razor sharp. "Doesn't it matter that while you were busy playing the white knight, your best buddy tried to rape Birgit?"

Brad frowned. "Aren't you being a bit dramatic? So, he had too much to drink, but to suggest that he'd harm Birgit is ludicrous. For Christ sake, we've been friends since college…" Brad turned to his wife for support, but was met with icy silence.

Clueless. For the hundredth time, the word popped into her head. All these years and her husband still had no inkling of what was going on with his and Bud's so-called friendship. "I never want to see either one of them again," she said calmly. "And if you do, it will be without me."

"Same here," Elizabeth echoed. "You know Mom felt that way about them too."

Brad was stunned. "What is this? A female onslaught? I'm sure the guy is as sorry as hell about it."

Elizabeth smirked. "Yeah, sorry I *interrupted* him."

Suddenly, Birgit felt drained—fed up with conversation that led nowhere, of Brad, her life, Florida—everything except Elizabeth. Had she truly thanked her for rescuing her and for the adult way she'd handled the situation? Tears welled up in her eyes as she turned to her stepdaughter and mouthed, "Thank you."

She had to give Brad one thing—he was trying hard to make up for his mistake. That Brad hated conflict was no secret—he desperately wanted things back to normal. To be honest, so did she. Could she forgive him? Maybe. Trust him again? Debatable. But he *was* her husband and she loved him.

The Kerrys had been gone for a couple of weeks and the three of them sat around the dinner table. The worst had blown over. "We have neglected our families," said Brad. He looked at Birgit. "I know you miss your folks and I wouldn't mind patching up my relationship with Mother. Since the house is ready, how about we have a family reunion?"

The thought seemed to excite him more than Birgit. She actually wanted to see her mom, but a meeting with Vera Svenson, self-conscious and uptight, and Brad's mom, the "ice queen"? The thought of the two women in the same room made her shudder. Their personalities alone would be bad enough. And on top of that a language barrier? Unthinkable!

"I don't think that would be a good idea," said Birgit.

Brad did not bring up the subject again.

Despite all, Birgit still knew she was a lucky woman, the envy of her female friends. Her husband, other than being incredibly handsome, was affluent, generous and a fantastic lover. Bud's assault on her even seemed to have increased Brad's libido. Their love life had never been better or love-making more frequent.

Whatever questions she had about him was swept away in those moments. Her body always responded to his touch, quieting all doubts. Still, afterward, she often sobbed for no reason. Brad never asked why.

§

"Are we expecting royalty?"

Brad, still wet from his swim, walked out on the terrace, picked up a chocolate-covered strawberry from the table and popped it in his mouth.

Birgit frowned at him. "Don't mess it up, please…no, it's only the Crawleys." *Was he making fun of her? Was she "overdoing" again?*

"Remember, no fuss," her friend Hunter had said. "Just throw some peanuts in a bowl." Even so, Birgit didn't feel good about the result. Was there too much stuff, too many dips? *What would Lindsey have said?*

Birgit scolded herself. *For heaven's sake, the woman is gone. Why am I keeping up a fight with a dead foe—especially when I keep losing?*

Brad sneaked another strawberry. "Are they due here soon? Do I have time for a shower?"

Birgit refocused on her preparations. "Forty minutes. But please hurry—I need your help setting up the drinks."

"Care to join me?

"Don't be silly! I already took a shower."

"How about getting dirty again?"

Birgit threw an olive at her husband and heard him chuckle as he walked away. She followed him with her eyes. He was perfectly proportioned—powerful shoulders, narrow waist, muscular legs.

She shook her head. She'd always despised men who objectified women, but here she was doing the same to her husband. Was she equally shallow?

A column of sandhill cranes flew over, so close their flapping wings almost touched the roof. Floridians were fond of these birds, but Birgit wasn't. The thunder of their wings and their metallic-sounding cry made her anxious.

Once the birds had passed, she breathed again. She was calm, but something in the back of her mind nagged at her. She wasn't sure what it was, but something was missing.

And then the answer came. There was no mystery, no secret, no void that couldn't be filled. "I want to have a baby!" she said out loud.

45

No matter how turned on, Brad always used protection when they made love. Early on, Birgit hadn't given it much thought—they were newly-married and she assumed he felt they needed time to themselves.

Lately, though, her own inner voice had started to whisper in her ear, softly at first, but over time it became louder and more persistent. The message it sent was nothing she wanted to hear. It raised doubts about several things—her life, her marriage…and Brad. Trying to silence the inner voice was fruitless. It showed no mercy—just kept pounding away, coming up with new, and often petty, accusations.

She felt a need to defend her husband, even in these increasingly regular conversations in her head. "Be fair! Maybe he should take more of an interest in Elizabeth's life, but he *is* a caring father…"

"So let's go to something else," replied her inner voice. *"Remember when Lindsey found out she had cancer? Whom did she tell first? Her sister. Have you forgotten when Big E said, 'I know Brad is shallow, but he can't be that shallow!'"*

"Well, that was her perception, not mine."

"*Isn't Ethel Hirschberg a woman you admire?*"

"*She is, but she never liked Brad…*"

"*Hmmm…Didn't Brad have sex with you, fondling your breasts the night after his wife had hers removed?*"

"*Yes, but he needed comfort and I was as much to blame…*"

"*So he's weak?*"

"*You said it. I didn't.*"

"*And what about the baby?*"

"*What baby?*"

"*The one you're planning on…*"

"*Brad and I haven't even talked about that yet.*"

"*Why not?*

"*There are many reasons. For one, we're not in a rush, and Brad might be concerned about Elizabeth's reaction…*"

"*Sorry to disillusion you, but he doesn't give a rat's ass about Elizabeth's feelings.*"

"*That's uncalled for…*"

The voice snorted. "*But there is that one thing you do remember,*" *it said.* "*The one thing you don't want to address…*"

"*What's that, wise ass?*"

"*That day in the hospital? The last time with Lindsey. You recall what she said.*"

Birgit turned cold. "*No, I don't! And whatever it was, it had no bearing on anything—she was all pumped up on morphine.*"

"*I don't care about that. I asked you what she said!*"

"*I don't remember. She was incoherent…*"

"*That's not true and you know it. There was one thing that happened that day which truly bothered you. And her dying wasn't it. Let's face it—you already had your eyes on the big prize. Her death would be so convenient, turning everything rosy…or so you thought. No, there is something she said that has stuck in your gut all this time."*

"Leave me alone! I told you that I don't remember!"

The voice persisted. "If that's the case, I'll refresh your memory."

Birgit wanted to protest, but found herself mesmerized by the sound of the voice in her head, and she couldn't block it out.

"Lindsay said that Brad never wanted children!"

§

The experience shook her, and her anxiety transferred to the bedroom. She tried not to wake Brad with her tossing and turning, but despite her efforts, she did.

"I tried to be quiet…" she mumbled when he began to stir.

"You were," Brad said sleepily, "But I could hear you thinking."

A flush of happiness swept over her. *I could hear you thinking! That was not the answer of a shallow man. He was aware, perhaps even sensing what was going on in her head. Was this perhaps the moment she'd been waiting for?*

"Brad…" she began softly, but there was no answer. Her husband had already gone back to sleep.

It could wait till tomorrow. She was happy and so relieved. "See," she whispered defiantly to the voice. "He is not as clueless as you think."

There was a moment of silence and then the voice spoke, almost sadly this time.

"Maybe not. But *you* are."

46

"He's a true gentleman."

Even before she heard his name mentioned, Birgit knew that Brad was the topic of the conversation. To avoid the appearance of eavesdropping, she quickly turned her back to the group.

The party had shifted into a higher gear after a messy start. The caterers had arrived late due to an incorrect address, and the host's teenage son had clipped the fender of a car in the driveway—a brand-new BMW. The guest and host had exchanged words and tempers had flared before cooler heads prevailed.

Now, with drinks served and food on the table, the general atmosphere had changed and turned into Kumbaya. Samba tunes by the group Brazil 66—one of Birgit's favorites—played in the background, and a few latecomers, whose sloppy grins indicated that happy hour had started early and elsewhere, had helped lift the spirit of the place.

Birgit tapped her foot to the beat, but the happy feeling from earlier had vanished. To hear Brad praised was nothing new. It happened often, but the thrill it usually brought hadn't come.

Her only reaction was mild curiosity. *Who'd made that comment? A man or a woman?* She drew a blank. *Had the drinks affected her?* She finally decided it was a woman—men seldom talk about each other in those terms.

Although she realized it was a crazy idea, she thought about trying to find the person who'd said it—not because she planned to make a scene, but because she wanted to know what the speaker believed made someone a gentleman. No one would question Brad's social skills—the way he'd been raised, his upper-class background and Waspish values had seen to that. He was exceedingly polite, held his liquor well, showed a self-deprecating sense of humor, didn't tell off-color jokes—at least not in mixed company—and was modest almost to a fault.

Birgit realized that it was that last part that she didn't buy. *How hard is it to be humble when there is nothing to be humble about?*

Suddenly, she thought of Bud's hands all over her and her husband's betrayal. And all it had taken was a casual comment by a stranger to make it all surface again.

§

The Fillmores were frequently entertaining or being entertained, but living in near proximity of one another, they repeatedly bumped into the same cast of characters. Socio-economic level usually dictated who was invited and who was not. Or, as Brad put it, "Birds of a feather flock together."

There were exceptions of course: a certain "savoir-faire" improved your chances. Miguel, the Venezuelan tennis pro was one such exception. A rumored affair with an under-aged female player was overlooked. His handsome features, flowing dark hair, and elegance on the dance floor more than made up for any indiscretions.

A similar case could be made for Mario, who, despite a pending criminal investigation, was also a fixture at social gatherings. His trademark purple shirt, opened almost to the waist, made him sexy, and he played guitar and sang in a smooth, pleasing baritone. His dark and brooding looks were interpreted differently by different people—men saw strength and danger, women sorrow and loneliness.

§

The place was packed, and the guests were mostly "monologuing," since the noise made it impossible to hear what anyone was saying. Around the table on the lanai, people nodded, smiled and nibbled hors' d'oeuvres, doing what people do when they want to be "seen." Birgit enjoyed dressing up and socializing most of the time, but her mood tonight had soured. She hoped for an early exit, but Brad was nowhere in sight.

She found herself pressed against a thin young man with garlic breath. He might have mentioned the word "investment," but it was hard for her to tell in all the chatter. She tried to look engaged, but a small piece of shrimp stuck between his front teeth was a distraction and a reminder of the lunch she had missed.

Excusing herself, Birgit worked her way toward the table when a woman in a floral dress leaped up, grinned, and pointed to her, reminiscent of a politician greeting supporters at a rally. Mercifully shuffled away by the crowd, Birgit managed to smile as genuinely as possible, but she was certain she had never met this woman before.

From now on, I must try the association game, she thought. *The one with the unfortunate hair color is…?* She scolded herself. *What is the matter with me? I used to be a people person!*

Across the table, she finally found someone she remembered—a banker from Philadelphia, who, despite his middle Eastern features, introduced himself as "Mike." She assumed that the chubby woman next to him was his wife. Did he say her name was Rose?

The music changed from Samba to tango. There was a sudden hush, as Miguel and his dance partner cleared the floor and put on an electrifying performance. The audience clapped wildly and a few "olé's" were shouted. Women couldn't take their eyes off Miguel's cute, tight behind.

Birgit finally caught a glimpse of Brad in a group of men talking about golf. She watched as one of them stepped away, took an imaginary swing, and then looked expectantly at her husband. His response was typical—a smile, a shaking of the head, a pleasant refusal to deliver advice, give instruction or show off.

So fucking humble. She mouthed the obscenity and it flew with surprising smoothness from her lips. She whispered it again, gleefully tasting its brutality. Brad glanced over at her, apparently having sensed her watching him. He pointed discreetly to the Rolex on his wrist as a signal. *Ready to go?*

She nodded. This silent communication between them was a part of what she had once loved. Togetherness, belonging, being a couple—a beautiful, popular couple.

She studied Brad as he said his goodbyes. *Such a good-looking man.* There was so much to love about him—how he carried himself, the way he threw his head back when he laughed.

There would be no reprimands on the way home—only concerned questions: "Was something wrong…Was she feeling okay?"

Her anger was gone, and so were her childish, petulant thoughts. What persisted was the unmistakable knowledge that she no longer trusted the man she'd married. *The man who did not want to have a child with her.*

47

Feathers flew everywhere and Birgit and Elizabeth lay on the bed laughing. The girl giggled and hit her once more with the pillow. "Shouldn't you be more mature? Remember, you're my stepmother!"

"Let's forget the step, okay?"

Birgit instantly regretted her words, fearful that Elizabeth would think she was trying to replace Lindsey. But the girl didn't seem the least bit bothered by the remark. Her cheeks were glowing.

"What do you want? *Mother?* In that case, you must have been about eleven when I was born. Isn't that a bit shocking even for a Swede?"

Birgit dove across the bed toward Elizabeth and attempted to tickle her. "Don't you badmouth my country! How about 'little sis' then? I never had a younger sister!"

Elizabeth grinned. "No-o-o, let's stick with Mom!" Although she was joking, she had no idea how happy she'd made Birgit feel.

The seam of one of the pillows was ripped all the way down one side. "I just bought these!" said Birgit. Elizabeth jumped up, grabbed another one and aimed for her head, and laughed uproariously. "Cheapskate!"

Birgit pinned her to the floor. "You little brat!"

Elizabeth rolled out from under her and sat up to catch her breath. "What will we do tomorrow? Go roller skating?"

"I don't know," said Birgit. "We'll see." She vaguely remembered something about a tennis lesson, but it didn't matter—it could easily be cancelled. Spending time with Elizabeth had suddenly become far more important.

§

An uneasy truce had formed between Birgit and Brad. She no longer brought up the subject of having a baby, and Brad, as with everything else, avoided it. He occasionally pointed to childless friends of his and commented on how happy and carefree they seemed.

Why didn't Brad want children? Did he have mother issues? Yes, Helen Fillmore seemed to favor Charles, but Birgit had always assumed it was because he was so needy. Was that the problem? Did Brad need no one?

Whatever the reasons, Florida had changed—or perhaps revealed—the man she'd married. The disciplined, hardworking man she'd once been wildly attracted to was gone, replaced by someone she did not recognize. Some mornings she woke up, sure that she was blowing everything out of proportion, but at the end of the day, the doubts were always back. Brad was civil, but the light teasing they had so often shared between them had ceased. They still made love occasionally, but both sought to satisfy themselves, not the other.

Talk of a family reunion reared its head again and then fizzled out and Birgit found herself wondering if she wanted a child for the wrong reason. Was she trying to save the marriage?

§

Curled up in the lounge chair on the veranda with a glass of iced tea, Birgit looked at some photographs Ruth had sent her. Her sister and Arne, arms around each other, smiled at the camera.

Mom had written that Arne no longer touched liquor and, if the picture told the truth, she was right. He was healthier and thinner and his face had lost its puffiness and bloat. He looked more like the young man her sister had fallen in love with. Tears filled her eyes.

Elizabeth wandered onto the veranda. "What's the matter? Are you crying?"

"No," said Birgit. She brought out a tissue from her pants pocket and blew her nose. "I think I might have an allergy."

The girl glanced at the photographs in Birgit's lap. "It's your family, isn't it? You miss them, don't you?"

Birgit thought for a moment and to her surprise, found what Elizabeth had said to be true. "I do."

Elizabeth pointed to a picture of Gunnar. "Who is this cutie?"

Birgit loved her nephew, but she had never seen him through the eyes of a young girl. She studied the photo. He had grown taller, had filled out, and was no longer the awkward little boy she remembered. "Gunnar, my nephew. He's your age and very smart."

"He doesn't smile like the rest of them. Is he always this serious?

"He's a deep thinker, but when he smiles his whole face crinkles." She looked up at the girl. "You'd like him."

Elizabeth pointed to the photo of Ruth and Arne. "And this happy couple?" To hear them referred to as "happy" was something new, but Birgit smiled. Perhaps they finally were.

"They're Gunnar's parents. My sister Ruth and her husband Arne."

Elizabeth sat down beside her in a lawn chair. "I know you were close to your dad. You told me a lot about him when he died, but I haven't heard much about the rest of the family."

Birgit meant for her response to be short but found herself talking and talking. She told stories about Ruth, Arne and his problem with drinking, and her mom. The stories about her mother made Elizabeth laugh.

"She sounds like a piece of work."

Birgit thought for a moment. "More an acquired taste," she said.

Time away from home had clearly painted her family in a different light. Mom was still quite a personality—hot-tempered, but funny. Ruth seemed less abrasive. Arne didn't pass the smell test just yet, but it seemed he was on the right path.

Was she embellishing or finally seeing the "better angels of their natures"?

"I'd like to meet them someday," said Elizabeth. "Especially Gunnar. Does he speak English?"

"As I said, he's smart. He's already had several years of English in school." She grinned at Elizabeth. "Of course, he speaks with a Swedish accent."

"That makes him even cuter."

Suddenly, Birgit visualized Elizabeth in Sweden. She could see her walking on cobblestone streets, taking the "shrimp boat" out to the islands.

She turned to her stepdaughter. "It's more rustic there than here."

"I do rustic well," said Elizabeth.

§

What would she tell him? "I'm leaving you" sounded less cold than "I want a divorce," but it probably didn't matter. She knew they would separate amicably—for once, it was good that Brad didn't tolerate "scenes" and unpleasantness well.

She prepared for the moment—what to say and what to do. She imagined that they would be calm and talk to each other kindly.

§

They sat at the table, dinner finished, a bottle of wine between them. Elizabeth had already gone to bed. There had been no provocation, no disagreement, no meaningful conversation.

"I'm divorcing you," she said.

Brad froze, as if waiting for a punchline. "Are you joking?"

"No. I wouldn't joke about a subject like that."

Clearly confused, he focused intently on Birgit's face.

"I know we've gone through a rough patch lately, but divorce? Isn't that a bit drastic?" He made a sweeping gesture at the house, the water, and the surroundings. "What could you possibly be missing?"

Birgit remained stone-faced and said nothing.

"You're walking away from Elizabeth, too? After all she's been through?"

She had no idea where the words came from, but when Birgit heard them pass her lips, they made perfect sense.

"No, I'm not walking away from Elizabeth. She's coming with *me*."

She watched as her husband's expression passed through a series of emotions she thought a true father would feel—disbelief, hurt, anger—but, then something else flickered in his eyes.

Relief.

When she saw it, a flood of thoughts passed through her mind. Clear thoughts, unlike any she'd had before. *Brad is not capable of love in the true sense of the word.*

He loved Lindsey's talents, her charm, her sophistication.

291

He'd loved Birgit's body and had from the first time he saw her.

He loved his bright daughter's wittiness.

But the only thing he really loved was the Femme Fatale. A silent wooden sea craft meant more to Brad Fillmore than his family and that would never change.

It would never excuse her behavior toward Birgit in other ways, but Lindsey had tried to warn her. She'd known it all along.

Only one question remained.

What would she say to Elizabeth?

48

Elizabeth bent down and picked up a shell. "If I live with you, can I still see Dad?"

"As often as you want," Birgit said. "You know he cares."

The girl had no illusions about her father. "Not enough."

They continued to walk down the beach. "He and I have discussed it all," said Birgit. "Holidays, summer vacations…"

"Not Christmas—I want to spend Christmas in Connecticut. You, me, and the relatives."

Birgit thought about the Sorensons and Hirschbergs and Helen Fillmore and wondered how they would react to the news. Lindsey's parents would probably say nothing and she thought she already knew what Big E would say. And, since the day Helen had come to help clean out Lindsey's closet, Birgit's feelings had softened toward her. She certainly acted like a snob sometimes, but there was one thing you could say about her—there was nothing she wouldn't do for her granddaughter.

Birgit took a deep breath. "You know that your grandmother doesn't approve of me."

"Which one? Jack the Knife?"

"I wish you'd stop calling her that."

Elizabeth shrugged. "Mom thought it was fitting. Besides, I only call her that behind her back."

"That makes it worse!"

They walked along in silence until Elizabeth stopped and squinted at Birgit. "Is this what you really want? I don't mean you and Dad. I'm talking about us. You and me. Don't you want to be free?"

Birgit looked at the girl's upturned face. No matter what, Elizabeth deserved the truth. She searched for an honest answer, both hopefully and fearfully. Then it came, strongly and clearly.

"I wouldn't be free without you," she said. "It might sound corny, but I love you, Elizabeth Anne Fillmore. Besides, I'm also fulfilling a promise I made to your mom. Her last words to me were about you. Before she died, she asked me to take care of you."

Elizabeth poked with her toes at some small smooth pebbles buried in the sand. She picked up a handful, examined them, chose the flattest one and threw it forcefully into the water. Tears streaming down her cheeks, she watched it skip—one, two, three, four, five times—before disappearing.

"You know, when Mom and Dad entered a room, they took it over. Sometimes it made me proud, but most of the time, it made me feel sad or angry. Why couldn't they just be ordinary, normal parents?"

Birgit knew that Elizabeth didn't really want an answer. To take her hand and walk in silence toward the pier seemed the right thing to do. When they reached it, they climbed up and walked to the end. Seagulls circled above their heads. Elizabeth shielded her eyes and looked up at them.

"So where are we going to live?"

"How about moving back to Connecticut?"

The moment she finished the sentence, Birgit found herself wrapped in the arms and legs of a gangly teen. "You mean to our HOUSE?"

Birgit nodded. "Yes. Dad is the one who suggested it. At least until you go to college."

"You know this was my dream."

"I know. But don't believe I'm just going to lie on a couch, eat chocolate, watch soaps and live off your dad. I am going to work. I want to build a career of some kind for myself."

"You'll still have time for gardening?"

Birgit smiled. "Absolutely!"

Elizabeth was quiet for a moment. "Don't think I am ungrateful," she said. "I love the boathouse and the canoe. There are definitely things I'll miss about this place."

"Me, too," said Birgit.

"But it just isn't home."

The girl peered over the edge of the dock at the brilliant emerald water and shook her head. "This shade of green is unreal," she said. "Doesn't it look fake?"

"Why don't you find out?" Birgit gave her a shove and Elizabeth plunged into the water. Sputtering and splashing, she came up yelling.

"Silly woman, I have my clothes on!"

Birgit laughed out loud.

"So do I. And here I come!"